EVERYONE LOVES
CORINNE MICHAELS!

"Michaels writes unputdownable romance."
—Helena Hunting, *New York Times* bestselling author

"Corinne Michaels is a master storyteller."
—Penny Reid, *New York Times* bestselling author

"Michaels's writing provides the perfect mix of humor, heartbreak, and sexy. It's a ride you don't want to miss."
—Claire Contreras, *New York Times* bestselling author

"Sexy. Heartwarming. Addictive. Michaels is at the top of her game in *Defenseless*."
—K. Bromberg, *New York Times* bestselling author

"Sweet, sexy goodness."
—Mia Sheridan, *New York Times* bestselling author, on *We Own Tonight*

"What an incredible ride! It's real, it's swoony, and it's 100% Corinne Michaels. It has heart and heat from the first page to the last, and I loved it every minute of it!"
—M. Leighton, *New York Times* bestselling author, on *We Own Tonight*

All I Ask

All I Ask

CORINNE MICHAELS

FOREVER

New York   Boston

Copyright © 2020 by Corinne Michaels

Cover illustration and design by Elizabeth Turner Stokes.
Cover copyright © 2020 by Hachette Book Group, Inc.

Forever
Hachette Book Group
1290 Avenue of the Americas
New York, NY 10104
readforever.com
twitter.com/readforeverpub

First Edition: March 2020

Forever is an imprint of Grand Central Publishing.
The Forever name and logo are trademarks of Hachette Book Group, Inc.

The publisher is not responsible for websites (or their content) that are not owned by the publisher.

The Hachette Speakers Bureau provides a wide range of authors for speaking events. To find out more, go to www.hachettespeakersbureau.com or call (866) 376-6591.

LCCN: 2019955892

ISBNs: 978-1-5387-4565-6 (trade paperback), 978-1-5387-4566-3 (ebook)

Printed in the United States of America

LSC-C

10 9 8 7 6 5 4 3 2 1

To those who love someone enough to
let them go.

All I Ask

prologue

Teagan

twenty-one years old

Fate. Hope. Love.

All words I think of as I stand at the front of this church in a gorgeous dress beside my best friend, Derek. It should be a happy day. One filled with tears of joy instead of tears of sadness.

No one knows that I'm not happy, though.

No one knows that he's the one I love.

No one knows that I wish I was standing in *her* place, hearing him proclaim his love to me.

"Do you, Derek Matthew Hartz, promise to love, honor, and obey Meghan Kimberly Aston from this day forth?"

I stand behind him as his best woman, as he so called me, unable to see his face, but I don't have to. I know what's there. His strong jawline will be set, because when he's serious he can't stop himself from showing the determination that fills him. His two-day stubble that covers his cheeks is there just to please her. The love, though, the love that's in his eyes should bring her to her knees. Because no one loves like Derek.

Another tear falls, but I plaster on a smile so people won't see how much I'm breaking.

Please don't say it, Derek, I want to beg. *Please see that it's me who you belong with. Just turn around. Just look to your left. See me. See us. See what could be if you'd open your eyes.*

"I do," he says with pride.

The ring slips on her finger, sealing their love, and I try not to feel the pain that's threatening to overtake me. I would give anything to be the friend he believes me to be. The one who loves him like a brother, wants him to be happy, and stand beside him on the biggest day of his life. Instead, I'm dying inside. I know I will never—*we* will never—recover from this.

I can't be his friend when I love him this much, and yet, I'm not strong enough to quit him.

"I now pronounce you husband and wife. You may kiss the bride," the pastor says with a triumphant smile.

Derek dips Meghan back, presses his lips to hers, and seals their union and my broken heart.

I follow behind him as he walks his wife back down the aisle.

Wife.

Another wave of emotion hits me, and I rest my hand on my very large stomach, trying not to be sick when the baby kicks, reminding me why exactly I could never have Derek anyway.

"Are you okay?" he asks as we exit the church.

Our eyes meet, and I use every ounce of strength to mask my emotions. "Yeah, sorry, just felt a little dizzy."

Meghan immediately takes my arm. "Here, honey, sit. Someone get Teagan some water."

"I'm fine! Really, I stood too long because Derek talks too much." He rolls his eyes, and Meghan smiles. "I mean it, the baby is doing the salsa in there and I'm fine. This is your big day, please don't worry about me."

He eyes me like the protector he has always been. "You don't have to be so tough around me."

Oh, but I do.

I shake my head. "I would tell you. I always tell you."

The lie slips from my lips so easily it's scary. Derek and I have been best friends since high school. I've always told him the truth, until now.

"Okay. Just know, I'm really happy you're here, Tea," Derek says as he tucks Meghan into his side. "It was a lot for you to travel and probably hard to be on your feet the entire wedding, but you're my best friend and I couldn't have imagined anyone else by my side."

The ache I had gotten under control is back to a steady throb. He has no idea why the wedding was hard. He thinks it's because my now ex-boyfriend knocked me up and then left me. Keith doesn't want anything to do with the baby, neither emotionally nor financially and now, I'm here, with a choice to make. I can fight him or run the risk of him exposing a secret that I never want out. I'm conflicted, angry, and my heart is decimated.

Yeah, this wedding is hard, but it has nothing to do with my ex and everything to do with Derek.

My chest feels tight, and I want nothing more than for it all to stop. I should've told him. So many times I could've opened my mouth, but it was one missed chance after another.

Then, it was too late. He and Meghan had fallen in love and were expecting a baby.

But he's my best friend and I'm glad that at least one of us will be happy. There isn't a person who deserves it more than he does.

"I love you, Derek," I tell him, wishing this was the confession where he understood my love was more than just friendship, but that opportunity is gone, and I would be the worst friend in the world to tell him now. "You're my best friend and I'm so happy for you and Meghan. You guys…you're both so…" The tears start again, and for the first time, I'm grateful for the pregnancy. "God, I'm such a hormonal mess!"

They both laugh. Meghan steps forward, pulling me in her arms. "We love you so much, Tea."

I know she doesn't mean it. She's always had issues with Derek and me, which if I were her, I would too.

Derek puts his arms around both of us. "My girls."

We break apart, and it feels like so much more than him releasing me. It feels like he's letting me go—letting us go.

I watch the two of them greet their guests, laughing, smiling, and completely in love.

It hits me like a bullet to the chest. Not only did I lose the love of my life today, but I also lost my best friend.

chapter one

Teagan

present

"Thank you, Mrs. Dickman, I'll definitely let you know if I get any more of the chairs in from that set," I explain with the phone to my ear as I try to tidy up the store.

"Okay, Teagan, you do that, but I'll call tomorrow to be sure."

She always does. It wouldn't be another glorious day in Chincoteague Island if Mrs. Dickman didn't remind me she still wants those damn chairs. I run an antique store, and our stock is whatever we find on any given day. But it makes her happy to check with us, so I smile and do my best to make her day a little brighter.

"Mom!" Chastity comes running down the stairs, her fabulous thirteen-year-old attitude already on display. "Why did you stick Mr. Stinkers outside again?"

I should've known the cat would be today's argument.

"Because I told you that we can't have a cat in the apartment."

"Grandma will let me. I know she will."

"She won't. I'm not about to ask her and piss her off when we need to live here."

We live above the store rent free, which means it's the only place we can afford. Even though Mom says my living arrangement is part of my salary. Chastity doesn't understand that I can't feed another living thing. Or that the car is about three thousand miles overdue for an oil change and needs new tires, which means I say a prayer each time I start it. I leave out the part that I can't afford to buy her new sneakers because I make minimum wage in my parents' antique store—as the manager—and that I haven't seen a dime from her father in thirteen years, since he signed his rights away. Not that my parents couldn't pay me more, but they feel that choices have consequences, so me getting pregnant, dropping out of college, and allowing Keith off the hook means I need to suck it up.

"The cat needs to be inside where he can be loved."

Yeah, kid, I need to be loved too.

"I'm sorry, sweetheart. I really am, but we can't have a cat or dog or any other stray thing you bring home."

She huffs. "Animals need me."

My daughter is really a great kid. She gets straight A's, always listens, still thinks I'm sort of okay, unless we're talking about animals. Then, she's a lunatic. As much as I'd love to give her what she's asking, it's not possible. I'm saving every penny so I can get us out of this town and into a better life.

"Yes, they do, and all of this is fascinating, but you're going to miss the bus and I can't drive you today, so…" I grip her shoulders, turn her about, and start to march her toward the door to the apartment. "…off you go, my Ace Ventura."

She shakes her head. "You're really lame."

"So I've been told."

"Do you think we can go see Dr. Hartz today? Maybe I can volunteer at the clinic or help with the animals."

Immediately I feel my chest constrict.

"You can," I say with a tight smile. "I'm sure he would appreciate the help."

Dr. Hartz is Derek's father, and even though I haven't spoken to Derek in over thirteen years, I still feel anxious just hearing his name. An unbreakable friendship that dissolved the day Chastity was born. I have no idea why or what happened to make him disappear. All I know is one day the phone rang and when we hung up, we never spoke again. It's been so long since it all happened, and still it hurts.

There was no more help or calls. No more late-night talks where I had my friend, my only friend. It was like he vanished, and I was left completely alone.

"Good, then I'll go see Dr. Hartz after school."

Derek's parents have always been kind to me. They've never judged me or made me feel small, which is great, because living in this tiny town doesn't lend itself to avoiding people. It's just that whenever we talk, it's superficial because what do two people talk about when the common thread between them has been severed?

"I'm sure that'll cure your itch regarding the animals."

"Not likely, but I think I could do some good," she says.

There's my girl, always wanting to help. Her heart is ten times too big for her body. She would do anything for anyone. At her age, my life revolved around Friday night football games, my stupid boyfriend, and my friends—who were, I'm ashamed to say, the mean girls.

Chastity is my polar opposite. And I'm so thankful for that.

"I know you could. Let me know how it goes with Dr. Hartz, okay?"

She wraps her arms around my neck, squeezing me tight. "I will! Thanks, Mom!"

I kiss the top of her head, grateful that she still thinks I'm cool enough to hug.

"Don't bring home any animals. Understood?"

Chastity smiles and I know that look. "I make no promises." She rushes out the door, avoiding any response I could toss back.

And I begin my mundane day.

Once I've had my coffee, I head downstairs to the store. It's the end of summer, which means tourists are gone and the town is going into off-season mode. The antique shop hours have dwindled, the beach crowd has thinned, and everything is a bit...calmer.

During the summer, the busyness keeps my mind off the things that haven't panned out the way I hoped. My parents are gone the entire time because they want to see the world, which is great for them—and me. My mother drives me to drink, and I enjoy every moment when she's gone.

It's much quieter and less judgy.

In a few days, they'll return, letting me know all the things I did wrong, reminding me that this is not the way I ever wanted my life to go. How much potential I had— and wasted.

It's super fun times. However, I will survive, like I always have.

"Teagan?" Nina calls from the back. "You down here?"

"I am."

She peeks her head over the lamp by the back entrance, waving her hand. "Hey!"

Nina is my best friend and has a glow about her. No matter how crappy things are, when she's around, you can't help but smile. Her energy is infectious, and she's the kindest person in the world. She loves, forgives, and every day I wonder how she found it in her heart to give me her trust.

"How was yesterday? Sorry I couldn't come by, but I had to handle Daddy and his doctor's appointment. He would not go willingly. Trying to say it was a bruise from hitting the side of the boat when he clearly has a gash on his arm that needs tending. That man is either hell-bent on making my life a nightmare or he wants to join my mama in the ground."

"Is he okay?"

Her lips purse and her eyes narrow. "Uhh hmm. He's fine, just stubborn and thinking he can still go out crabbing. The man can barely walk on steady land, but he thinks he can navigate a boat?"

Nina's father is the sweetest man. However, he's old and refuses to believe he's old.

"Well, at least he's feeling good, you know?"

She sighs. "I know. I prefer him this way, but I'd also prefer he listen to what we tell him. Anyway, what's new with you?"

It's been a day since I've talked to her. "It's Chincoteague, what could be new?"

Nina sits on the old sofa that's been here since 1973 and will never sell. It's probably the ugliest thing I've ever seen, but there's something ornately beautiful about it. The sofa may not have the best upholstery, but the bones are there. The frame strong, withstanding countless times of being sat upon, and the cushions aren't dented, regardless of the number of asses that have been there. If I ever get my own home, I plan to buy it because someone should see it for what it could be.

"Maybe some handsome stranger rolled into town to see the wild horses and realized you're the fairest maiden in the land, professed his undying love, and now you're getting married. Of course he only granted you a chaste kiss, after which you fell helplessly in his arms and wanted to stay there."

Oh Lord. "You're reading historical romance novels again, I see."

"I always do. One day I'm going to find a man like the heroes I read about. Mark my words. Until then, I refuse to settle."

I love my friend, but her head is always in the clouds. She's beautiful, smart, and any man would be lucky to have her…she just won't even give them a chance. I don't know what it is that has her so afraid to love, and she won't tell me. I've tried many times to get her to open up, but I've never been able to crack her.

There's no secret as to what my issue is. Keith is the biggest piece of shit there is, my ex–best friend abandoned me, I'm broke, and I have a teenager who is my priority number one. As soon as I tell any potential date I have a kid—poof—they're gone. Which is fine by me. I've had enough disappointment from men unwilling to commit.

"Well, I would like to meet a man who isn't married, like the last asshole, or unwilling to deal with the fact that Chastity is my life. I'm tired of having to even explain that."

"You shouldn't have to."

No, I shouldn't.

"My love life is a damn disaster."

"There's a hero out there waiting for us, Tea. I know it. We just need to find him."

"Well, so far I've gotten the antihero that you can't even grow to like."

"At least you know what it felt like to be loved," she challenges.

"Keith didn't love me. He didn't love anyone but himself."

Keith is still the town hero here. No matter what he did to me, it doesn't matter. While Nina knows the truth, sometimes I wonder if anyone else would believe it if they found out. Of course, his version paints me as the whore who tried to trap him into marriage.

Each freaking Sunday during football season, I have to hear his name, see his stupid face across the television screen, know how much money he makes while I can't even buy school supplies for Chastity.

Nina's eyes go soft and her lips tighten. "I wasn't talking about him, honey."

"Well, I sure as hell hope you weren't talking about Derek."

She lives in a world where impossible things happen all the time. Like a man waking up and realizing that it was you he wanted all along. I don't have time for fantasies because they're just that—fiction. I would much rather have my head on straight and focus on what's real. Like bills and teenagers.

"I still think that..."

"I know what you think." I sigh. "He got married and

had a kid and somewhere in that equation, I didn't fit. That's what happened. He knew I was terrified, alone, living with my parents, and freaking the fuck out and he felt that I wasn't worth the time."

At least that's all I can come up with at this point. Why else would he bail? Why would the guy who was supposed to be the only one I could rely on just stop talking to me completely? Maybe it wasn't me, maybe it was his wife, but at this point in my life, I can't keep debating it in my head. Derek made his choice and I had to go on with my life.

"It was a long time ago, Tea."

I roll my eyes. "And a long time that I haven't heard from him. My phone number is the same."

I say that last part and I feel so pathetic. I've given up on a sudden call or appearance at my door. Believing that he was different and would come around was only hurting myself. Now, I'm just numb.

"Okay, no more talk about Keith or Derek." She raises her hand. "Have you painted anything new? I've been dying to see if you added to your collection."

I shake my head. "I haven't had much time to paint, but I'm going to head out to the beach this weekend." My hands have been itching to hold a brush. Painting allows me the time to just…breathe.

"Good. I'm excited to see what you come up with."

"Me too. In fact, I might head out there a little early."

Nina smiles, probably happy that the conversation shifted a bit too. "That makes me happy."

It does the same for me. At least I have something of my own, even if only two other people in the world know about it.

chapter two

Teagan

present

"Teagan, we're back!" my mother announces as she opens the door dramatically.

"I see that. And so *early*!" I say with a smile even though I feel like screaming and throwing a fit. "How was Europe?"

"It was fabulous. Your father was so tired, he went straight home, but I wanted to come see you…and the store, to make sure it was still standing. I'm never quite sure what will happen in my absence."

My parents are wonderful people. No one can deny that, but my mother has a way of cutting me down. It's little comments that let me know how much of a disappointment I am.

No one is more disenchanted with the way things have gone than me.

In high school I was voted most popular, most likely to succeed, most outgoing, and best smile. I was captain of the cheerleading squad, dated the captain of the football team. We were the all-American couple that was going to set the world on fire.

Being a single mother with no money, working and living in this town, was never in anyone's version of my future.

"Why wouldn't the store be okay?"

She touches my face. "You never know, darling. Things don't always go to plan."

"Yeah, plans, daughters, who knows what might've happened…"

Mom ignores my jab and walks around. "I see you sold quite a few big pieces?"

I close my eyes, release a breath and nod. "I did."

"Good. How's my granddaughter?"

"Going to ask you if she can adopt a cat or a horse or maybe even an entire zoo."

"I think it would be hard to keep a horse in the apartment." Her smile is wide as she shakes her head. She may not be the most wonderful mother, but she is the best grandmother. Chastity is the one thing I've done right.

"Yes, but you know her, she loves animals more than people. She's going to be volunteering with Dr. Hartz, cleaning out cages and whatnot. She's really excited about it."

My mother clasps her hands together, and her eyes brighten. "Oh, that will be wonderful for her."

"I agree."

"And Dr. Hartz is such a good man. He'll definitely teach her responsibility, how to deal with people, and other great skills. Things that she's probably missing out on at home."

Oh, Mom, please feel free to keep telling me what a bang-up job I've done so far.

"What does that mean?" I ask, unable to stop myself.

"Nothing, but the girl doesn't talk to anyone, Teagan. She has no friends, no social life, she doesn't do anything but read and talk to animals."

God forbid she doesn't act the way *my mother* thinks she should.

"She's fine. Chastity is a wonderful kid with fantastic grades. She's happy, smart, respectful, and I'm glad she's nothing like me at that age."

Now it's her turn to look horrified. To her, I was everything she ever wanted in a daughter. My popularity furthered hers at that time. People thought she had some secret as to why I was "perfect" and sought her out for advice all the time.

Except I was far from perfect.

"You had your chance, Teagan Berkeley. You had everything right there in front of you and then, I don't know what happened."

"Why do we do this, Mom?" I ask with sadness in my voice. "Why do we always go back to this? You just got home and instead of us catching up about what happened while you were away, you showing me photos, telling me that you're happy to see me, we're arguing about twenty years' worth of shit?"

I watch the fight drain from her. Neither of us want this animosity between us, but it feels like it's all we know. "I just want you to be happy. I want Chastity to have the life that you could have had. That's all."

"I'm glad that she's not boy crazy or trying to fit in with the popular kids, because those popular kids grew up and are still mean. They stayed in this town, where it's safe and they're loved by all. None of those girls are making a difference in the world, and you know what? I want that for Chastity. I want her to go, live, experience, and be passionate and happy. I will do everything I can to make sure she doesn't end up like me."

"You had friends. You were happy."

"And look at me now!"

Mom rubs her forehead. "A lot of this was your doing, sweetheart."

As though Keith wasn't an active participant in the whole thing. I should've been more careful. I should've never asked him to give up a career in football, money, or his freedom because I got pregnant. If I had understood what he needed, I could be married and raising a child, but I didn't do that.

Me, me, me. It's always me. Women don't exactly make a baby on their own, but we're sure expected to deal with the consequences.

"Right, Mom. All my fault."

"Yes, Teagan, I think some of it was your fault. You had a baby, but then you could've had a life. You made Keith sign away his rights, and that left you here—in this town you despise so much. You made your bed, so to speak, now you choose to lie in it."

Her thoughts on all of this will never change as long as I continue to keep the truth of what happened to myself. I could make all this stop, but to protect Chastity, I keep my mouth shut. The worst part is that I can't fight back too hard, because if she ever wants us out, I'm screwed. I can't afford to lose my job or my home.

"I wish I didn't disappoint you so much, Mom. I really do. I'm trying, and maybe someday you'll see things differently and see the woman I'm raising, even if she doesn't fit into your mold."

"I'm not saying that." She tries to soften her tone. "I want Chastity to have a life outside of books and animals as well. She needs real people who converse back with her. I want her to have love like I have with your father. She could be happy living here, just like I am. I want her to have more."

No matter what my mom thinks of me, she loves Chastity. She's her first, and probably only, grandchild and she's nothing like me or even her. My mother was the homecoming queen, captain of everything, and ruled the school. She met my father, they married, and lived the small-town life. It fit for her. She's truly happy with her life, but she doesn't understand that people—that Chastity and I—might want more.

"She has us."

My mother nods. "She does."

"Believe me, Mom, that girl is going to do big things. We just have to let her find her way."

She smiles, touches my arm. "I believe you, honey. It's my job to worry, you understand that?"

There is a part of me that gets it. I worry constantly about Chastity. I worry I'm not giving her enough, loving her as much as I should, or that I'm not able to provide the opportunities she needs.

Could my mother be right? Maybe by not pushing her to be social I'm screwing her up. God, I hope not.

"I do understand. Does the pit in my stomach ever go away?"

Mom shakes her head. "Never. I worry about you all the time too. I worry you won't find someone and all I want is to see you happily married to someone who will help take care of you."

"I don't need anyone to take care of me." My voice sounds much stronger than I feel. I may not need it, but it would be nice.

Mom sighs, turns her head with a frustrated sigh. "We all need someone, Teagan. Love is the most basic need. I had hoped...I thought maybe Keith and you would be forever, like your father and I were."

"Keith was never my forever," I say with defiance.

I always knew this. I never wanted to live the rest of my life with him. I loved him, but he never *got* me. Keith wanted a girl who would be his constant cheerleader, not someone who wanted a career or had goals outside of him.

I wanted Derek to be my forever.

"Yes, but as a professional football player, he could've at least given you a nice life."

"One filled with regrets and probably a few mistresses."

She lifts her shoulders and then drops them. "Regrets are better than loneliness and solitude. Surely, you could've found someone else by now."

I huff. "I don't want to talk about my dating life."

"Well, it would be hard to, since you don't have one! When is the last time you went out with anyone? Two years? More? If you at least became a nun I could understand it."

"What's the point? The tourists are here for a week tops, the local people are...well, not my type, and what do I have to offer, Mom? What part of my life screams: date me?"

She tilts her head to the side with a sad smile. "You were pretty in high school."

"Were?"

"You still are. If you put some more effort in, it might help."

My jaw drops open. "Gee, Mom. You're really a great ego boost."

"You know I think you're beautiful. Everyone says you look like me."

I'm glad for a break in the conversation. I can handle this version of my mom. "Yes, we could be twins."

Mom lifts her shoulder and turns her head with a smirk. "I mean...we have gorgeous hair."

I laugh and sway my head side to side, allowing the blond locks to have that authentic beach wave. "That's totally going to be what wins them over. Our hair is every man's dream."

Mom moves closer, pulling me into her arms. "I love you, darling. No matter what you think. I know I'm hard on you"—she leans back, and her voice softens—"but it's only because I want better for you than what you have right now."

I fight back the emotion bubbling up in my chest. "I'm really okay."

"Promise?"

"Promise." I lie because it's easier than telling her the truth. She won't understand that nothing in my life, other than Chastity, is okay.

I'm falling, and it feels like nothing will stop the descent at this point. I just don't know how badly I'll be broken once I reach the bottom.

* * *

"How was school today?" I ask Chastity as we sit at the table for dinner.

This is the one tradition from my childhood that I will always keep. As a kid, I hated it, but as a mother, I get it. No matter what we have going on in our lives, we always sit down and have dinner together.

"It was...fine."

Totally not buying it. "Just fine?"

She shovels food in her mouth, probably trying to keep me from asking her more, but she should really know better.

"Chas?"

Her eyes lift and then she shoves more food in. "I hate that nickname."

Okay, it's going to be like that.

The one thing I've worked extremely hard at is our relationship. I try not to keep things from her, and tried to emulate being both a friend and a mother at the same time. She's always been an open book, so this is strange for her to hold back.

"Would you rather I shorten it to Titty?"

She snorts. "If I had any that would be better."

I fight back the smile and wait for her to laugh, but I get nothing. "What has you so angry?"

"Nothing."

Right, this glowing new version of herself is clearly a product of nothing.

"I'm going to keep asking," I warn her. "I have no boundaries."

"Oh, I *know*."

"So, you should probably spill it."

"There's nothing to say, people are stupid." Chastity pushes the food around on her plate. "I hate people."

"We know that's true. Is it a boy?"

She drops her fork and glares at me. "Really, Mom?"

"What?" I raise my hands in surrender. "Most of the time, when a girl is this…*fine*…it's usually about a boy. They're kind of dumb, you know?"

I can't make out what she says under her breath but I swear it was something about mothers are too.

"It's not a boy."

"Is it your teachers?"

Chastity is often frustrated by them, since she's pretty advanced. She's in the gifted program and still she's bored. It's one of the things I despise about living in a town with very few kids, a lack of options—and funding.

"No, Mom, stop. I'm fine. I just…I had a bad day and I *really* hate people."

I can understand that sentiment.

"Hopefully tomorrow is a better day."

She huffs and starts eating again.

I start to eat my meat loaf and a few moments pass before Chastity slams her fork down. "You know what I hate? Girls. They're so mean."

And here we have it. "What happened?"

"She thinks she's so perfect and pretty. She's not. She's not perfect!"

Chastity has never fit in. No matter how many play-dates I set up or sports I tried to get her to try, she never enjoyed it. Instead of makeup, she'd rather study the ingredients of makeup to let me know all the hazardous things inside of them. When I tried to get her to do cheer-leading, we quickly learned that clapping and doing any other motion at the same time was not her strong suit.

I've always described her as an old soul. She doesn't

understand why things fascinate the kids her age. She wants to talk about politics, animal rights, and spend her time learning instead of gossiping.

Her hand taps on the table, reminding me I haven't asked her who she's talking about.

"Who?"

"The new girl."

Someone new? How did anyone move into this town without a bulletin going out? "We didn't have anyone new move in."

Her eyes narrow. "Yes we did, and the mean girl is in my class."

"Who?"

Chastity ignores my question and starts a rant like I've never seen from her. "I offered to let her sit at my lunch table and she laughed and said she'd rather not be a loser on day one. Do you believe that? How would she even know that? Why am I a loser, because I'm *nice*?"

Now it's my turn to feel an extreme amount of guilt. Many moons ago, I would've said something like that to Nina if she had offered for me to sit with her. In fact, I probably did.

I was the mean girl or at least friends with them all. So many times I would say things because I had to. It was better to fit in with them than be on the outside. I regret it.

My heart breaks a little that my daughter is on the receiving end. "You're not a loser."

"I know that. And I'd rather be a loser than a horrible mean girl. I'm so tired of them acting like they own the school, prancing around with their perfect hair and perfect makeup. I hate them! Someone needs to tell them that they're not going to be popular forever."

"Most mean girls only act mean because they're afraid to let other people see their flaws."

Chastity knows the stories of my...reign. "You can't defend her, Mom. After lunch, she was telling people how I tried to get her into my cult. Cult! Then—" Chastity pauses, and I nod to encourage her. "I don't want to say it."

"Why?"

She traces the wood grain in the table and I keep quiet. She does this when she's mulling over something uncomfortable. I used to push, but I realize how the introspective moment helps her focus and handle the excess of emotion.

"Because it's about you."

Like I haven't heard it all? "Believe me, sweetheart." I wait for her to look up. "There's nothing that can be said that will hurt me."

"She said at least her mom didn't have to trick her dad to have a baby."

This town needs a damn hobby. I don't know why Teagan bashing is still the cool thing.

"And you said she's new?"

"Yeah, they just moved here yesterday and she started school today."

"I guess my mistakes of the past precede me even for out-of-towners. Not that you're a mistake," I tack on. "You know people like to make up their own versions of the truth."

She groans. "This is why I didn't want to tell you!"

"I'm not upset, Chas. I hate that it's affecting you, that's all."

I couldn't care less about what people think of me anymore. I sleep just fine at night with how things happened with Keith. There was no tricking or missed birth control. I didn't drug him and screw his brains out while he was unconscious. That happens to be one of my favorite stories, though. I weigh 110 pounds soaking wet, and he's over 250 pounds. If someone actually believes I could maneuver his dead weight, arouse him to the point of having sex, and impregnate myself, they have bigger problems than I do.

"Why are you smiling?"

"Oh, I'm reminding myself of all the rumors I've heard."

Chastity shakes her head. "Why can't these people get over it?"

"My sentiments exactly."

"This is why I like animals. They're not stupid."

Sounds like someone I used to know and be best friends with.

I release a sigh, knowing that animals are for her what painting is for me. "And why I paint, because it's not stupid."

"You paint because you say it calms you," she says with a shrug.

It does calm me. I started painting after Chastity was born. I never really considered myself artistic, but Nina made me go to some wine-and-paint thing and I kind of liked it. Now, it's what I do when I feel like the walls are closing in.

"Doesn't working with animals do the same for you?"

"Yes, and I do it because people are horrible and animals love you no matter what."

"I can't argue with you there, but at the same time, you can't defend me or worry about what people will say. Unfortunately, the man who gave me you is famous. He's never going to fade away, and whether your father starts to suck at football or wins the Super Bowl, we'll have to hear about it. I wish I could change things, but I can't. You can't. We have to suck it up."

"I hate sucking it up."

I nod. "Me too. So..." I grab my fork. "What's this new girl's name?"

Chastity leans back in her chair and crosses her arms. "Everly Hartz. As in Dr. Hartz's granddaughter, so I can't even avoid her in my happy place."

And suddenly, I feel like I'm going to be sick.

chapter three

Teagan

fifteen years old

"I need two volunteers for peer tutoring," Mrs. Mathewson asks the class.

I really don't want to do it. Between cheerleading, Keith, and my own homework, I don't have any extra time. Then I remember how much I need more volunteering on my transcripts. Getting into college should not be this hard.

"Anyone?" she asks again.

Then her eyes meet mine, and the look says it all. I'm being voluntold. "Fine, Mrs. Mathewson, I'll do it," I say with reluctance.

Just one more thing on my plate.

Keith laughs and elbows one of his idiot friends. "She won't do my homework for me, but she'll help someone else."

"Come on, Tea, you should help your man out."

I roll my eyes. "I help him out plenty."

Keith nods. "Yeah, you do, babe."

"Thank you, Ms. Berkeley. Your student will be waiting for you today."

She hands me a paper and I could cry. The peer tutoring happens during my study hall, but maybe I can still use some of the block for getting my own work done.

The bell rings and I head to the cafeteria, where during class hours it's meant to look cozy for studying. It doesn't. It looks—and smells—like the cafeteria.

Keith tosses his arm over my shoulder. "You coming over tonight?"

"Maybe."

"I miss you."

I let out a small giggle. "You can't miss me if you're with me right now."

He stops, pulling me into his arms. "You know what I mean."

And I do. He means he wants to fool around again. I've been trying to come up with reasons as to why I don't really want to do it, but Keith is relentless.

Keith's the most popular boy in school and a god on the football field. He's funny, can be nice when he wants something, and everyone loves him.

The whole town basically falls at his feet.

And he expects my panties to do the same.

"I'm not ready for more, Keith."

"I didn't say we have to have sex, Tea. But you can at least give me a blow job before the big game."

"Oh, I can?" I say as I push against his chest.

"Look, it helps me relax. After the last time I threw the most touchdown passes I've ever had in a game. I think that's because of you."

A small part of me likes to think I had something to

do with it, but then I remember he only wants what he wants.

"Well, since I'm all about statistics," I say with a coy smile. "How about we test that theory?"

He nods, thinking he's got me. "Hell, yeah."

I run my fingers around the captain patch on his chest. "Tonight, you don't get one, and if you outdo your last passing yards, we'll really know." Before he can respond, I lean up and kiss his lips, drop back down, and run off. "Good luck!"

"You're so cold, Teagan!" he yells after me, but I'm already down the hall.

When I turn the corner, I run smack into Nina Banks. My books fall to the ground, papers go flying. "Ugh!" I groan. "Watch where you're going!"

"Sorry," Nina says, bending down, trying to help me. "I didn't see you."

"Obviously."

"Look, I said I was sorry," she says and her lip trembles.

I didn't mean to make her cry. Damn it. "I was in a rush—" I start to explain that I was in a hurry and didn't mean to snap, when two pairs of shoes appear on either side of me.

I look up and see my two best friends, Lori and Kelly, standing there, glowering at Nina.

This is so not going to be good.

"Did Stanks knock you down?" Lori asks, using the horrible name they've given her to let her know how much she smells.

"No, I turned the corner and lost my footing. Nina was helping me pick up my stuff."

I've known Kelly and Lori my whole life, and they can be cruel beyond belief. However, the three of us do everything together and it's been that way since we were in kindergarten.

"Still," Kelly huffs, picking at her nails. "She should... shower...or something."

I look at Nina, who is clearly on the verge of tears. I want to say something, tell them to stop, but I don't. I never do. I hate myself for it. I don't want to be this way, unwilling to speak up for those who can't, but I don't want to be on the other side of their friend-card either.

A year ago, Lauren Evans was our fourth best friend. She was by far the nicest one of all of us. Whenever Kelly and Lori got mean, Lauren would never join in and was always uncomfortable around them. Then, she decided she didn't want to do cheerleading anymore, and she was booted from the group because she was "too busy" for us. You would think that Lori and Kelly would want her to be happy, but they don't. In fact, they make fun of her more than anyone else in the school. Lauren can't fight back either because they know some of her secrets. Which makes me terrified to be like her, because they know *all* of mine.

The bell rings and I jump up. "Shit! We have to go. Thanks for helping, Nina."

Kelly and Lori scoff. "Shower, Stanks."

"Guys," I say with frustration. "She didn't do anything."

"She exists."

"And she's gross," Lori tacks on.

There's no stopping them, and if I push back, it'll make it worse for Nina.

"We'll see you after school?" Kelly questions.

"Yup! See you later."

I rush off and enter the cafeteria before the bell rings. I head over to the teacher who is stuck chaperoning the group and he points out the table where my peer student is.

Derek Hartz? Really? It has to be the one kid who seems to think I'm the biggest bitch?

"Hey," I say as I sit.

"Oh, come on. *You*?"

"I'm not any happier about this than you are," I assure him.

Derek is…odd. When we were younger, it was fine, but he never changed. He still wears out-of-style clothes and never talks to anyone.

"I just need help with a few math problems."

"Okay. Show me where you're stuck."

We go over them, and I show him a few tricks I've learned when it comes to equations. The next twenty minutes fly by as he starts to master the steps a little more.

We chat a little about his father and the wild horses that he found wounded on the island. I can't imagine seeing them hurt. They always seem so mystical to me whenever we do see them.

"They're cool," he says. "I like the fact that they're wild, but the more people who come around, the less the horses will be willing to show up."

"Really? I feel like this island was built for the wild horses."

"I agree, I'm hoping more land gets preserved to protect them."

I nod. "Me too." We both sit here, looking at each other and I wonder why I've thought he was so weird. He's not. He's actually pretty normal and funny. I'm having an off day if I'm thinking of Derek Hartz this way. I need to get back to the math so I can get my head on straight. "Okay, let's try this problem."

I laugh when he gets frustrated because it's the same part I've shown him twice, but he keeps trying.

"What if you try it like this?" I spin the paper around and show him how to draw it out. "Does that help?"

"That actually does."

I smile. "Good. I'm glad. It's really easy once you get the right order. Is there anything else I can help with?"

"You know, when you're not around the two super-bitches, you're not all that bad."

"What?"

Derek shrugs. "Bitch one and Bitch two. You know, the ones who seem to think they're perfection walking."

"Lori and Kelly aren't bad."

His brow raises. "They're beyond bad, and you know it."

Okay, maybe I do. "Still, they're my friends."

"Lucky you." He chuckles.

"Next you're going to insult my boyfriend, huh?"

Derek laughs, his head falling back, and I can't help but think how free he looks. I don't laugh like that. I can't let it fly and not worry that someone might see me. I don't ever feel comfortable enough around people to not have to keep some sort of control because people are always waiting to see me fall.

Other girls want it more than anything. To see the queen bee fall from grace.

The guys want it to either date me or take something away from Keith.

If I could be invisible or part of the background, no one would care.

I glance around the room, looking at everyone going about their lives, not watching him, and jealousy rears its ugly head.

"I could never insult Keith. He's...a god amongst men. I would be shunned, hung in the town square, beaten for speaking out against the king."

"Just a little dramatic?"

"That's what this town thinks."

I lean back in my seat. "And you don't?"

"Hell no. He's a dickhead. Who cares that he's great in football? Not me."

"Well, a lot of people do," I challenge him.

"Good for them. I'd be impressed if he used his time to do anything good for anyone but himself."

"And what do you do, since you're all about putting everyone else down? I don't see you out there saving the world."

Derek leans forward, arms on the table, his face is closer, and I wonder if he knows that he's really cute. His eyes are a deep blue. They have tiny flecks of green, though. His hair is cut short, and his smile is warm. *Did I seriously just think he was cute?*

"That's because you're not looking. I help people, animals, and I use my time to better the world. I don't care that people, like you and your idiot friends, think I'm weird. I'd rather be weird and make a difference than fit in and believe I'm better than anyone else. Because you're not...and neither are your friends."

The words slap me in the face. "I don't think I'm better than anyone."

If he only knew what I really thought of myself. How much I hate everything. I don't understand why people talk to me when I feel so unworthy. I hate that I have to treat people a certain way or I'll end up being attacked by people meant to be my friends. All I want is to get out of this town and start over.

"Then prove it. Come to my house tomorrow and help volunteer."

"With you?"

"Got other plans?"

No, but...I don't get why he's asking me. We're not friends. Hell, I don't even think he likes me at all. There's a challenge though. I say I want to start over, be someone else, and right now Derek Hartz is offering me a small opening.

"Do you want me to come?"

"Do you want to?"

I might beat him with a stick though. Maybe this isn't the fresh start I was hoping for. "Are you trying to be obtuse on purpose?"

"Do you always answer a question with a question?"

I chew on my thumbnail and glare at him as I wrestle with the decision. I never back down, but at the same time, Derek isn't exactly the kind of person I would normally hang out with. Although, this is volunteering and not really a social thing.

Ugh. Why is this so hard?

He taps his fingers on the table and I sigh. "Fine. I'll be there."

He smirks. "Good, but don't think this means we're

friends or that I'm going to want to talk to you outside of helping others."

Now it's my turn to laugh. "Don't you know, everyone ends up loving me."

"Yeah, we'll see about that."

chapter four

Teagan

present

"What do you mean Derek is back?" Nina asks as she sips her coffee.

"Just what I said. I don't know when or how. Last night, Chastity said a girl named Everly Hartz was giving her a hard time. Derek is an only child, and his mother has mentioned her granddaughter with that name in passing, so it would only make sense that he's here."

"And you didn't hear from him?"

If I did, I wouldn't be freaking out right now. "Nope. Do you think maybe it's just his daughter that's here? Like, maybe she came to live with his parents or visit for a while?"

She shrugs. "I don't know, I haven't heard a word about him in years. I know his parents went down to South Carolina for a visit recently, but that's all anyone has said. You know how they are, very quiet and don't like the rumor mill, which means we know nothing."

Nina has her ears to the ground for all the gossip. If she

knew, she'd tell me. She's also the only person who knows
I was desperately in love with him. To everyone else, we
were simply best friends. Two crazy kids who clicked one
day and never looked back.

I fell in love with him before the end of our senior year,
and it never stopped. Just the idea of being near him makes
my heart pound so hard in my chest I worry I'll bruise.

"I can't see him," I say as I pace around.

"You won't have a choice if he's really here."

My shoulders drop as I turn to look at her.

"What?" She raises her hands. "I'm just being honest,
Tea."

I know this, but still. "I'm saying that I can't handle it.
It's been over thirteen years since we've spoken and the
last time wasn't pretty."

Nina touches my arm. "You think after all this time it'll
still be awkward?"

I don't think it'll be awkward. I know it will be. If he
wasn't angry or hurt, he would've called or talked to me.
Instead of pretending I no longer existed. It's not easy to
forget your best friend.

"Yes."

"Why? It's been so long, maybe it'll be like falling into
an old routine."

"You can't just…walk up to someone after that long…
someone you loved more than anything and have it not be
awkward."

Nina sits in the chair beside me. "He doesn't know you
loved him."

"Which makes it even worse."

"Look, you don't know that seeing him will be bad. It
could be fine and you'll smile, hug, and that's that. Thir-

teen years is a lifetime to most people and it's not like you still think about him that way, right?"

I look up at her from under my lashes.

"Teagan." She sighs. "You can't possibly still think you have real feelings for that man."

That's the thing, my feelings for him have never faded. I've never dated any guy who I haven't compared to him and who doesn't pale in comparison. It's always been Derek in my heart.

"If he's here with Meghan, I really won't be able to handle it," I tell her. "I'll have to move."

It's been one thing to lose him to her. I've sort of come to grips with that and I think it's because I don't ever have to see them. There's no running into each other at the store or having to watch them walk down the street like the perfect couple.

"Yes, you will be able to handle it," she says with conviction. "You're not the same girl you were back then."

The phone rings and I groan. "I swear, someone has to explain what an antique store is to Mrs. Dickman."

I grab the receiver and brace myself for the same conversation that happens every single day.

"Island Antiques, this is Teagan."

"Hello, Teagan, this is Mr. Beeson from the middle school."

"Oh, yes. Hi, Mr. Beeson, is everything okay?"

He takes a small pause. "I'm going to need you to come down to the school and pick up Chastity."

"Okay? What happened?"

"There was an incident with another student and I'm afraid the school has very strict policies regarding bullying."

My poor daughter. This kid doesn't deserve to be picked on by anyone. She has never gotten in any trouble, and I can only imagine how much this upsets her since she prides herself on having a perfect record.

"Did she come to you about it?" And then it dawns on me that they want me to pick her up. "Why would I have to get her? Is she hurt?"

"No, she's okay, just come down here and we can sort everything out."

"Okay, I'll be right there."

I hang up the phone and tell Nina what he said.

She clutches her chest. "Poor thing, I'll stay here until you get back."

"Thank you! I'm sure my mother will stop by. Let her know I had to get Chas."

"Just go!" She shoos me out the door.

On the ride to the school, I go over a million scenarios. Did someone make her cry? Did they hurt her? I wish I could go back in time and slap myself for the way I treated others or stood by and watched when my so-called friends bullied anyone they didn't deem worthy. I was as culpable as they were. Now my daughter is on the receiving end of other people's cruelty and I can't help but feel this is some sort of karma.

I park the car and go inside to find her sitting in the office.

"Chastity," I say her name and she leaps up, running toward me. Her arms wrap around my middle and I hold her close. "Don't let them see you cry."

She looks at me, nodding her head in understanding.

There's nothing that vile people thrive on more than the pain of others.

"Ms. Berkeley," Mr. Beeson calls my name. "Please, come in. We'll ask you to join us in a few moments, Chastity."

I touch her cheek, leaving her in the front office as I walk down the long hall with Mr. Beeson.

"As I said on the phone, we take bullying very seriously here."

"Yes, I hope that whoever was harassing my daughter will be punished," I say as we move toward his office.

"I think you're misunderstanding." Mr. Beeson touches my arm, stopping me from going forward.

"I'm sorry?"

"It wasn't Chastity who was being bullied, Teagan."

No. That makes no sense.

"You're confused," I say with a short laugh. "My daughter is the farthest thing from a bully. She's kind even when people have been horrible to her. She's dealt with constant ridicule her entire life thanks to this town and now you're trying to tell me that she was the one bullying someone?"

Of all the ridiculous things I've ever heard, this tops the cake.

"I wish I could say it wasn't the case. Chastity has always been a model student, but I saw this with my own eyes."

"Mr. Beeson, you've known me my whole life. You've known Chastity since she was an infant. Do you really mean to tell me that you saw her being cruel? Isn't there a chance that maybe you saw something else?"

I babysat Mr. Beeson's youngest daughter. I've sat next to him at church every week since I was eight. Probably because my mother thought maybe I would behave if I thought my principal was watching. He knows us. He knows the hell I've been through and he has seen my sweet girl never hurt a fly.

"Chastity has admitted to it all."

My jaw falls slack as I clutch my throat. This can't be. I truly don't believe it. "Well…"

"Let's go in my office, we can talk about it further there."

I'm in shock. That's the only way to describe it. I've fought so hard to teach her how to be nothing like me and now she's bullying someone. My heart is breaking and I feel even more like a failure.

Mr. Beeson opens the door and someone gets to their feet. Nothing could've prepared me for this.

No number of pep talks or knowing this was possible would've been enough.

Time stops. My heart races and everything inside of me is tight.

There, standing, looking out of the window in a pair of dress pants, a crisp white button-down, and an opened tie is a man I haven't seen in forever. A man who I can still feel beneath my fingertips if I try hard enough. A man who knew me better than I knew myself and the only man I've ever truly loved.

My lips part as the name I've tried to keep off my tongue slides out. "Derek."

chapter five

Derek

present

I should've known it would be her daughter.

This was the moment I was dreading when I decided to move back here. I knew that we'd have to see each other eventually. In this town, avoidance is damn near impossible and it's part of why I didn't come back here sooner. I fought as hard as I could to stay in South Carolina. This place holds too many memories for me. Too much pain and now I have to come face-to-face with it.

Teagan stands there, unable to mask her emotions, and even though so much time has passed, I can still read her. She's confused, happy, angry, sad, and there's a hint of disappointment under it all.

I cut ties with her years ago because it was the only option. Now, I'm face-to-face with her all over again.

Time has done nothing to dull how beautiful Teagan is. She stands there, her eyes full of confusion and apprehension, and yet, she's breathtaking.

Teagan.

God help me to keep my distance from her.

"I really hoped it wouldn't be you," I say as she stays quiet. The hurt flashes in her eyes and I realize how what I said might sound to her. "I mean that it wouldn't be you as the parent of the child who was harassing Everly."

"Right. Not that Everly didn't possibly start it, right? Because I was a shitty kid, I must've given birth to a shitty kid."

"Everly has never had issues before."

"And neither has Chastity."

Mr. Beeson explained as much, but yet here we are. Her daughter is harassing mine when she's been through hell.

"My point is," I continue, "this is the last thing that she needs. With losing all she has, we really hoped that this would be a safe place for her."

Teagan runs her fingers through her long blond hair and sits in the chair. "I don't know what you're talking about, but we've lived here forever and not once has Chastity ever been in any trouble. She's kind, honest, hardworking…in fact, she works with your dad."

"I heard."

My father sang the girl's praises for an hour over the phone. He said how she's the polar opposite of Teagan as a kid. And yet, here I am because on day two in the new school, she's harassing my daughter.

"I'm sorry, but this is crazy, Mr. Beeson. Again, Chastity isn't a bully. In fact, she said yesterday that she was being bullied by Everly. So, what now? Why is she the only one in trouble?"

The sad part is, I don't doubt that Everly was bullying Teagan's daughter. She's the opposite of me as a kid, but not so different from her mother. Meghan was popular, beautiful, smart, and adored—like Teagan.

Mr. Beeson takes his seat and motions for both of us to sit, but I remain on my feet. "It seems that while you two may have been friends a million moons ago, they haven't taken to each other quite yet. Chastity did explain that Everly was making fun of her for…her parentage. I only heard Chastity's rebuttal."

"Just like us," I say with a huff. "We didn't like each other in the beginning." Flashes of the past fill my head. The way Teagan and I could barely speak to each other…seems our children are following in our footsteps.

"So." Teagan crosses her arms over her chest, leaning back in the chair, clearly ignoring my comment. "We're going to punish Chastity for defending herself? I thought you were always an advocate of standing up for yourself."

"Why don't you hear what your perfect daughter said to mine, and then maybe your tone will change?"

There are lines that no one should ever cross. Whether Everly started it or not, there are only so many things my kid can handle, and this isn't one.

Teagan glares at me. "Why don't we hear the entire story, Derek?"

"Sure." I mimic her posture, only standing.

"Okay," Mr. Beeson says while clearing his throat. "According to Chastity, she was at lunch and Everly started making fun of her regarding you." He looks at Teagan.

"Her?" I ask.

He nods in response. "Yes, I'm paraphrasing here, but she said something about…at least not having a slut for a mother who couldn't even trap her boyfriend right. Something about her not being smart enough."

Teagan gasps and my stomach drops. "How…where… where would she even have heard something like that?" I ask.

This is crazy. Everly doesn't know anything about Teagan.

"Probably from her father," Teagan suggests.

"I've never said anything negative about you. I sure as hell wouldn't say anything like that!"

The fact that she thinks I'm even capable of thinking that way is ridiculous. I was there. I saw how that entire pregnancy went down. There was no trapping. Hell, she didn't even fucking like Keith by the time she was pregnant. I still think there's more to that story than she ever let on. Our friendship ended for other reasons, but I never would've said anything about her like that.

"It seems she learned it somewhere," Teagan says while shaking her head.

"Regardless of what Everly said, which I will definitely deal with, that didn't give your daughter the right to say what she did."

"What did Chastity say?"

I brace myself to contain my anger. Everly doesn't deserve to be put through any more pain—she's had enough of that in the last six months. I have to control myself and remember these are kids.

Mr. Beeson shifts, looking uncomfortable. "Chastity said her mother may be all those things, but at least she didn't have to die to get away from her."

Hearing it again is no better.

Teagan gets to her feet. "I don't…I don't understand."

Her eyes meet mine, filled with confusion. "Die? Meghan is dead?"

I don't know how she could possibly have not heard. This town hasn't changed in twenty years, and everyone talks. "You mean to tell me you didn't hear? I had at least four people stop me on my way into school, not to mention the five who brought food to my mother's since we arrived."

Her lips part and she keeps shaking her head in quick movements. "I didn't know…I swear."

Teagan's hand covers her mouth and tears form in her eyes. She didn't like Meghan, and Meghan sure as hell hated Teagan. No matter what the two of them tried to feed me in the beginning. But seeing this girl, who I once loved more than anything, grieving over the woman who destroyed that love, makes the emotions I've smothered come back to life.

My heart aches, my chest tightens, and I suddenly, for the first time since Meghan's death, want someone to comfort me.

Of course it would be Teagan that is my undoing.

"How? Why didn't you call me? God, why didn't anyone tell me? I would've come, Derek. I would've, even though we…I would've been there."

When the tear falls down her cheek, I break.

For the first time in six months, it all hits me.

chapter six

Teagan

nineteen years old

"I met someone," Derek says as we're sitting at our monthly dinner.

I try so hard to look happy but I hate it. "You met someone?"

"Yeah, she's great. I met her in my econ class."

"Well, that's great, Der." I pop a fry into my mouth to keep from scowling.

It's not great. I hate her and I don't even know her name. Regardless, she's not good enough for him. He's the best and he doesn't even see it.

Gone is the goofy kid who I couldn't even imagine ever kissing two years ago. Now stands a very, very attractive man. He's filled out in all the right places, found the gym, and he's still the same sweet Derek I love.

Love.

God, I'm so stupid. I have to try to get this under control because loving him is the dumbest thing I could do…but yet I do.

I love him so much it hurts. Every month I have to remind myself that he's my best friend, not some guy to lust over.

Plus, he doesn't see me that way. He never has.

"I think I'm in love with her."

My drink goes flying out of my mouth.

"Jesus, Teagan!" he complains as he wipes his face.

"Sorry, but love? How long have you guys been together?"

He sets the napkin down. "Six months."

"Six months?" I shout. "And you're just telling me now?"

What the fuck? I tell him everything and he's keeping things from me like this?

"Calm down, I know how well you react to…new people."

I roll my eyes. "No, I just don't like the girls you bring around."

"Yeah, because the dickhead you've been with for the last four years is a fucking winner."

"We're not talking about Keith. Besides, we both know how I really feel about him."

Now it's Derek's turn to be irritated. "But you won't dump him?"

Because then I wouldn't have an excuse as to why I can't be with you.

I don't say it because I'm ridiculous. Derek and I are best friends. He's the man I know one day I'll be with, but right now, I can't until I get my life straight. I'll be ready to admit the truth, just…I need more time.

Keith is comfortable, and he doesn't expect anything from me other than to be at his games, which I have to be anyway, thanks to my cheerleading scholarship. Then there's the fact that Keith is safe. He's not a bad guy, he's just the guy. Derek goes to school two hours from here whereas Keith is at the same school as me. It's nice having someone close. I don't feel so lonely all the time.

"I know it doesn't make sense to you, but it works for us. You're not around, and he is."

"You need to stop being so dependent on him. It's okay to be alone."

"Says the serial boyfriend?"

Dating someone new has never been a big deal before. He usually lasts about two months with a girl before he realizes she's not for him, they break up, things go back to normal, and I rest easy again. He's never dated anyone longer than four months. Until now.

Derek leans back, watching me with curious intent. "Why are you upset anyway?"

Because I don't want you to be serious with anyone.

Because it's you I see in my future.

Because you should love me.

"I'm not. I'm hurt. You should've told me. We talk all the time and have dinner once a month. You've forgotten to tell me about the new girl or you didn't want to tell me?"

He crosses his arms and releases a heavy sigh. "I knew you'd act like this."

"Like what?"

"This! Like I've done some horrible thing and betrayed you. I really like Meghan. I love her, Teagan. And as my best friend…" He may be saying it as though I'm important, but right now, I hear the words as much more. He's reminding me of my place in his heart. I'm only the friend and I'd do well to remember it. "I would think you'd be happy for me."

I close my eyes, shoving down my feelings for him and focus on how many times he's been there for me. How many nights he held me when Keith said something mean or I've gone back and forth about leaving him.

Countless shirts I've soaked over stupid things with my family or friends and Derek has always been there. He has always been my rock, and I'm being selfish.

Slowly, I lift my gaze to his. "I am happy for you, if you're happy. I was just taken by surprise, that's all."

"You'd really like her, Tea."

I doubt that.

"If she likes you, she clearly has good taste," I say with a smile.

Derek laughs. "Yeah, I'm such a catch. I don't know how the hell I convinced her to date me. She's beautiful, funny, smart…a lot like you."

My chest constricts. "So, she's amazing?" I try to joke it off.

"She could be the one."

So could I, if I wasn't so afraid to tell you and hope you felt the same.

chapter seven

Teagan

present

"I'll give you two a moment," Mr. Beeson says as he walks out.

Derek turns his back, hiding the pain so clear in his eyes. "Derek." I call his name, but he doesn't move. "I'm so sorry."

He shifts, his head shaking before lifting toward the ceiling. "Don't say shit you don't mean. We all know how you felt about Meghan."

"That's not fair."

"No, none of it is fair," he agrees, but not about the same thing.

I didn't love Meghan or even like her, but I would never wish her dead.

I move closer to him, not sure what to do. If this was back in the day, I would wrap my arms around him, clutch him until he cried it out. I would know exactly what to say or do because he was the other half of my brain.

This man, I don't know.

So, I go with the truth.

"I have a million things I want to say, but all of them sound stupid in my own head. It's been so long and we've both changed. I am sorry, though."

Derek turns to face me. "It's been—hard. Everything is hard. I shouldn't have snapped at you."

"I understand anger."

More than most people. That's typically the emotion I feel most attached to. It's easy to be angry. To look at the world around me, wishing I had a better job, money, a house, a man who didn't fuck me over, so being angry just feels good. It's better than self-pity or sadness. Anger is intense and so much easier to hang on to.

"Yeah, I would assume you do."

I was angry for a long time after Keith threatened me and I felt it was the best choice to let him off the hook. I took it out on everyone, including Derek.

"I know you don't believe this, but Chastity...she's truly the kindest person. She's nothing like me as a kid, and I don't even understand what could've gotten into her to say something so cruel. But know that I will not accept that behavior from her."

"I appreciate that, but it doesn't surprise me that Everly said anything to provoke it, if I'm being honest."

I didn't expect that, and then I think about what she must be going through. Losing her mother, moving to this tiny-ass town where she knows no one. I would be pissed off at the world and everyone around me.

"Regardless..."

"Yeah, regardless..."

There is so much I want to say, ask, and hold on to. As much as I was upset, the truth is, I've missed him. He was more than just the man I loved, he was my everything. He knew all my truths and lies. Derek was a part of my soul and when I lost him, he took it with him.

My eyes study him. He's so different and yet the same. His hair is a little longer and has a hint of gray, but his eyes are kind and make my heart stutter. There's a warmth under all of that hurt. I wonder if he can still see through me? Can he see that I've missed him? Does he know how many times I've wanted to call? Does he know how many times I've wanted him to call me?

Does he see that I love him? Not only as someone I've always loved but also for who he is at his core or at least who he was.

I open my mouth to say something but Mr. Beeson enters. "Have you two talked?"

Derek nods. "I think we can handle this without the school intervening. Everly was wrong to say what she did, and I'd like to give the girls the opportunity to work it out. Especially since I'm staying here permanently."

Permanently? I'll never be able to avoid him. I'll have no choice but to become a damn hermit if I want to survive.

It's clear that too much time has passed and we'll never be friends again. Besides, how can I be friends with him when everything I'd ever felt for him is clearly very much alive?

"Are you sure?" Mr. Beeson asks. We both nod.

His lips turn to a flat smile. "I think that's the best idea. Everly and Chastity will need to figure out a way to co-exist and I'd like to not have the rest of the student body feel the need to involve themselves. Besides"—Mr. Beeson looks to both of us—"if they're anything like their parents, they might need a little push to be great friends."

"Well, friendships change," Derek says, his eyes filling with regret.

"Yeah." I sigh. "And sometimes they're never what we thought."

* * *

"Teagan, are you okay?" Nina asks as I sit on her couch, drinking a glass of wine.

"Huh?"

"You're off in another world."

I have been since I got home. Chastity is now grounded, which honestly isn't much of a punishment at all. She'll beat herself up about what she said enough without me having to do anything.

We'd talked about kindness in the face of cruelty although the other side of me, the mama-bear side, is proud of her. She stood up for herself.

Still, she hadn't exactly acted like the child I raised her to be.

"I'm just...processing."

"It was a lot today, huh?"

I look at Nina. "Can I ask you something?"

"Of course."

"Do you forgive me? I mean really forgive me for how I treated you in high school?"

Nina places her glass down. "Why would you ask that?"

Because I was a wretched bitch and I hate myself for it. I wish I could go back in time, change how I was and what I thought was acceptable behavior. There's no excuse and if I were her, I would never be nice to me. Let alone be friends with me.

"We both know I wasn't a good person."

"You weren't a bad person either. You were just around people who didn't bring out the best in you, but you weren't mean to me."

I huff. "Yeah, okay."

"You weren't! You didn't purposely go out of your way to be a bitch."

"But I was a bitch and now Chastity is saying shitty things that remind me all too much of myself."

"Now you're being silly." Nina rolls her eyes. "That girl doesn't have a mean bone in her body. And I'm sorry, but what Derek's daughter said to her warranted a response. She doesn't know you or what you've been through and why say it? It was meant to provoke. Chastity is kind and didn't deserve to be spoken to like that."

I agree with her, but it's still hard to see her getting in trouble for something even a little like I did. My regret regarding how I treated Nina and others is something I struggle with to this day.

"Still, I was not a great person and I want to say I'm sorry—again. I'm so sorry."

Nina and I have had this talk many times. I know I'm not the same person I was back then. Not even close, and she's over it, but there's still times I feel her holding back. I don't blame her. I wish I had a way to make it up to her. I should've never listened to my friends back then. I called her names and I'm not proud of my behavior.

I didn't really change until I became friends with Derek.

"Stop apologizing, Tea. We were kids. You were not even half as mean as Lori or Kelly were. Those girls I'd like to see tarred and feathered, but you were kind."

"When no one was looking."

"You're so upset with yourself at sixteen. The bigger question isn't whether I've forgiven you." Nina pauses, waiting for me to look at her. "It's whether you've forgiven yourself."

"I don't know that I ever can."

She touches my arm. "Then my forgiveness, which I granted you a million years ago, means nothing. None of us are like that anymore. It would be ridiculous to hold on to all that for this long. Plus, you've atoned for your mistakes, don't you think?"

"Just...it feels like time is going in reverse."

"Because Derek is back?"

That's probably exactly why. I see him and now I'm thrown back in time. How we would sneak out, hang out at the beach for hours talking about a future neither of us ever lived.

Derek made me believe I was good.

He made it sound so easy to leave behind the parts of myself I didn't like. When I was with him, I felt...real.

I didn't have to hide my fears because he didn't make me.

Now he's back and everything inside of me is unsettled.

"You should've seen him, Nina," I say with a wistful sigh. "He was...the same and then not."

"I can't believe his wife died. Do you know how?"

"I don't. We didn't really talk much."

She squeezes my hand. "You guys have a lot that probably needs to be said. You know, like how you were in love with him and he broke you."

Each time I thought the time was right, it wasn't. I was with Keith. He was with some other girl. Then, when I was finally ready, I found out I was pregnant. I didn't care about his relationship with Meghan because it was supposed to be me. At least, that's what I thought. I was young, dumb, and naive, but I wanted that. I felt like, if he could just see me as more than a friend, the rest would be so easy. It was right there in front of us.

Then, everything in my world came to a halt.

"There's really nothing to say anymore."

"Really?"

"What exactly would I say at this point? Hi, I was in love with you since I was seventeen but I was too big of a chicken shit to ever tell you and see if you felt the same way. Then, you broke my heart in a million fucking pieces when you married Meghan." I sigh with a shake of my head. "He chose her, Nina. He knew…he had to have known. There's no way he didn't see that I was madly in love with him."

She leans back, watching me as tears start to form. "So you think he knew and didn't care?"

The tidal wave of emotion crashes over me. The current is so strong and the more I fight against it, the more it's pulling me under. Right now, my legs are tired from kicking, trying to get out for the last thirteen years.

"No. He chose who he wanted in his life, which says everything I already knew…I wasn't the one."

chapter eight

Derek

eighteen years old

"I hate college."

"Everyone hates their first year of college."

"No, but I really hate it," I tell Teagan as we're wrapped up in a blanket back in Chincoteague.

It's freezing, but I don't care, I have my best friend with me and life makes sense.

"You only hate it because I'm not there with you." She nudges me and then rests her head on my shoulder.

If she only knew how true that statement was. We're only a few hours away from each other, but it feels like an entire ocean separates us. In high school, it was so easy to see her every day.

I miss her.

"So transfer schools," I encourage her. She'll never do it, but I can't help but ask.

"You transfer schools."

"We both know I can't."

The scholarship I got was highly competitive. My tuition is practically nothing compared to everyone else in the veterinary program. While my family isn't poor, we're not loaded either. Dad came out of his college with enough loans to drown in and my mother works for him. They've saved a little for me, but not nearly enough to cover the costs.

"I know, but I miss you."

Sometimes, when she says it, I can almost pretend she means it in a different way. Then I remember she's with Keith and slap myself out of that delusion.

"I miss you too."

She sighs and snuggles closer. "I'm freezing."

"Well, it's December."

"We really need to pick a new spot to meet at."

Never. This spot is where our friendship formed. "Not likely."

Teagan lifts her head and smiles. "It's special to me too. This is where you realized what an amazing person I am and how lucky you are to have me."

"Is that so?"

She's correct, but I'll never give her a win that easily.

"Yup. You had no idea I was this extraordinary, did you?"

"Nope. I still don't either."

"Liar."

I shake my head. "Did you ever think that you're the lucky one out of this friendship?"

Her eyes sparkle in the moonlight. "I know I am."

And it's moments like this, when she's not the perfect cheerleader or student, that she takes my breath away. She looks at me as though I'm the one person in the world who makes her happy, and I don't know how to keep fighting against wanting more.

"I was thinking…" I start.

"That's scary."

I laugh once. "Shut up. I'm serious. I was thinking about what it would be like if…" I want to say: we dated. The words are on the tip of my tongue, desperate to get out, but then the fear becomes too much.

This is Teagan, my best friend, and I don't want to lose her.

"If…?"

"If we were at the same school."

She purses her lips and moves my arm to go over her shoulder. "It would be the end of me and Keith, that's for sure."

"Yeah, God knows we wouldn't want to upset him."

Like I give a shit about Keith. Stupid asshole.

"Stop, you know he's just jealous…and an idiot."

He's completely undeserving of her. She's a prize and he's a thief that's stealing something that shouldn't belong to him.

"Yet…you're still dating him."

Teagan grumbles. "I know, but it's freshman year and I figure if I can get through the next year, then I can dump him."

Her logic is ridiculous. "You need mental help."

"So you've told me…many times."

And she never listens.

"Besides, it's not like I have anyone else beating down my door."

I would. I would tear the door off the hinges if I wasn't worried about her rejecting me. Instead of taking the chance, I stay where it's safe.

Teagan twists, pulling the blanket over her shoulders, and faces me.

"Tea!" It's fucking freezing. "Share the blanket!"

"Tell me something real," she says as she stares at me.

Not this game. Not now.

I can't do it.

"Tea." I say her name as a warning.

"I'll give you the blanket back, but I want something real."

I'm freezing and my head is fucked-up with thoughts of her eyes and her lips are close. "I can't think…I'm frozen."

She grins. "Try."

I love you.

There, that's my something real. I love her and I know it's crazy and stupid, but I do. I dream about kissing her. I think about the way her lips would fit with mine. How she would feel in my arms as I held her tight. My nights are filled with fantasies of making love to her until we both can't take any more. I love her and I will never tell her.

Because she's not mine. She's someone else's.

My teeth start to chatter when the cold air hits me. "I *really* want that blanket back," I say as my something real.

"No way, buddy! You can't cheat!"

"Then you give me something real and I'll give you one, if I don't die of hypothermia."

"Fine," Teagan tosses back with a hint of anger. "I really don't ever want to know what life is like without you in it."

I'm stunned. I literally can't move or speak. I have so much I want to say back to her because it's as though she and I might actually be on the same wavelength. A few years ago, it wasn't anything more than friendship for me.

Sure, she was gorgeous, but we were always just friends. All I wanted was for her to see that she was more than her popularity.

The joke was on me, though. *I* saw it. I saw how special she was. I saw her donate her time to helping others during the food drive and then again with a fisherman who needed help with his boat. She didn't know how to fix an engine, but Teagan read every manual she could. I saw how much she wanted others to see her for who she really was but was too afraid of the way it would change her world.

Then, I saw her stop caring about her fears and embrace the woman she was, making it impossible not to fall for her.

"Derek?" Teagan says my name slowly. "You okay?"

"Yeah, sorry."

"I was worried maybe you froze to death…like Jack and Rose."

I roll my eyes. Only she would make that stupid movie reference at a time like this. "That fucking movie."

"You love it. I know you cried."

"I cried because it was three hours of my life I'll never get back."

Teagan steps forward and wraps the blanket around me, hugging me at the same time. "More like sixty hours, since I made you watch it every day."

The things we do for the girl we want but can never have.

"You make me smile," I say without thinking.

Her eyes lift, meeting mine with curiosity so deep. "What?"

"That's my something real. You make me smile."

To that, her lips turn into a huge grin. "I'm glad we were forced to become friends."

"Me too."

She snuggles into my chest and I rest my chin on the top of her head. "I miss you, Der. So much."

I swear I hear her sniffle, but she coughs quickly after that so I'm not sure. "I miss you too, but we're never really apart."

"No, I guess not."

I lean back, press my finger under her chin, and lift it. "You will never have to know what it's like not to have me, not unless you decide I'm too much of a pain."

She smiles softly, the moonlight shining down on us. "Never."

She's my something real. Hell, she's my everything that matters.

chapter nine

Derek

present

"You will not behave like this!" I tell Everly as she rolls her eyes.

"Whatever."

"I'm serious. You don't know these people. You show up and the first day you decide to be nasty just because?"

Everly picks at her nails and then slams her hands on her bed. "You moved me here! *You!* You don't get to tell me that I have to be nice to some dork! She actually thought I would sit with her? *Please.* Like I want to be friends with the losers on day one? No thank you."

When did my sweet girl with big brown eyes and a smile that could melt even the coldest of hearts turn into this?

While I would love to say her newfound nasty attitude started when Meghan died, that would be a lie. She was already becoming this creature I didn't recognize before then; I think her mother's death sped up the transformation. Suddenly, Everly had every excuse to be mad. I watched her go from one extreme to another, unable to help stop her anger.

"You have no idea if she was a loser, she was being nice! Besides, how do you know anything about Teagan anyway?"

She shakes her head like I'm an idiot. "Don't be dumb, Dad. I heard Mom talk about her."

I jerk back, confused and pissed at the same time. "When did…?"

"If she hated her, then so do I."

I close my eyes and count to four. I need to be calm. "Your mother didn't hate her."

"Not what I heard."

"You're thirteen! What could you possibly hear anyway?"

"Mom always talked about your slutty friend from back home."

Anger begins to fill me, but also guilt. I let this happen. I allowed Teagan to be the villain in our story. It wasn't Teagan who did Meghan wrong, it was me.

At first, I did as Meghan asked, letting Teagan go, focusing solely on my marriage.

I pushed aside the conflicting emotions I felt for Teagan because that's what I needed to do to keep my wife.

When I think back, I remember the pain in my chest when I made that last call to Teagan. The way I pictured her face as she cried and begged me not to do this. I let her think it was her fault. I didn't tell her it was me who was weak and ashamed.

I didn't tell her that I had feelings for her and I needed to make the right choice, even if it hurt us both.

Meghan would've left me if I spoke to Teagan again.

So, I kept my promise to my wife, cut all ties, told Teagan I couldn't be there for her anymore since I had my own family. Which wasn't the case at all.

But Meghan is gone now, and no matter what happened between me and Teagan I will not allow Everly to hurt anyone like this.

"You don't know anything about the past, and you will not treat that girl or her mother with anything less than the highest respect," I say as I take a step closer. "So help me God, Everly, if I find out that you say anything again, you'll regret it."

"What are you going to do, Dad? Move me from my home? Take my friends from me? Maybe take away my life? Well, too late!"

"You think this is what I want?"

I had a great practice in South Carolina. We had a beautiful home, friends, schools, and the life that people dream of, and I had to leave it all behind.

Not because we lost Meghan, but because my father needed me.

Everly crosses her arms and shifts away from me. "Just go, Dad."

I'm completely inept at dealing with her. Talking does nothing but lead to a fight and neither of us are willing to bend.

Maybe giving her space is what she needs. "Fine, but you need to stop thinking you're old enough to understand things you should've never heard. You're not an adult, contrary to whatever you think, and I won't put up with you bullying anyone, understand?"

Her head turns and she glares. "Completely."

I have a feeling she and I agreed on something else, but I'm too exhausted to push her.

"Good night, Ev. I love you."

I want her to at least hear that.

Her eyes soften, but I know her too well to expect her to give in. She's always been more like Meghan when she digs her heels in. "Whatever."

I close the door and lean my head against the wall. No one ever told me how hard parenting really is. It was different when it was Meghan and I. We were a team when it came to Everly and where one was a little weaker, the other was strong.

Now, I'm just weak and completely freaking lost.

My parents are sitting in the living room that hasn't changed in the last thirty years, doing their best to pretend not to have heard all of it.

I sit on the sofa that still has the bloodstain from when I cut my arm when I was six. The photographs on the wall haven't been changed out and I cringe at my braces and long hair.

"Are you going to tell us what all that was about?" my mother asks while continuing to knit.

"Just me failing as a parent."

My father chuckles once. "That's a perpetual state, son."

"Thanks."

"I'm just being honest. If you ever feel like you're doing a good job—worry."

My dad is the main reason I decided to head back here. Mom told me that his memory has been failing of late and that he needs help with the practice. I suggested he finally retire, but she said he won't even consider it until he found another veterinarian to take over.

However, it's not like there's anyone else around here.

He's the only one people call.

Which meant, I was the only option he had.

"How are you feeling today, Dad?"

He shrugs. "Horses were giving me a bit of trouble. You know how stubborn they can be."

"Much like teenagers," I toss back.

"Everly is in a lot of pain, Derek. You should remember that. Losing a parent is very difficult." Mom's voice is soft and full of understanding.

"Doesn't give her the right to be a little shit."

Dad pushes the paper he was reading down. "Mouth."

"I'm almost thirty-five."

"I don't care if you're seventy-five. Around your mother we don't use that language."

My mother smirks and rolls her eyes because he's so hell-bent on protecting her delicate ears when she has the worst mouth in all of Virginia. Mom cusses like a sailor thanks to her father, who was one.

"Whatever you say, Pop."

He grumbles and goes back to his paper. Mom shares a secret look with me and I smile. She and I have always been close, and right now, I need her help. I was fortunate to grow up with a loving, sweet mother who baked a cake once a week but who also loved poker and taught me how to cheat. She's the oxymoron to every situation. My friends would look at her and see this version of June Cleaver, only to find out she was really Peg Bundy.

"You know what always helps me clear my mind?" she says, drawing my attention. "A walk on the beach. The salt air is great to cleanse the soul. Don't you think, honey?"

It's been a long time since I've been close to the water.

We lived on the Georgia border of South Carolina. I've missed the waves and the mere idea of seeing the wild horses.

"I hear you, Mom."

She smiles to herself and goes back to her knitting when I stand.

The walk to the shoreline takes about ten minutes, but it's ten minutes of total peace. There's no one out, since it's September and all the tourists are gone, leaving the locals back to their little slice of heaven. It's still warm enough that it feels like summer, though. The breeze tonight is light, just enough so the air's not stagnant.

I make my way over the dunes and see her.

Her back is to me as she sits looking out to the ocean. There's a bottle of wine beside her, and I'm thrown back in time.

How many nights did we meet this way?

When the world was asleep and we wanted to pretend all our dreams were within reach.

Teagan was my world and my fantasy, wrapped up in one perfect person. I stand here, unsure of what to do. So much time has passed and I'm not ready to deal with the things between us.

So I do what I did thirteen years ago, I turn my back on her—again.

chapter ten

Teagan

present

I know he's here. I can feel his presence, even in the dark with the wind and sounds of the ocean, I can sense him.

If only I didn't, maybe his being back in this town would be tolerable. Time has done nothing to diminish the connection I have with him, and that is the saddest part.

The seconds pass and I wait to hear his arrival. There's no doubt he saw me, but as the numbers climb in my head, he still doesn't appear.

I turn, shifting to see where he is, and that's when I see him walk away. "Derek!" I call his name without thinking.

I'm frustrated because I should've let him go. It's clear he didn't want to talk and I don't have anything to say—well, that's a lie. I have a million questions I want answers to, but this place, this beach, is where we came when we needed to think.

Which we both clearly are grappling with.

Derek starts to walk toward me so I get to my feet, heading to meet him.

"Hi," he says as we stand a yard apart.

"Hi. If you want the beach, I can leave," I offer.

If he needed solitude, I'll grant him that. I've been here for an hour already and feel no better than when I arrived.

"No, no. It's fine, really. Not like the beach isn't big enough for the both of us."

"Then why did you leave?"

He straightens his back and looks off to the left. "I don't know."

"You saw me, right?"

"Yes."

"Oh." The air escapes my chest in a huff. "I get it."

He steps forward. "No, you can't possibly because I don't get it."

I don't know what he means, but my pride can only take so much. He was my best friend. He knew me. He was the only person on my side and he walked away.

He let me down.

"I'm truly too spent for riddles or anything. I'll head out, take the solitude."

When I start to walk away, he grips my arm. "Stay." Derek looks as shocked as I feel. "We don't have to talk, but I'd like you to stay."

My heart is racing, and as much as I want to be the one to walk away this time, I can't. I'd never been able to before, and it seems I'm still not. It's clear that things are weighing on him.

"Okay."

We walk down to the shoreline, allowing the water to lap over our feet.

This isn't the time to ask the one question that weighs on me so heavily...how?

Not why, because I know why. It's obvious that Meghan forbade him from talking to me. Something happened, I still don't know what, but we went from some kind of mutual understanding to radio silence.

At first, I thought maybe she knew that I loved him. Although, not a soul was aware of that, so it always seemed impossible.

Then I thought she suspected something was going on between us, but again, it made no sense. Yeah, he was coming to see me once a month, like he did the entire time we were in college, but that was part of our thing.

So it isn't the why that has kept me up at night, it's how.

How could he do it?

How could he turn and walk away when he was my best friend?

I look at his face as we walk, but he keeps his eyes down.

"I can practically hear you screaming at me in your head," Derek says with a sigh. "I said we didn't have to talk, not that we couldn't."

I cross my arms over my chest to hold myself together. Instead of asking about what happened all those years ago, I decide to start small. "What brought you out here tonight?"

"Everly."

"Teenagers will do that to you." I try to make a joke, but he doesn't laugh.

"She's not handling things well."

"I would assume not. Losing her mother isn't easy, I would imagine. She's probably full of anger and then moving...to here...I would be pissed too."

Derek huffs. "Oh, she's angry all right."

"And you're bearing the brunt of it?"

"Every day."

I feel bad for him, but there's a childish part of me, the wounded part, that's kind of happy he's getting shit. "Well, I'm here to tell you that single parenting sucks."

"Gee, thanks for the encouragement." Derek nudges me a little deeper in the water.

Thankfully, I don't fall.

"I'm just being honest. I've been taking the hits since Chastity was born and it doesn't get easier. You are always the bad guy and very rarely the good guy. Nothing you do will ever be right because...again...you suck."

Derek lets out a laugh, but then turns his head. "I've felt that way for a while."

"Welcome to the club. I'm the owner."

Then both of us are quiet as we walk at a glacial pace. I'm not in a hurry, even though the proverbial elephant is between us.

"Everything I want to say to you right now seems so trivial," he admits.

"I know what you mean."

"Do you?"

We both stop walking, and watch each other.

It's apparent that we're both dancing around what we want to say, but I don't know that I'm fully ready to hear it all either. Once I know, I'll have to decide how to handle it, whatever the outcome. In the past, I haven't been known for my fantastic decision-making, but when it comes to him, I'm even worse.

I give him an out. "You never said, how did Meghan die?"

Derek's eyes break from mine. "It was a car accident.

She was running late to get Everly to cheerleading. They were arguing because Meghan was overwhelmed since she got her new job and kept forgetting everything. Including when she had to pick up Everly. I was in surgery and couldn't get her this time."

The tightness in my chest grows because I already know the ending. The tragic part is coming and there's no alternate ending.

"Everly was in the car?"

He nods. "She was on her phone, apparently texting her friends about her mother being a bitch, and a car ran the red light. They hit the driver's side, Everly was in the back passenger side."

I gasp. "I can't even…"

"It was horrific. I've never seen anything like it. I don't know how Everly walked out of that wreck."

"How long ago?"

His eyes are filled with unshed tears. "Six months."

"I really didn't know," I say as I shift closer. "I would've called or gone to you. Your parents never said a word."

He nods. "I asked them not to."

My back straightens and I eye him curiously. "Why not?"

"Because I knew you'd come. I knew that if you thought I needed you, even with me being an ass the last time we talked, that you'd be there for me. Isn't that ridiculous? That I would rather suffer than have had you comfort me?"

There's nothing I can say. The tears that don't fall from his eyes descend from mine. It hurts to know that he didn't want me there. I loved him, sure, more than I should've, but I would never have hurt him. I kept my mouth shut, dealt with standing beside him during that fucking wedding, and never said a word.

I struggled so he wouldn't.

And he'd kept his wife's death a secret.

"What did I do to you that was so wrong?" I blurt out. "What did I ever do, Derek? Because I don't understand how thirteen years ago you could walk out, and never tell me why."

I didn't plan to say anything, but small talk will only go for so long. There are big issues between us, and while I wish we could pretend things didn't happen, wish we could sweep them under the rug and ignore what happened in the past…we can't.

I can see that he's either not ready or can't say what he's thinking, and I really don't feel like playing this game.

I muster the courage to speak first. "We need to talk about this."

"Yeah, it probably would make things a little less awkward." His foot carves a line in the sand, the water rushing over and flooding it. "It's funny how things happen. You dig the hole only to have the space you thought you made fill right back up."

I stay quiet because I'm not sure if this is going to relate back to us or if he's just talking.

Derek continues after a moment. "You can't stop it or control any of it, it just…happens. Which is sort of how I feel about the way things went down with us."

"You couldn't stop it?" I ask.

"I couldn't control it."

I shake my head while releasing a heavy breath. "You're talking in riddles."

"Meghan."

The single word hangs out there.

"Meghan?"

Derek takes a step back, allowing more space between us, and although he's only moved a few inches it feels like miles to me. He takes a deep breath.

"Meghan found my journal."

chapter eleven

Derek

twenty-two years old

"We've only been married two months, Derek! How can you be so unhappy?" Meghan asks with tears streaming down her face.

I wish I could tell her the truth, but that would be intentionally cruel.

Meghan hasn't done anything wrong. She's been a great wife and she was a good girlfriend. We've had our spats and arguments—mostly over Teagan—but we've found a way through it.

But the last two months have been hard. I'm trying to be a good husband, give her the support she needs, especially since she's four months pregnant, and yet...I'm failing.

I'm torn between driving up to see Teagan and being here for Meghan.

Because ever since I found out Teagan was pregnant, I realized: I'm madly in love with her.

Since the night it hit me, three days after my wedding

when I was staring at my new wife, wishing she was Teagan, I can't look at myself. I hate myself more than I can express. I married Meghan in spite of what I thought I felt for Teagan. I love Meghan, but there was this moment when I was looking at Teagan, wishing it was my child she was carrying.

How fucked-up am I?

Then again, I didn't have a choice because she was with Keith, trying to figure out if they had a future, and by then, I was engaged to Meghan. What choice did I have?

"Talk to me!" Meghan pushes her hands to my chest. "Please."

I can't. I can't tell her because she really doesn't want to know. It's my job as her husband to fix myself, and she doesn't deserve this.

I grip her wrists, holding them, focusing on the fact that it's Meghan here. She's my wife. She's having our baby. "I'm just…nervous, Meg. I'm worried that I'm not going to be a good dad and husband." Which isn't a lie. "I'm still in school and I don't know how I'm going to take care of you guys and still finish vet school."

Meghan's eyes fill with empathy and a bit of relief. "You're going to be a great dad and you're already a good husband."

No, I'm not.

I'm not a good man, let alone husband.

"I'm…in my head."

Meghan sighs and then lifts her hands to my chest, softly. "You don't have to do that. I'm here too and I'm just as nervous as you are. I'm having a baby in five months and it's a lot of changes all at once. There's so much uncertainty, but we can do this, babe. We're Derek and Meghan."

I feel sick to my stomach because this is the first time she's said that where I don't believe it.

Because I'm a fucking piece of shit.

She leans up, pressing her lips to mine, and I force any thoughts of Teagan out of my head. Meghan has given me everything.

Meghan has been the one who has loved me.

She chose me and continues to do so.

Whatever is going on in my head needs to stop. It's not real. It's fear because everything is changing. It has to be that because otherwise I'm not the person I thought I was, and I can't accept that.

I cup her cheeks and kiss her back. After a few seconds, I rest my head against hers and feel calmer. Meghan is my wife, and I love her. "I'm sorry."

She lifts her head. "Just talk to me. You don't have to do this alone, you know?"

"I know."

"I get being scared, believe me, but when I start to feel that way, I remember that I have you and as long as we're together, we'll be okay."

"You're so much smarter than me," I say with a smirk.

"I'm glad you learned this early."

I pull her tighter to me, and she wraps her arms around my middle. This is what I need to focus on. Her. Us. Our family. Not a delusion I've conjured up with someone who doesn't feel the same about me.

* * *

It's been a long week. I've had a bunch of tests, one I know I bombed, but I couldn't focus. Meghan and I are having dinner tonight, though. I promised her that once I got through my exams, we'd have more time together because I'm determined to make this work.

She is my wife, and for better or worse, I'm going to be here beside her. I just have to get it together.

"Meghan?" I call out as I open the door to our apartment.

She doesn't answer.

I toss my bag full of textbooks onto the floor and drop my keys on the entry table. Her keys are there, so I know she's home.

"Meg?"

Still no answer.

Weird.

I head into the living room and she's sitting on the couch with her legs crisscrossed and head down.

"Hey," I say as I make my way to her. "Sorry I'm late."

When her eyes meet mine, I stop moving. They're red and puffy, and the pain in them is clear as day.

"What's wrong?" I'm instantly worried about her and the baby. "Are you okay?"

She shakes her head. "I'm not."

Worry fills me, pushing me toward her. I tug her to me and hold her tight. Her body starts to shake, and my own fear grows. Something is terribly wrong and whatever it is has her devastated.

"Talk to me."

Meghan shoves out of my embrace. She reaches behind her and pulls out a leather-bound black journal.

Time stops, because I know now what has her devastated. I've written in that journal the last two years—including last week.

"I want to talk." She sniffs. "I want to talk and ask you things, but I don't know that I need to because it's all here."

No longer is worry my primary emotion, now it's mixed with anger. Those are my thoughts and feelings. I write because I have to get it out in a place that's safe.

"In my private journal."

"It was sitting on the counter, and I didn't know what it was."

A part of me doesn't believe her because I'm never careless. I keep it in the same place so that it would never be found.

Hell, I've never told anyone other than Teagan I even keep a damn journal.

But now Meghan knows, and she read it. Without my permission.

"And then when you figured out what it was, you just kept reading?" I push.

A tear falls from her face, and my heart continues to pound to a beat that is so loud in my ears. I stand, needing to get some distance from her.

"I...I wasn't...I know it was wrong!" She gets to her feet as well. "When I saw some of the...the things you said. Is this really what you feel? You want her? You wish Teagan was pregnant with your child?" She screams the words and the tears fall down her cheek.

I thought I felt that way. I thought maybe it was really what I wanted, but it's not. I was confused. I wrote it down so I could get it out of my head and move on. At least that has to be the truth because otherwise I'm a fucking failure of a man.

"No! I was dealing with so much and I was fucked-up in the head. It's not like that!"

"You wrote it, Derek!" She throws the journal at me. "You wrote it all here. You said you love *her*!"

Meghan's pain is so deep, I can almost feel it. She's hurt by what I wrote and rightfully so. I didn't explain that after I wrote about it, I realized I was crazy.

"I do, but not that way! She's my best friend."

"No. No she's not. You're in love with her and I would bet my ass she's in love with you, and *you*...you wrote about it. You want her."

"I don't," I say as I step closer to her. "I want you. I married you! I love you, Meghan."

She shakes her head in disbelief. "You said..."

"I know what I said but it wasn't like that. I was so confused and mixed-up." If I could just explain it to her, maybe she'd understand. "I saw Teagan for our lunch last week and it was different. I was different, and talking about the baby with her, she started crying, and then it was just...I don't know, but I had to get it out and work through it. It was just my fears and being irrational."

Meghan steps back. "Do you love Teagan that way?"

I can't tell her. I can't lose her and as much as it pains me to lie to her, it's the only way I can spare her feelings even a little.

"No."

"Have you ever?"

My eyes widen and as much as I want to deny it and protect her, I can't.

"I did or I thought I did. I don't know."

A heartbreaking sound releases from her mouth. "I...I can't...you..."

"I thought I did but it could never work and I had you.

It was never a question with us. I knew I loved you. I loved you from the beginning."

"But you loved her."

"This isn't about her. It's about you and me."

"No." She throws her hands up. "No, it's always about her. I've tried so hard to understand your friendship and accept it, but I can't do this. I have to go."

"Go?"

"Yes. Leave. I'm leaving."

"Meghan." I move in front of her. "Don't do this. I swear, it's not like that. I love you, damn it. I love our life. Our baby. Everything we have. Please, you can't leave."

She wipes the tears that paint her face. "I can't be the third wheel in my own marriage, Derek!"

"You're not."

"No?"

I've fucked this up so bad, but the idea of losing her proves that what we have is real. It's not a fantasy I've made up in my head. Meghan is my life.

"I don't know that I can do this. I don't know that I can be around her."

My heart begins to race even faster. I know where this is going. "Around Teagan?"

"I don't trust you now. I don't trust her and you. I can't be worried all the time. Those words will be in my mind forever. Seeing how you feel about her is too much."

"I don't feel that way," I try to remind her, but she isn't hearing that.

"Even if you're telling me it's not true now, there was some part of you that thought it was. I feel like you betrayed me and our marriage."

Jesus Christ. I wrote about my feelings because I wasn't

strong enough to put them aside, and I hoped putting them down on paper would make them go away. I hurt Meghan when she did nothing wrong.

"Meghan, please, I would never cheat on you."

She points to the journal. "You did. In your heart, you betrayed me."

My own tears fall because I despise myself for hurting her. I look at the pain in her eyes, wanting to take it all away, willing to do anything to make this better. "What can I do? What can I do to prove that it's you I love?"

Her eyes are no longer sad, they're filled with determination. "If you want this marriage to work, you have to cut her out of your life. Completely. It's me or her, you choose."

chapter twelve

Teagan

present

"I'm still not understanding. She read your journal and that was reason enough to stop talking to me? Was she mad because…?"

Derek looks uncomfortable, and I'm truly confused. He's kept a journal since he was in high school, writing his random thoughts, making plans for things he wanted. It's not like it held the key to his soul.

"Because I talked about you…a lot."

"Oh," I say, taking a step back. "So she was jealous and you just dropped me? Not an explanation, not a… 'I'm sorry, Tea, I need some time.' Just a vague phone call that said you thought it best if we stop speaking, and if and when you thought the time was right, you'd be in touch."

What Derek doesn't know is that his call that night sent me into labor. I was so distraught, I couldn't breathe. I cried with such force, knowing that my person was no longer mine and I was truly on my own. Not even his wedding had made me feel so alone and destroyed.

"No, that's not it. I mean, she was jealous, but because I had written stuff about you...about us...and she almost left me."

I cover my chest with my arms as a feeling of emptiness fills me. "What could you have written about us? We never dated and we were never inappropriate."

"I know that."

No, I don't think he does. "There's nothing that ever crossed any lines, Derek. We were just friends."

He closes his eyes, releasing a heavy breath. "It wasn't like that. You and I...we were different. We were more than *just* anything."

"Clearly not. You threw me away so easily. You were the only person in this world I ever could truly count on and you abandoned me. You took what should've been a night that I smile over because I had a baby and it became tainted with losing you."

His hand grips the back of his neck and he paces. "I'm sorry I did that to you. I'm sorry the whole damn thing happened, but understand that I was faced with the choice of you or my wife. My pregnant wife who I was married to for only two months. I loved you both, and choosing almost killed me."

I was a friend. Of course he chose her.

My life was such a mess and I didn't know if what I felt at that time wasn't desperation for someone to love me.

Keith sure as hell didn't. But I believed Derek did.

I thought that even when he got married, he would still have room for me in his heart.

"Well, when you chose, it did kill me. I had no one,

Derek. I had a new baby, no friends, living in this stupid town that I hated, and was in the middle of the worst experience of my life and you chose to completely cut me off."

"It wasn't that simple."

I'm trying to be mature, but the broken girl inside of me is screaming to lash out. "I don't care that it wasn't simple for you, and maybe that makes me a bitch, but there's nothing that Meghan could've possibly seen in that journal. Hell, I read it how many times?" I yell. "You wrote random shit, weird notes about your plans for the future and song lyrics. So, I'm so sorry your new wife found some lame-ass excuse to finally be rid of me."

Because that's what it was. She hated our friendship, even if she pretended otherwise. I mattered, maybe even more than she did at some points, and it bothered her. But she couldn't understand the depth of our friendship.

He was the first person to see me as more than some immature girl who wanted to be popular.

I was selfish and stupid back then, but with Derek...I could be anything.

He believed in me, thought I was worth more, and gave me the courage to be better.

"I promise you, Teagan, it was not lame."

"It doesn't matter, does it? In the grand scheme of it all, you did what you did and I had to learn to live without you. I struggled, was depressed beyond words, almost lost Chastity in childbirth, and you weren't there. I did it all alone."

"I knew you could."

"Please," I huff. "I don't need your praise. I needed your friendship. I needed you to be the one man, other than my father, to actually be there and not turn your back on me when things got rough. Do you have any idea what I went through with Keith?"

He shakes his head.

I don't know whether to laugh or cry. All these years I've waited for this moment to call him out and I can't even do it. I can't tell him that it wasn't about me doing it on my own, it was about doing it without him. I still can't say the words: *I was in love with you.*

The fact is, it doesn't change anything.

"I went through complete fucking hell. I watched someone I thought I knew become someone I couldn't even recognize. All because of his new life. But what about my life, Derek? What about my needs? What about Chastity? None of that mattered because I was irrelevant in the grand scheme of things."

The things I did in my youth were…stupid. If I could go back and talk to my nineteen-year-old self, I would bitchslap her. I would tie her hands to her books and force her eyes forward.

As an adult, I have the beautifully cruel gift of hindsight. I see the errors, and the way I made excuses for my poor choices. I gave Keith every possible opportunity to hurt me and then wasn't even surprised when he took them.

I let my desire to be popular keep me from seeing that I was loved by the few people who mattered. Keith told me he loved me, that I would be on his arm like a queen in high school, but only if…

If I did this.

If I gave him that.

If I allowed him what he wanted.

Everything came with an...if.

"I'm sorry. I know it's not enough for you and I know I let you down, but know that I didn't want to do it."

"I'm not even angry anymore," I tell him as I start to walk because standing here, looking at him as regret fills his eyes, is too much for me.

There's this part of me that has spent so much time loving Derek, longing for him, that I want to pull him into my arms and forgive it all. Then there's the other side that's hurt and disappointed. If he loved me, he would've fought for me. Regardless of her reading silly things written a million years ago in a journal.

"Then what are you?"

I turn my head toward him. "Used to it."

Derek's eyes close and the breath expels from his nose. "I thought about you, Tea. I wrestled with calling you every single day."

"But, what? You couldn't? You really thought Meghan was going to leave you?"

He takes a few steps closer, eliminating the distance between us. "Yes."

"I'm trying to understand here. I'm doing my best to get what the hell could make it that *easy* for you. You didn't even try after that. I was...am...angry and I hate this."

"I hated it! I hated it and then I hated you for making me hate it."

"Me?" I gasp. "What did I do to deserve your anger? I woke up one day and realized that you didn't want to ever hear my voice again. You never wanted to see me, know anything about me, and I was to act as though you were dead! Dead, Derek! You told me to go on with my life as though you had died because that was what I was to you—dead! And I didn't do anything wrong!"

"I know that!"

"Then please, tell me, what was my crime?"

Derek's breathing is labored and he throws his hands in the air. "You made me fall in love with you!"

Time seems to cease around me. I feel the air stop moving, and I can't hear anything other than the words he just said replaying in my head.

He *loved* me?

He loved me the way I loved him and his way of dealing with it was to completely cut me out.

I romanticized for years over hearing those words from his lips. I dreamed of how he would take me in his arms, kiss me, tell me he was a fool and loved me. It was supposed to be this magical declaration.

Not out of anger. Not telling me that he hated me for making him love me.

I'm tired of being the bad guy.

I loved him too. I loved him so much that I was willing to suffer through his fucking wedding, stand by his side, and give him the little bit of peace I could. I didn't use my love to hurt him. It stayed bottled up where I allowed it to eat me alive, and protect the relationship we were allowed to have.

I look up in his blue eyes, and a tear falls. "That's the cruelest thing you could've ever said to me."

And then, I walk away, leaving him like he left me.

chapter thirteen

Teagan

twenty-one years old

"What are you saying?" I ask as tears start to stream down my face.

"I'm saying I don't think we should talk anymore."

My heart hurts. I'm confused and I don't understand why Derek is saying these things. I haven't done anything. We talked yesterday and everything was perfectly fine. What the hell changed?

"Why?"

"Because, Teagan, I don't want to."

This is crazy.

"I don't believe you."

He lets out a sigh and I imagine him pacing, like he does when he's dealing with things that stress him out. "You don't have to. It's the way it is, you'll understand someday."

"I don't understand any of this!" I yell and sink onto the couch. My stomach clenches and I rest my hand there. Why is he doing this? Why is he pushing me away?

"It's just time. I'm married now and having my own family. I need to focus on Meghan and the baby."

My mouth opens and then closes because it still isn't computing. "What does that have to do with me? I'm your friend, Derek. You promised." I choke on the word as a tear falls. "You promised you'd be here for me. You said you wouldn't let me be alone after everything with Keith!"

He's silent. If it weren't for the sound of his breathing, I would think he'd hung up.

"You have nothing to say?" I ask.

"No."

"No? After all these years? After everything we've been through, you offer me no fucking explanations?"

His voice is angry when he responds. "What do you want? I'm doing what's best for my marriage!"

My heart aches because I did what was best for his marriage too. I stood there a few weeks ago, watching him marry her, and didn't say a word. I hugged her, told her I was so happy for her when I wanted to tear my own heart out because it was dead anyway.

For him, I did that.

Now, he doesn't want to speak to me anymore?

"What happened?" I ask.

"Nothing happened, Teagan."

"You have never lied to me." My voice is filled with hurt. "We've always told each other the truth, tell me so I can fix it. We can find a way but I can't lose you. Please..."

"We can't," he says and the crack in his voice tells me he's crying.

"So this is it? No real explanation? Just, we can't be friends...it's not me, it's you?"

I feel like I'm going to throw up. My stomach turns again, pain radiating from the front to my back as I wait for his answers.

"This is the way it has to be. If you were married to Keith and he told—you realized what it was doing to him, you can't say—"

"I would tell him to fuck off!" I yell. Now I'm pissed. If Meghan has an issue with me, then she could've talked to me. Instead, she makes him cut me off? Fuck them both.

"You wouldn't." He sighs and then sniffs.

He doesn't get to cry. I'm the one breaking. "Well, I guess there's nothing more to say," I say and then wince. "You clearly have made your decision, screw me and the baby you promised to be there for."

"I'm sorry, Teagan. I hope you and the baby will be happy. I want nothing more than for you to find everything you want. I wish there was another way."

The tears won't stop and I wipe them away. "There's always another way. That's what's *real*, but apparently our friendship wasn't. You want me to stop calling and talking to you, fine. Just do me one favor, don't ever contact me again because I can't...I can't even breathe right now. I thought...well, I thought wrong and I'm done. I'll be happy because what choice do I have? You're a fucking coward and I don't ever want to hear from you again! Goodbye, Derek."

I hang up the call, throwing the phone against the wall, shattering onto the floor.

Another stabbing pain hits my stomach and I stand up, only to have a gush of water fall to the floor.

My water broke, just like my heart.

chapter fourteen

Teagan

present

"I don't want to go to school," Chastity complains as I try to get her ass out of bed.

"Well, you have to."

"Anyone ever tell you that you suck?"

I laugh. "Daily. You've met my mother, remember? Now, get your butt up and get ready."

She sits up, groans, and then flops back down on her pillow. "Where were you last night?"

"In my bed."

"No, I looked for you before I went to sleep and you weren't there."

My mind immediately goes back to the beach. The words Derek said and the way he said them. How much disappointment filled me and is still there. I'm... unlovable. That's all I can come up with.

Two men, one who I loved with my whole being and the other who I should've never given a chance, both found the idea of loving me so disgusting they cut me out. I'm winning at life for sure.

"I was at the beach."

Chastity nods. "I should've figured."

"I needed perspective."

"Did you find any?"

"Nope," I tell her as I get to my feet.

"Maybe you should try a park next time."

I really would like to throttle her some days. "Maybe you should get to school before I call the cops for truancy."

Chastity gasps. "You wouldn't."

"You're right." I sigh. "I'll just call Grandma."

She throws the covers off, mumbling about mutiny and treason, but I grin. When Chastity is like this, I can't help it. I love that we can verbally spar in a way I never could with my mother.

I head into the kitchen of my tiny apartment and once again, hate my life. There is only one bedroom, which is Chastity's, and then I took the dining room and made it into a bedroom.

She emerges from her room wearing a T-shirt that says: DAMN THE MAN.

Okay, I really do love this kid.

I love that my thirteen-year-old quotes *Empire Records* on her clothing.

"So, today you need to get along with Everly," I say as I sip my coffee.

"You act like I'm the bully here. That girl is mean and I defend myself and get in trouble? I hate this town."

That makes two of us. "I know, but you're going to have to be the bigger person. Her grandfather is the town vet that you're working for and now people are going to be watching how you act more."

Chastity rolls her eyes. "I can't wait for college."

"You've got a few years there, sweetheart."

"I could get in early."

"You're not Doogie Howser, settle down."

Her eyes narrow and she looks at me like I've sprouted two heads. "Who is Doogie Howser?"

I feel old.

"Just…go to school and try not to get in trouble. If I have to leave work again, your grandmother will ask questions."

She snorts. "She'd probably be proud I finally acted a little like you."

"Hey!" I protest.

"I'm serious, Mom. She's always talking about how popular you were. Which is code for you were *so* cool. But I know what *popular* and *cool* mean. You were probably just like Everly."

I'd love to deny it, but that would be lying right to her face, which I've always avoided. Chastity is a good kid and while I don't overshare with her, I don't hide things either. We're a team. She doesn't judge me for my past and is appreciative for how I keep our lives together with duct tape and chewing gum.

"It's nothing I'm proud of."

"I don't know how you could be like her."

Oh, how I wish I could go back in time.

"Girls like her are usually scared. They're often insecure or afraid that people they thought were their friends would turn on them. Bullies are sort of in the mentality of bully-or-be-bullied."

She shovels a spoonful of cereal in her mouth and shrugs. "Whatever."

"I'm serious. Her mother died, she moved to a new

town, and her entire life is a mess. She probably feels like her life is out of control so she's searching for a target."

It doesn't mean that Chastity should be the object of her anger, but I get it. Everly's got a lot to be pissed about.

"So you knew her dad?"

Sometimes having a really observant daughter sucks. "I did, a long time ago."

"Grandma said you guys were best friends."

I cross my arms over my chest and wonder why she asked a question she already knew the answer to.

"What?" she asks.

"I'm curious what you're trying to find out, since you knew who Derek was."

"I wanted to see what you'd say."

"What else did Grandma inform you of?"

Chastity shrugs and puts her bowl down. "She was just giddy to tell me juicy info about you."

"I'm sure she was. She's also a pathological liar."

My daughter laughs and rolls her eyes. "Yeah, okay."

"I used to like you."

"You still do. Also, you suck as a liar."

I'd like to flip her off but that would be inappropriate. "Back to the conversation. What did Grandma tell you?"

"She said you two were in love but too stupid to see it. Oh, and she was not happy that he was back either. She kept saying something about your head in the clouds and now you'd end up floating away."

Why my mother disapproves of him, I'll never know.

Derek volunteered with his father, caring for animals and doing other good deeds while I was making out with Keith under the bleachers.

"What the hell does that even mean?"

"She also thinks that if I have to spend time around him, that I would like him much more than you."

I laugh. "Well, that's interesting."

"Why?"

"Because it's true."

She smiles. "Well, I'll let you know the verdict after I'm done working with Dr. Hartz."

"They're both Dr. Hartz," I inform her.

"He's a vet too?"

"Yup."

"Great, now if I defend myself when his awful daughter is being a bi—" She catches herself. "Big mean person, I won't get to work with the animals." I see the disappointment in her eyes.

I touch her cheek. "You'll find a way to be nice."

"I am nice! It's her! I just want to be around the animals. They're not cruel and don't make fun of me, or say stupid things. The cat walks around being a cat and the pig doesn't care that the other pig is fatter than him. It's why I want to be homeschooled!"

"It's a good thing that you're not a cat or pig."

"Yeah, god forbid I get to be happy."

I've never seen her be so unforgiving, but clearly Everly has gotten under her skin. Much like Everly's father is under mine.

"Happiness is overrated, babe. Best learn it early in life. Now, go to school and be a human—a nice one."

* * *

Nina walks toward the counter with a grin. "You missed your favorite caller."

"She's like clockwork."

We both laugh because the one day Mrs. Dickman didn't call, we didn't know what to do with ourselves.

Nina and I stared at the phone that day, waiting for it to ring. After two hours, I had the worst feeling and walked to her house to be sure she wasn't injured or sick. It turned out her grandson was visiting and she forgot all about the chairs. Which seemed so impossible, since it's basically her life's mission to get the chairs back.

"Yes, she really is, but it's rather cute, isn't it?"

I nod. "I wish we could find these chairs. I know it weighs so heavy on her."

Nina sighs. "I wish someone would love me that much."

"Well, if she hadn't sold the ugly chairs to begin with she wouldn't need to search the world for them."

Not that I blame her at all. Those chairs and the ugly couch must've come from the same designer back in the early 1900s. Still, Mrs. Dickman won't rest until the set is back in her possession.

"You would've done the same!" Nina giggles. "Look at the true testament of love, though, willing to sit on those hideous things just to feel closer to the man you loved."

We both grin as we each remember the story that we've heard a million times.

Nina sits on the ugly couch and sighs. "It's so sad that he passed last year."

"But you're right, it is sweet that she still looks for the chairs."

Mrs. Dickman may drive me bonkers with the chair call each day, but it's a beautiful testament to the love they shared. No matter that he's gone, she still wants to get back the dining set because her heart needs them.

The first time I heard the story I was so moved I went on a mission to find them. We called pretty much every possible antique store and furniture place possible, but came up empty-handed.

"I think she irritates me so much because I feel like I'm disappointing her each time she calls."

I nod in agreement. "I want to find them so we can give her some peace."

"We will. You never know what you lose that will come back." Nina's eyes are studying mine. "You know, lost things tend to find their owner."

"Why do I think we're not talking about the chairs anymore?"

"Oh, I don't know why you'd think that. Did something recently return to you that was gone?"

I'm not ready to talk about last night. I'm too emotional and raw to actually be able to describe what I'm feeling aloud.

In my head, I'm battling whether I'm being irrational or not. Derek and I were kids to some extent and we made choices we thought were right. It's not even so much that he basically cut me off, it's the reason. I didn't do anything wrong, and now I know that it was something he did—or wrote—that caused it.

Yet he never talked to me. He didn't tell me he felt anything more than friendship. Neither did I, but he was engaged.

And I was pregnant with another man's baby. There wasn't exactly some prime opportunity to confess my undying love. It all could've been so different for us. For everyone, really. Had we just talked to each other, we might've found a way.

Nina clears her throat, apparently wanting an answer.

The bell above the door rings and I smirk. "Saved by the bell."

Nina eyes me. We both know better. She's like a dog with a bone when there's information she wants. There's no way she'll let this go just because a customer is here. Then, her grin looks like it could split her face. "Sure. Something like that." Then she turns back toward the door. "Well, well, well, look what the cat dragged in. If it isn't Derek Hartz."

chapter fifteen

Derek

present

I'm not sure why I'm here, I just knew that I needed to talk to her. We're going to be in the same town and I don't want it to be uncomfortable for everyone.

Also, I hate that I hurt her.

The look on her face lets me know I've managed to do it again by showing up.

"What are you doing here?" Her voice is full of venom as she glares at me.

Nina slaps her arm. "Stop it. He's welcome here. It's good to see you, Derek, or should I call you Dr. Hartz?"

I always liked Nina. She was kind and would do anything to help someone in trouble. It's good to see she and Teagan are friends.

"Don't you dare call me doctor anything." I pull her in for a hug as Teagan glares at me. "It's good to see you too."

"I heard about your wife, I'm so sorry."

"Thank you."

"How are you holding up?"

There's the honest answer and then the one that everyone wants to hear. I'm sure I could tell her how I'm falling apart, not only because I do miss Meghan, but because I don't know what to do. I don't know how to be a dad without her. She was the one who told me to go talk to Everly or pick up things. I was…an accessory to parenting. Now, I'm everything.

I don't know how often I need to take Everly for a haircut or if she should be shaving her legs. I really pray that's already taken care of and I don't have to think about it.

Then I wonder about all the girl shit that I know absolutely nothing about.

So, I'm not holding up anything but a prayer because I'm hopeless.

"I'm doing the best I can," I say with a sad smile. This answer is really all anyone wants to know. "It's been an adjustment, to say the least."

"I would assume so. How's your father? Your mother, bless her heart, told me he was having a bit of trouble lately."

It's hard to talk about. My father has always been a hero to me. He was strong, smart, able to make things happen without looking like he tried. When my mother called to tell me that he was forgetting things, I thought it was because he's getting old, but it's more than that and I'm struggling to cope with it.

"He's doing the best he can."

Teagan takes a step closer. "Your dad is loved in this town."

I nod. "He'll be okay. I'm here to take some of the pressure off of him, which I think will help."

Nina touches my arm. "Anything that you need, just ask. This town may be full of loony people, but we all care when one of our own needs some help."

Teagan scoffs. "Right."

"Oh, you stop it," Nina scolds her with a wave of her hand. "I'm going to head into the back and see about some of the new stuff that was brought in. It's like Christmas each time Mrs. Berkeley goes on a road show trip. She comes back with a crate, we open it up and see what she thought was a good find."

"I'll have to take your word on it."

"I've got that." Teagan jumps in. "I'll go back there and handle it, you and Derek catch up. You know how much I love the crate opening."

From the sound of her voice, she's full of shit. What she would love is to get away from me.

She starts to move but Nina shifts around her. "No, no, we both know he's not here for me. I'll go, you guys…you know…be adults here and work your shit out."

Teagan hisses at her, but I can't understand what she's saying.

Nina, who is always polite, throws me a smile and then kisses Teagan's cheek before exiting. "It was great seeing you, Derek. Be sure to stop by again."

"Thanks."

After a few seconds of silence, Teagan's shoulders slump. "What are you doing here, Derek?"

"I came to talk."

"Then talk."

The whole point to this unexpected visit is to lay out what happened better, but now that we're here, looking at each other, I don't know what to say.

How do I explain that my feelings for her were so deep I contemplated how to leave my pregnant wife? I don't know if I ever would've left, but I know I had to walk away from Teagan to make sure I didn't hurt everyone involved. It was the only way to save my marriage and even give Teagan a chance at a life that I couldn't give her.

The thing is, even after all the time that's passed, I still love her.

I've always loved her. From the first time we met on that beach after she tutored me when I was barely sixteen, I knew my life would forever be altered by Teagan Berkeley.

She had this light inside of her that cast a glow around you. You couldn't help but want to bask in it, and when I was with her, I did.

It wasn't just that she was beautiful, it was also how she made me feel when I was around her. Once she let me in, I never wanted out.

Now I've injured her, and I want to make it right.

"I didn't mean to hurt you."

"I appreciate that wasn't your intention, but it doesn't change the fact that you did."

There's one part of this that has been bugging me…why did she walk away on the beach last night? Was it because Meghan asked that I stop seeing her? Or was it because I chose my wife? If I'm honest, I suspect it was my confession that I fell in love with her that made Teagan walk away.

"Why, though?"

"Why what?"

"Why did you say it was cruel to tell you the truth?"

Teagan shakes her head. "You were never stupid, Derek. Don't pretend to be now."

"You were also never this closed off and unwilling to tell me things."

She bites her lower lip and looks away. "I wonder what could've made me this way?"

I deserved that. I've given her every reason to distrust me. "Why did me telling you the reason I had to end our friendship upset you so much?"

"Why do you need to know?"

"Because it doesn't make sense."

"It doesn't matter."

That's where she's wrong. "It matters to me. Why, Tea?"

Her green eyes study me. It's as if she's trying to see through me so she can be sure I'm not really this dense. "Because you say you realized you loved me, and your solution was to walk away from me. So easily. That's not love. Not real love in a way that was actually meaning-ful."

"You would've told me to leave my pregnant wife for my best friend who didn't even like me that way? That would've been your solution?" Teagan's arms drop as she pushes off the counter. Her head lifts to the ceiling and I can practically feel her anguish. "Tea?"

"I more than liked you, Derek. I loved you. Not just as a friend, but I *loved* you."

My heart rate accelerates and I rack my brain for any indication she felt the same. There were no signs or even a hint that her feelings were more. If anything, she made it seem the opposite. Someone would joke that eventually we'd realize we were desperately in love, she'd laugh and say we had a better chance of hell freezing over. To me, it wasn't even a possibility.

"You never said a word."

She throws her hands up. "No shit I didn't! I had all these plans to tell you and then something or someone else would be in our way. There was never a chance to say anything."

Now it's my turn to be pissed off. "You had plenty of chances."

"When? When you told me about Meghan and that you were already in love with her? Or maybe when you were dating someone before her? Or what about right after I found out I was pregnant? No, none of those times worked because I would've been the worst person alive to have told you. I would've destroyed everything that made you happy. What would that have made me?"

"The person who loved me enough to tell me!"

The real answer is…*hers*. It would've made me hers. I'm livid. I'm not just angry she didn't tell me. I'm pissed off at everything and everyone. I'm mad because if Meghan didn't die, I wouldn't be hearing this. I'm angry because if I could handle Everly and my dad wasn't sick, I wouldn't be here.

Then I could've spared us all of this hurt—again.

She crosses her arms over her stomach. "No, I loved you enough to let you be happy and not fuck your head up. I stood by your side at your wedding, wishing it was me in front of you. I wanted to beg you so many times to love me, but that would've been unkind. I didn't think you felt the same and I wasn't going to risk everything we had, not when I needed you."

Now it's my turn to step back. My jaw falls slack at her confession. "I never thought…"

"I wouldn't let you. So you want to know why it hurt so much last night? Because after all these years of imagining you telling me you felt this way, I find out that it was a way for you to resent me. As if I ever did anything to deserve your hostility." Teagan takes a step closer with unshed tears in her eyes, but they don't fall. "I did everything to protect you so that I wouldn't lose you. Having you as my best friend, even if I loved you more than you would ever know, was more important to me."

"I didn't want to lose you," I tell her as I move closer. "I never wanted that."

"You were the one who walked away."

"I had no choice."

"There's always a choice, Derek. In fact, it was *you* who told me that. You chose to marry Meghan and that's okay."

It wasn't okay. I did choose Meghan. I had to. I loved her, and she was my wife. That was the hand I was dealt and chose to play. I couldn't fold and I wasn't allowed to draw.

"What would you have done if you were me?"

A tear runs down her cheek. "I would've done what felt right, which, knowing you, is what you did. You had a family to think about, and I'm not angry at that. I get it. I wished so many times that someone would choose me."

"So you're upset that I chose Meghan?"

She shakes her head. "No, it's not about Meghan."

"Then what's it about?"

Teagan looks like she's at war with herself. "Everything. I went through hell, Derek. I have never felt more alone than I did after you cut me off. I had my parents, which was actually worse than being alone. The town judged me—still does most days. Then there was the fact that I had this baby I didn't know how to take care of. I was so scared. I had to go through this court hearing to relinquish Keith's paternal rights. Can you imagine how crippling all that was?"

No one ever saw the amazing person she was, even in her faults. I did though. I run my hand through my hair, pacing. I know all of this and the guilt I felt was monumental. She counted on me and I walked away. "It wasn't easy for me to let you go! I didn't want you to go through any of that. I would've been there. I would...I should've...I didn't want any of it!"

"But I did do it alone! And somehow, I survived, but none of what I endured held a candle to the amount of hurt I felt at losing you. In a matter of a few months I lost *everything*. My life, college, my parents were so angry, Keith was selfish, and then...the only person in the world I loved and I knew would love me...was gone. So when you ask me why that hurt me so much...I'm hurt that you loving me cost me the only thing I cared about. I lost you because you fell in love with me. Once again, I destroyed my own happiness, without even knowing it."

Teagan deserves so much more than she'll ever know. "You didn't lose me because I fell in love with you, and you didn't destroy anything, Teagan. I did."

She huffs and wipes the tears under her eyes. "That's not true. The minute you realized you loved me is the minute I lost you. But the thing is, I had a part in it too! I loved you so much and I let you go. I did it for you. I watched you walk away and I was too afraid to stop you. We are both culpable."

We both fall quiet. The room is charged with so much emotion it's hard to breathe. How far we've fallen...

Once upon a time she and I were envied by many. I don't know that anyone would look at us now and hope to become what we are to each other.

Feeling sad that this is the current state of things, I confess my own shame. "There were so many times that I wished I never wrote those words down. If I had kept my feelings to myself, nothing would've changed. I could've been there for you and we could've gone on without anyone knowing." Admitting the words aloud for the first time is difficult. I've thought them, plenty of times, but never allowed myself to speak them.

Teagan releases a heavy sigh. "It would've happened at some point."

I look at her, surprised that she would say that. "What would've?"

"One of us would've said it. We never kept secrets before, I don't know how we managed to do it with something this important." Teagan moves toward me, and for the first time since I showed up, she's not filled with apprehension. "I never would've put you in a position to choose me or Meghan because you should've—and would've—picked her. So, I would've sat back, watching you live and love her, hating it, wishing it was me. And if the truth did reveal itself, I would've denied it, not wanting to ruin your life. Maybe...I don't know."

"Maybe it was for the best?" I finish her thought.

"Maybe."

"No," I tell her, wanting her to understand. "It wasn't. I should've been there for you too. You needed me and I failed you."

So many times I wanted to ask my parents about her, but I didn't. I wasn't strong enough to know she wasn't okay, so I made myself believe she was happy, married to someone, raising their kids together. I would've never stayed away had I heard otherwise.

"I failed myself," Teagan says as she sits on the ugly sofa that's still here.

I move over and sit beside her. "I think we both had a part in our own destruction."

She sniffs. "I guess we did."

"How did we get here?"

"I have no idea," Teagan confesses.

"This wasn't going to be us. We were better than this. We were supposed to be indestructible."

"No, we could've been that, but I was scared and stupid. Neither of us were willing to see the truth until it was too late. And then I got pregnant."

"Why did you stay with Keith, Teagan? Why didn't you end things?"

She turns to look at me, tears filling her beautiful green eyes. "I thought if I held on to him, then I could let you go. In the end, he not only threw me away, but he cost me you. Funny how that worked, huh?"

"I don't think anything regarding Keith is funny."

"I would agree with you there. He made his choices, though." Teagan sighs and wipes her eyes. "He gave up the best thing he ever did in his miserable life. Chastity is bigger and better than any dream he could've had. He walked away from her without ever understanding what a gift having a child is."

Losing Meghan was horrific, but the fear I felt knowing Everly was in the car was—crippling. It was a terror like

I'd never known. Thinking I could've lost them both was too much to even comprehend.

It made me feel sick to have any relief at the time of the accident, but all I kept thinking was, thank God it wasn't Everly.

For a father to give that up willingly, is beyond my understanding.

It goes to show what an asshole Keith was. He cared about only himself and football. Teagan knew it, and it never made sense to me why she stayed with him.

But it was irrelevant because in the end, we made our choices and have to accept them.

"I really did come over here to apologize. Not to drum up old shit and fight."

Teagan shakes her head with a smile. "Well, you've always sucked at apologies."

"And you sucked at accepting them."

Maybe she and I will find a new way to coexist and maybe I can have my best friend back because I could sure use her.

chapter sixteen

Teagan

present

"I *still* want to be homeschooled," Chastity announces at dinner…with my parents. She's been a bear the last four days and I can only assume it's because of Everly and whoever she's found for her squad of bitches.

"Well, I love you, but not that much," I say as I shove a forkful of spaghetti into my mouth. "We've already had this talk and my stance hasn't changed."

"Why would you want to be homeschooled?" Mom asks, unable to stop herself from seizing the opportunity to pry.

"Because I hate the stupid girls there! I'm not going back."

I look at her and shake my head. "Yeah, you are."

"You can't make me."

"Oh, but I can."

"Maybe we should talk about it," Mom suggests. "She's clearly upset."

I didn't want to come here tonight, but I did because

Chastity wanted to see her grandparents. Now I'm starting to wonder if this isn't an ambush. My parents are getting ready for another road trip. The summer tourists clean us out each year and then we spend the winter finding treasures to restock the store.

"Mom, you're not helping."

She touches Chastity's arm. "She's upset and needs support."

"Well, I'm upset and could use some too."

"We're not talking about you."

"We're not talking about Chastity and homeschooling either," I emphasize.

Dad clears his throat and grabs his phone as if he's reading. Glad to see I have his help on this one.

"Why can't we just discuss it?" Mom asks.

"Because there's no reason to. I have no help as it is and taking on tutoring my daughter, who is pretty much smarter than me at this point, isn't possible."

"So you'd send her to school with those horrible girls?"

I laugh once. "You want to teach her to run away from them?"

I try not to ask for much from my parents. The apartment is the only thing they help with, which isn't really help. It was vacant and it was in shambles. I lasted a whole two months in my parents' house after Chastity was born before I decided cleaning, painting, throwing out whatever I could to fix it up was worth it.

After negotiating with my father, I had a fair rent set up, which is deducted from my paycheck, a clean place for me and Chastity, and a job. Of course, it was meant to be a two-year plan and I've extended it…a lot, but whatever.

Going back to school is really hard when you have no money or time.

"You should at least hear her out," Mom chides as she takes a sip of her wine.

"No, because I'm not homeschooling her. Besides, when exactly would I do this? I work at the store six days a week, for minimum wage I might add, and…if I'm going to work on top of doing schoolwork, it would be for me."

Chastity leans back in her chair. "You?"

"Yes, I would like to go and get my degree since I dropped out."

"You want to go back to school?" My daughter stares at me like I have two heads.

Have I really never said it? "I guess. I mean, once you're off to college it would be nice to have a plan."

Since I doubt painting is ever going to be anything more than just an outlet, a backup seems necessary.

"Why haven't you mentioned it?" Dad asks.

"Why would I?"

"Because we could've helped."

Now I'm stunned. "Helped how? You and Mom have been going on and on about me being independent and caring for Chastity on my own, which I've managed to do. Why would I think that was an option?"

"You have been the one that demanded handling Chastity on your own, honey."

Is he crazy? "How?"

"You moved out of this house, for one," Mom says with a sarcastic laugh. "You wanted nothing to do with us and having a built-in support system. You couldn't sign those papers fast enough releasing Keith from—"

"Don't!" I slap my hand on the table. "Don't talk about him in front of her."

This is the one thing I've done my best to shield Chastity from. She knows who her father is. She sees his stupid ass on television and hears all about what a hero he is for this stupid town. I don't lie to her, but I don't talk about what happened between him and me.

"Mom, it's fine." Chastity tries to calm the situation, but there's not a chance of that.

"None of your life had to be this way," Mom says. "You could've had a different future, but you were so damn sure you could do this on your own."

And here it is. The talk of how I did this all to myself. That I signed away the right to be pissed at him.

"Yes, I know, Mom. Keith is the saint who did the right thing by all of us out of the kindness of his heart."

"Well, it definitely wasn't for your own good. You were always so thick-headed."

I shake my head. "What about the fact that he could show up at any point? He knows where we are. I see his mother once a week, right? It's not like they don't know that Chastity is their granddaughter, but...it's me."

My mother busies herself with her food. "They're honoring your wishes."

"My wishes?" I yell and slam my fork down. "*My* wishes? Are you serious?"

None of this was my wish. I didn't wish for him to never pay a dime after she was born, and then once the paternity was established—as if there was any doubt he was the father—tell me that I had two choices, thanks to his fucking agent. Either he would fight me for full custody and make my life a living hell or I let him out of all responsibilities and never have to worry about any interference from him again.

I was ready to fight him. He was signing his big football contract in a few weeks. That's when the floor dropped out. I had to choose, either I let him walk away from all parental rights or they leaked the tape that I regret more than anything, ruining my life and having the shame follow me and Chastity for our entire lives.

"Mom, please." Chastity stands. "Please, I really don't care. He doesn't care about me and I don't even think about him."

Protecting her has been the only thing I've ever given a shit about. "I'm sorry," I say to her. "I'm sorry that you have to deal with anything regarding him."

"Well, you made that her reality when you got pregnant." My mother's words feel like a slap across the face.

I start to say something, to defend myself, and demand that she stop this. I can take the fault for a lot, but I'm tired of the blame for getting pregnant being completely on me.

My father clears his throat. "I think we all need to calm down. Meredith"—he turns to my mother—"Teagan has done a good job raising Chastity, we should at least acknowledge that much. She's handled her situation better than most and I, for one, am proud of her."

"Yes, but think of how much *easier* it would've been if she hadn't pushed Keith away."

I shove out from the table. "I need a few minutes," I say as I get to my feet. "Please excuse me."

"Mom."

"No, it's fine." Her brown eyes, the ones that match her piece-of-shit father's, stare back at me. I see the displeasure in them and give her a reassuring smile. My daughter shouldn't feel bad. "I'm okay. I just need...to think."

I don't wait for a reply, I head out the back door and go to the only place I can ever feel any sort of peace...the beach.

* * *

I wish I had my paint. There are so many emotions at war inside of me and painting is my vessel that allows me to extract them. It's cathartic to feel pain and paint with red to emulate the hurt. Each color gives a visible voice to what I feel.

I need to find my voice.

My house is close and I rush there, grabbing the canvas and paints, not looking at what I grab, not caring because every color on the rainbow is appropriate.

I'm moving quickly, needing that release because if I don't, I might burst.

Painting has calmed me since I started. It was something Nina talked me into trying a few years ago, but it quickly became my form of therapy.

I get to the shoreline, tossing my supplies on the blanket, and sit.

With my eyes closed, I grab a color.

Blue.

How appropriate, since I'm feeling quite blue.

As soon as I dip the paint, my world shifts. I'm transported to where I can just...be.

The color glides against the canvas, creating another variation of the ocean I always paint.

Each time, the hues are different, the lights shining off the water in a different way, but the perspective is always the same.

I'm in the ocean, looking at the shore, wondering where in this great big world I fit.

I don't know how long I'm here. Time is irrelevant, but the sun is setting and the air is chilling.

"We have to stop running into each other this way." Derek's voice a little way back causes me to jump.

Shit. I quickly try to clean up what I was doing. There are only two people in the world who know I paint... Chastity and Nina. It's something that's mine and I've never wanted to share it. I dump the paints and dirty brush in the bag. "I was here first."

He's at the beginning of the dunes and it'll take him maybe thirty seconds to get here. I get the bulk of things put away, but I don't know what to do with the canvas. I really love the blues and purples in this one and don't want to ruin it and yet I don't want him to see it.

I turn my head and see him closer than I thought. Jesus, is he running?

I stand, put the canvas against my knees, and wrap my blanket around me, hoping it doesn't completely screw it up.

"You were here first, but you were always good about sharing."

"It's a big beach, you know?"

"I do."

"And yet you keep finding the exact spot I'm at." I purse my lips, wondering why that is. I specifically chose a little farther down the shore for this reason. I truly wanted solitude and to just...paint.

Right now, my emotions are too raw and close to the surface to be around anyone.

"Maybe I was looking for you..."

So many freaking times I wanted to hear that or something like that. I wanted him to find me, fix me, love me, but he never did.

It was stupid and immature, but when it came to Derek, I hoped, because he always came through for me.

"And why would you be looking for me?"

"Because I figure the more times I see you, the less awkward it will be."

I nod once. "Well, okay then."

Not sure that it'll ever be that way, but we can hope. Our lives were on a course, and then we took a detour, but never ended up back on the same road. I don't know that our friendship can be salvaged, which is sad, since he's still the best friend I ever had. Even though Nina is a close second, it's not the same.

"Truth?" he asks after a second.

"Always."

Derek runs his hand through his hair, which used to be his nervous habit. "I'm struggling."

My chest aches because I don't like to see him hurting. "I'm sorry."

"I'm completely fucking up this parenting thing."

I laugh because I can relate. "We're all throwing spaghetti at the wall to find out if it's done, only to watch it fall off. Parenting, from what I've learned so far, is trial by fire."

I'm in a constant state of anxiety and pretty much always wrong. There's all these books, advice columns, and people who will offer infinite amounts of crappy wisdom that doesn't work.

"Good to know."

"I'm saying you're not alone and you had a wife, who probably did a lot more than you knew."

Derek sighs, letting me know I was right. "Everly hates me. And sometimes—okay, often—it feels like she's purposely trying to make my life a living hell."

"She's a teenager. That's her sole mission. And from what I've heard, your daughter seems to be a bit less like you and more like…"

"You!" He says with a laugh. "She's you!"

I try not to take that as an insult, but looking back at myself at thirteen…it's not a compliment.

"Well, I think I turned out all right after fucking things up pretty good. There's hope."

"From what my parents say about Chastity, you've done pretty amazing."

"Yes, well, you didn't think that when we were at the school."

His laugh is soft. "I was pissed. My father and mother told me how she volunteers at the clinic. Then, Nina was raving about how smart she is. Not to mention the people in town talk about what a great kid she is when I'm doing vet calls."

His compliment washes over me and I try not to smile like an idiot. I've done the best I can. Chastity is a smart, kind, and giving kid. She's filled with sarcasm and fire, but uses it only at me. I think she's beautiful, even if she doesn't, and she won't waste her life away like I did.

"So you talk about me when you're on vet calls?" I ask.

"Anytime I see anyone they bring us up or ask if I've seen you. I'm proud of you, Tea. You're raising her with very little help and I've got my parents and I'm floundering."

"I know you're a little in over your head, but you'll find your footing." I let out a little giggle. "Just in time for the floor to move and you're wobbling again."

"Great."

"Yeah, I love my daughter more than anything in the world. I wouldn't give her up for anything, but since Chastity came along, I never feel like I have it together—ever. I doubt myself constantly and not a damn thing goes smoothly. There is nothing more rewarding or scary than being a single parent."

I shift a little and the canvas falls. Shit. I rub my hand over my face and groan.

"What's that?"

"Nothing." I try to shift to hide the painting again. There are some secrets that a woman should be allowed.

"No, there's something on your face," he says as he steps closer. He reaches his hand toward me and I freeze. I'm not even sure that I'm breathing because I don't trust myself completely.

Derek and I were never afraid of being physical when we were younger. We were always snuggling up together, hugging, and whatnot, but it's been years. It's been so long that I don't know how to keep myself in check. I no longer have the shell that I built up to protect me. And now I know…there was something between us all along. How do I fight him now? How do I protect myself because while Derek hurt me once, we were just friends then. This time, knowing what I know now, losing him would destroy me. My heart wouldn't recover.

Not to mention, while there might be this illusion of

something more, it could never work. There's been too much time that's passed and whatever feelings we might have had before aren't real now.

We don't even know each other anymore.

His finger lightly grazes my cheek and my skin burns from his touch. What is wrong with me? His wife died not too long ago and I'm standing here with my heart pounding. I shouldn't be relishing the idea of his touch. I should be completely immune because my feelings for him have changed.

Haven't they?

As quick and monumental as the touch is, it's gone just as fast.

"Paint?" Derek asks as he smudges the blue between his fingers. "Why do you have paint on your hands?"

"No idea."

"Really?"

I can either lie to him or fess up and lose my secret.

Lie it is.

"I must've touched something at the store."

Derek's brow rises, just the one, letting me know he clearly didn't buy it. "And after sitting out here for how long…it's still wet on your hand?"

"It could happen."

"It could, but it's not very likely."

Now his curiosity is probably piqued. Sure enough, he looks down at the ground and tries to see around me. I shift, trying to keep it hidden, but that gave it away, and now I'm so screwed.

Derek acts as though he's going to move to the right and I move that way to block him, but he adjusts quickly and reaches to the left, grabbing the canvas.

"Please..."

I'm not sure what I'm asking him. It could be please don't, please tell me you love it, please don't judge me, or please give it back and we'll never speak of it.

But what I really mean is, please give me back my heart.

chapter seventeen

Teagan

present

"This is amazing, you painted these?" Derek asks as he stands in what I pretend is a gallery, which is really a closet in the back of my parents' store that they don't use and never go in. This is my safe place. It's where I hang my paintings to dry. My favorite ones are still hanging because I can't bring myself to take them down.

"I did."

"I can't believe how beautiful these are, Tea."

There was no getting out of telling him once he grabbed the painting, although it had sand on it and wasn't exactly a beach scene anymore. However, as imperfect as it is, I'm sort of in love with it.

It's messy, much like my life. It has texture—I've never thought to add sand to the paint before—but it's also still vibrant.

"You don't have to lie," I say with a bit of nervous energy. "I know they're amateur and not that great, but painting is my outlet."

"Why do you think I'm lying?"

"Because you're not cruel and don't want to tell me they're shit."

His eyes go back to the painting. "I'm not lying, Teagan, they're really beautiful. I haven't seen paintings with this perspective before. Have you ever tried to sell any?"

Or maybe he is cruel. "No. No one even knows I do this. This is my hobby that I don't talk about, and now that you know what I was hiding, we can never speak of it again."

"Why?"

"Why what?"

"Why do you always do that?" he grumbles.

"Do what?"

"That!" Derek says with a growl. "You answer questions with a question—still. I figured you would've grown out of it by now."

I grin, liking that it irritates him. I don't even realize I do it. It's just easier than trying to guess and be wrong. If people were more forward and didn't beat around the bush, I wouldn't have to keep asking them to clarify.

"It's a habit." I shrug.

"Yeah, it's annoying."

"So is you pointing it out."

Derek huffs but I catch his grin. "Well...too bad."

This is the first time it feels a little like old times. He's giving me shit and I'm giving it right back.

"So what did Everly do that is making you question your life choices?" I ask as he stands in front of one painting for too long.

"I don't stand for bullying and I heard her"—he shifts uncomfortably—"on the phone...making plans."

It's not hard to guess what—or who—the plans are for. "She's trying to make her place in the pack."

"Excuse me?"

"You're a vet, you should get what I'm saying."

Derek rubs his temples and I try not to laugh at him. "You mean they're a pack of animals?"

He has no idea. "Wolves would've been my first choice of words, but yes. Teenage girls, well, the bitchy ones, tend to live in a pack mentality. Remember me with Lori and Kelly?"

"Oh, how I wish I could forget."

We were truly awful and I hate when I look back at myself during that time. I can only hope that Everly is more like me and less like Kelly. She was the orchestrator of it all. Each horrible thing came from her devious mind.

"Well, what were the plans for Chastity?"

"You don't want to know."

"That's where you're wrong, the best way to beat them is to know the plan. Can you imagine if every person Kelly wanted to destroy knew beforehand? They could've taken countermeasures."

Derek takes a step closer. "I squashed it. You don't have to worry."

"That's not likely."

"Seriously, I wouldn't let it happen."

He is cute that he thinks he has that type of control. "Still, I think the more information the better. Do you want to see Chastity caught up in this? Don't you think she's endured enough?"

Whether he tells me or not, I'm going to prepare my daughter.

"Of course she has." He sighs and moves back. "It's

just that so has my daughter and I'm not going to betray her."

I can understand that, but I'm in the same boat. "And what about protecting my daughter?"

"I would never hurt your daughter or let Everly hurt her," Derek says with conviction. "I need you to trust me."

Trust. That word means so much. "Once upon a time I did trust you, and we're a long way from that right now."

"I know and I'm sorry. I think you need to have some blind faith then. I really like Chastity. She's a smart girl, by the way. Way smarter than even you were back then. I enjoyed having her assist me today."

I forgot that today was the first time she worked with him. She's been going over there, doing tasks for his father, but she told me that Derek was who she shadowed today. I had to bite my tongue to keep from asking a million questions.

Was he nice to her?

Was he funny?

Did he ask her about me?

Did he smell nice?

The last one was way over the line of appropriate to ask my teenage daughter, so I figured it was probably best to not ask anything and let her lead the conversation.

"Yeah, I hope she's smarter than me in every possible way. She loves animals and would happily be with them more than people."

"I can see that. She helped clean out more crap in those stalls than I would've at her age and still asked to stay a little longer to play with the animals."

I smile to myself. "Reminds me of someone else I used to know."

"Well, I didn't have a choice. I grew up on a zoo thanks to my dad."

"But you loved the animals."

He nods. "I still do."

It's crazy how much Chastity is like him in some ways. "I feel like our kids were switched at birth, don't you?"

Derek lets out a small laugh. "You'd think, considering how close we were and how well I could manage you, that I'd do a better job with her," he says and then his eyes go back to the painting.

I walk up behind him, allowing myself to look over his shoulder to see which he's fixated on.

Of course it would be that painting.

I remember that one so distinctly. I painted it on my thirty-first birthday. It had been years since I had allowed myself to remember him in any sort of wistful way. I learned that thinking about him only made me sad.

But that birthday was different.

I was so lonely. We had made a pact that if by our thir-tieth birthdays we weren't married, we would marry each other.

It was stupid and it never really would happen, but there I was, seventeen again and laughing with him after prom.

I sat at the beach for four hours. With each stroke of my brush, a tear would fall, mourning the loss of him over and over. All the feelings of sadness I'd pushed aside washed over me. I was sitting, watching the waves crest and re-treat, painting them with the sun from a different angle.

He turns, our eyes lock on each other, and my heart begins to race. He looks at me like he's seeing straight through my heart.

Derek doesn't say anything. He watches, searching deeper inside of my soul than I give him permission to. It unnerves me and I feel exposed.

Too many feelings fill me.

Too much of…all of it.

I turn my head, and start to walk away, but he grips my wrist. "I'm sorry."

My eyes snap back to his. "For?"

"Everything."

Each breath I take is heavy and my head is spinning. When I paint, I'm raw with emotion. Now, being in this room with him looking at my work, saying these things, has me feeling vulnerable.

"It was a long time ago. It doesn't really matter, does it?"

His lids fall, and I know that wasn't what he wanted to hear, but it's all I can give. I need to build my walls back up because Derek is the dream that will never come true for me.

"I'm still sorry."

"I am too." For everything.

"Do you think we can ever be friends again?"

We've lost too much, hurt each other too deeply to ever be more than…this.

Indifferent old friends who won't be able to get through the mucky past, which is filled with quicksand. I can't afford to step in it and get sucked under.

Chastity needs me to be strong. I can't become this weak woman who is heartbroken over him.

"I hope so. I hope we can be a different kind of friends. Ones who are older, wiser, and honest. Do you think that's possible? Considering our history?" I ask.

Derek shifts to the side. "History doesn't always have to define the future."

I ponder that for second because I don't think that's true. "It usually does."

"Sure, it has before, but we're the ones who get to decide if that's the case for us."

I smile softly, wishing if I believe it hard enough, it could be true. But wanting something doesn't make it a reality.

Sometimes, shit happens and you have to make the best of it.

"What if something else has already made that choice for us?" I counter.

Derek shrugs. "Then I guess we'll have to figure it out."

"As friends."

"Good friends," he tacks on.

"Friends who will coexist in this ridiculous town and encourage our daughters to find a way to get along."

His eyes turn back to the painting. "I hope we're able to do more than coexist. I guess time will tell."

Yeah, I guess it will.

chapter eighteen

Teagan

present

"I don't know how you can talk to my mom," Chastity says to Nina as we put away my mother's newest finds.

"Why?"

"Because she was mean, like Everly." The name comes out as a sneer.

It's been a week since Chastity's brought up Everly and I'd hoped it meant Everly had moved on, but apparently not.

"Have you tried to talk to her?" I ask.

"You can't talk or look the Devil in the eye, Mother. You'll go straight to hell."

Nina snorts. "It's so hard for me to imagine that girl being anything but nice. Derek was such a good guy—still is, so I'm surprised his offspring isn't."

"Dr. Hartz is the best. He's so nice and lets me do way more than the other Dr. Hartz."

It eats me alive a little bit knowing she spends so much time with Derek. Each day, she heads there, works with him, and then comes here to tell me how much she likes him.

I'm jealous that my daughter is hanging out with a man I want to see, which makes me the worst mother ever. I'm the picture-perfect image of maturity.

"He's a good guy."

"You two were best friends, right?"

I nod. "Once upon a time."

"What happened?"

I would throw myself off a building to avoid this conversation.

"Nothing. We drifted apart."

Chastity nods. "Sad that it happened, since he's pretty cool. Even if he was responsible for creating Satan's spawn."

I burst out laughing. "You're so dramatic. You also have no idea what that girl went through."

I watch my daughter's eyes narrow in disgust. I know she hates Everly, and rightfully so, but exercising compassion is never a bad thing.

"So that gives her the right to be nasty to me?"

"Of course not, but I don't think she's inherently mean."

"I know what it's like to only have one parent and I don't treat others that way." That statement wasn't meant to be a dig at me. I know this. I can rationalize it, but it still bugs me that she doesn't know the love of two parents.

"Do you think that's because you never knew what it was like?" Nina asks.

"I also don't know what poop tastes like, but I know I don't want to try it."

"Chas, that's not exactly what we're…"

"All I'm saying is just because you got knocked up with me from that guy who wanted nothing to do with either of us, doesn't mean she gets to make bad choices too."

"So I made a bad choice?" I ask.

"Mom," Chastity says and moves toward me.

"No, no," I tell her with my hand up. "I get it. Mean girls for the win, right?"

Nina touches her arm. "I think what your mother is saying is that Everly's mother was killed in front of her. We know that your father is…well…but you didn't know what it was like to have him, lose him, and then be taken from all you know."

I need to send Nina a gift for that one. We would've headed down a very different road had she not intervened. I refocus on the issue instead of on my own issues. "Exactly, being nice to her is more of a statement about you than her."

Chastity shakes her head with an eye roll. "And I would feel bad if she didn't think making me cry was so much fun. If she was more like her dad, I wouldn't hate her."

There's no point in going on because she's right. However, I think that Everly's in deep pain, and lashing out is the only way to get through it.

"Speaking of, have you seen Derek lately?" Nina asks in a seemingly nonchalant way that isn't at all nonchalant.

She knows damn well I haven't. "Nope."

"Really? I saw him yesterday and he mentioned you. He was saying something about coming by to catch up."

I glare at her. "I haven't seen or heard from him, but I didn't expect to."

Nina nods with a smile. "I see. Well, in this town it's bound to happen."

Chastity looks between us. "Am I missing something?"

This girl is too smart for her own good. There's no way with Nina's subtlety of an elephant marching through the store that Chastity isn't going to catch on. Nina is hoping for some kind of grand reunion that I'm not ready to think about. Right now, I'm fine with friends. Friends are safe and leave no room for hurt.

"Nope."

"Really? Because I feel like there's something you're both talking about that I don't know about."

"Just that your mama—"

"Doesn't really want to see Dr. Hartz because his daughter is mean to you," I cut her off with my brows raised.

My friend is going to die today, it seems.

"Right. I would believe that, but you said that I should be nice…"

"Don't you think we should set your mama up?" Nina says out of nowhere.

"Set her up?"

"Yes, like on one of those online dating things."

"No," I say before this gets out of hand.

Nina grins and her devious little mind is hard at work. "I think it's a great plan, Teagan. You're clearly ready to start dating."

"Clearly? What's clear about it?"

"You mentioned the other day something about a man, didn't you?"

I mentioned Derek, not dating some random guy. "Nope."

"I think it's a great idea, Mom."

Of course she does. "I'm fine with my life as it is."

"What about dating someone local?" Nina appears to be focusing on sorting the plates, but she's not fooling me.

Dating always ends up the same way. I find a guy who's not my type, I'm forced to sit with him for hours, and go home and eat my emotions. The last guy Nina set me up with was the worst and I vowed to never let her interfere again.

"There's no one local and I really don't want to date anyone."

"Why not?" Chastity interjects.

"Because there's no point."

"You're going to die alone. Like a spinster in my romance novels." Nina used to be my friend, until today when I had to kill her. "Do you want to be a spinster?"

"I want to beat you with your own arms," I say with a fake grin. "Aren't you single?"

"I'm not a spinster. I'm more of a modern woman making choices." She smiles at me, and Chastity laughs.

"Well," Nina says as she claps her hands together. "Let's make good choices and get you a date!"

Chastity squeals and grabs my phone. "I already made her an account. We've got this!"

"I hate you both," I grumble and rip the phone back from her. "At least let me look first."

"Deal, as long as you promise to try and date at least one." Nina's fingers grip the top of the phone and she stares me down.

Maybe they're right. Maybe I need to try and see if there's someone out there. If I want to move past this silliness with my old feelings coming back, this would be a good way to start.

I release a heavy sigh and nod. "I promise."

"Good." I see the pride in Nina's eyes.

Chastity wraps her arms around me and squeezes. "I want you to be happy, Mom."

I look down at her, my heart filled with so much love for this girl who has brought me so many unexpected changes that have fulfilled me in so many ways. "You make me happy, Titty."

We all burst out laughing and she rolls her eyes. "Never call me that again."

I shrug. I can't let her have all the fun. Between these two it's a wonder I haven't pulled all my hair out. All I need is my mother to complete the party.

"Girls!" She yells from the back.

Jesus. I'm being punished for my past sins, that's all I've got.

"Talk about looking the Devil in the eye…"

"Be nice," Chastity warns me as though I'm the kid.

Mom and I have barely spoken since my outburst at dinner. It's been very…polite. My father probably laid into her and forced her to back off.

I've wondered, if they knew the truth about why Keith relinquished his rights, would their opinion of me change? I'm not sure and that keeps me playing the role they've cast me as and finding solace in my choice. I never want my daughter to be ashamed that I'm her mother. Her father is in a public role and that tape would've made headlines. She lives in a small town that would chew on the scandal for years. People might talk about me now, but Chastity would never escape that level of embarrassment.

"I'm always nice."

Nina snorts. "We're back here, Mrs. B."

"There you are." She sighs as though she'd searched high and low. "I have some new furniture in the truck that needs to be unloaded."

"Mom, we're running out of room."

"Then we'll have to make room."

Great. She should star on an episode of *Hoarders*. The only excuse she has is that she sells her junk.

We all start to move toward the front, but she grabs my arm. "You stay with me."

"I should help—"

"They can manage, we need to talk."

Mom tosses her coat on the back of the chair and motions for me to sit.

"We don't have to do this. All is fine in our world, Mother."

"I think we do."

In other words: I have no choice.

I don't doubt that she loves me, but I don't think she likes me. It's hard because years ago, I was her pride and joy. When you go from being loved so much it's stifling to being the shit on someone's shoes, it's heartbreaking. I want her to see that I'm not a total disappointment. Chastity is my one great thing.

"I'm sorry about the other night."

My jaw falls slack as I try to decide if this is reality or not. "You're what?"

"Don't be so dramatic, Teagan. I'm sorry that I said those things."

"Did Dad make you say this?"

Her eyes narrow. "No. He did not, thank you. I don't

want us to have this sort of relationship anymore. You're my only child, and regardless of your choices, I still love you."

There are two things here and I'm not sure which one is going to win out.

First, she said she was sorry. That has never happened.

Second, she still found a way to remind me that my decisions are a disappointment. Which makes me wonder if she's sorry that I'm her daughter or that she can't find a way to see past the things she doesn't like.

"So what exactly are you sorry for, Mom?"

"All of it. I'm sorry that we fight so much. I'm sorry that we haven't found a way to accept things as they are."

"I've accepted it. That's the thing."

She sighs. "I just wanted more for you."

I can understand that as a mother. I want the world for Chastity and I will be sad if her life doesn't include college, a career, happiness, and everything she wants, but I won't make her feel bad for it. That's the difference.

"I did too, but I wanted you to stand by me, be there for me, and not make me feel small all the time."

"That was never my intention. I thought I was giving you the truth to see that you're better than this."

She has never been good at emotions. I can't remember seeing her cry or being overly joyful at anything. It's why I pushed so hard as a kid to be everything she wanted. I thought that maybe she would really love me. Each accomplishment was just another rung to get higher on the social ladder. It was never good enough for her, and I don't think it ever will be.

"I think you mean well, Mom. I really do. I have always wanted to make you proud. I hope that one day, I will."

A long breath escapes her nose and her lips are in a thin

line. "I'm already proud of you, Teagan. I know I don't show it. I'm not perfect, and I hope you understand my heart was in the right place. You're so smart, beautiful, and have a wonderful heart, I…I went about it wrong, but my intentions were always good."

I have to accept that the way my mother loves me will never be the way I want her to love me. We may never see eye to eye, but maybe we can start talking heart to heart.

"I want for us to stop cutting each other down. I love you, Mom."

She nods once, wiping at her eye. "I have some dust in my eye." Her voice quivers.

"It's probably because I didn't get a chance to clean the shelves this week." I give her an out.

"Oh, yes, it's very dusty in here."

"Definitely."

"You'll do the shelves today," she instructs and straightens her back.

Emotions and my mother are a funny thing. "Of course."

"Now that's settled. Let's get this store in order because it's in total disarray."

I laugh through my nose. "Sure, let's get to work."

* * *

I sit at the bar, waiting for my date to show up, silently cursing Nina to hell.

Last week, I let her convince me to put a profile up on an online dating site after she and Chastity ambushed me. I don't know what the hell I was thinking, but she was so insistent that I needed to live again and that it would make

Chastity feel better. I had no idea anyone would actually contact me.

In seven days, I had a ton of messages, some creepy as fuck, others seeming like genuinely nice guys.

After listening to her badger me to reply to someone, I did, and he wanted to meet—tonight.

"Is this seat taken?" Derek's voice says from the left. *Great.*

"Yes, actually. I'm waiting for someone."

He smiles. "I see. Big date?"

"If you must know, yes."

"Ahh, well, leaving a beautiful woman alone at the bar is never a good idea."

I start to reply but the jackass takes the seat I was saving for Gavin or Gary or…shit…I need to look at his profile and remember his name.

"By all means," I say with a flair of the dramatics. "Have a seat."

"Thanks."

I roll my eyes. "That was sarcasm."

Derek's deep chuckle fills the air around us. "And here I thought you were just being polite."

He doesn't get to come here, take my date's seat, and gain my conversation. I use this opportunity to ignore him and look for what's his name's name on my phone.

Gavin. Phew. I was right.

I look toward the door, waiting to see if he's who just came in, but it was just another town person. I really should've picked another location. It's not like we have a plethora of options around here, but this was not my brightest idea.

I wanted somewhere I could easily escape from if I

had to, though. I know every exit from the Crabhouse. Lord knows I've snuck both in and out of here—many times.

"No such luck, huh?" Derek asks and then hides his smile with his beer.

"I'm sorry?"

"Your date. He's late?"

I straighten my back and look away. "He'll be here."

"Have you guys gone out before or is this a first date?"

"Don't you have anyone else to annoy?"

He grins. "Nope."

"Lucky me."

"Chastity mentioned your big date tonight."

I turn with my mouth gaping. "She what?"

Derek shrugs as if he didn't say anything of consequence. "I heard you were meeting some guy off a dating site and I thought someone should be here in case you go missing. You know...chaperone."

"And you thought *you* should do it?"

Meeting Greg—dammit—Gavin was going to be hard enough, but with my ex-best-friend-could've-been-more here it is going to be impossible.

"Why don't you head home and I'll let you know if I need help?" I suggest.

Derek leans in close. "But by that point, he could've buried your body. This way we're able to make sure it doesn't get to that point."

"They make these amazing things nowadays called... cell phones." I shake my phone at him for emphasis.

"I'm much faster than having to hope you have service."

"If I remember correctly, you're not very good in a

fight. Gary—Gavin is a big guy, he could kick your ass and then take us both."

Derek's eyes fill with mischief as he smirks. "I work out now, I can handle Gary or Gavin or whatever his name is."

I really want to kiss him—I mean kill him—and my daughter for her big mouth. She's the one who pushed me to do this. Nina was of course no help. I know they love me and were trying to help, but this night is definitely not going as planned.

Being in a relationship isn't that important to me.

Nina, however, disagreed with my priorities. She believes that the more I keep myself closed off, the more I'm holding on to the idea of being with Derek.

Sure, I love him. I always will.

But I don't want him that way.

I'm pissed at him, in fact.

I'm going to have to give up all the resentment and pain, and I'm not sure I can. Trusting him cost me my heart once before. He has the power to hurt me deeper than anyone. While some may not understand my reluctance, I'm doing what I feel will protect me.

My head and my heart are at war. Both wanting different things, but not knowing if they can trust the other to make the right choice.

"While I appreciate the concern," I say with my voice layered with sarcasm, "I will be fine without you here to ensure I don't get murdered."

I release a heavy sigh and look around. If this guy stands me up, it will be worse than getting murdered. Either way, I'm going to die of something.

"I'd rather not take the chance. Chastity needs you."

"And I don't need you."

He laughs and raises his now-empty bottle toward the bartender, who bites her lip as she does a hip sway. Jesus, doesn't anyone in this town remember how much they thought he was a dork and not worth their precious time? Now it's like the second coming of Christ since he's back.

Derek is so great.

Derek is a wonderful man, being a widower and all.

Oh, Derek, just…bless his broken heart.

I'd like to break something on him.

Instead of giving him the satisfaction of my would-be poor reaction, I open the stupid app again to see if my date messaged me.

Sure enough.

> Hi Teagan, I'm really sorry but I can't make it out there after all. I hope you forgive me but an issue came up at the office I can't ignore. —Gavin

Unreal. I bet what came up is his wife found the dating app he thought he'd hidden. I'm so stupid. I knew this was a bad idea.

"What has you so sour?" he asks after the bartender gives him a beer. "Why aren't you on pins and needles for this big date?"

I turn, my hand on the bar, gripping the edge. "Why are you here?"

"I told you."

I don't need him to swoop back into town to save me. I'm not a broken dove. I've done just freaking fine on my own the last thirteen years. He wasn't concerned about my impending murder then.

"We're not friends anymore, Derek. I don't need you to protect me. I've managed on my own with guys that were probably ten times scarier than this dude."

His body tenses enough to notice it. "I know we're not friends anymore, Tea."

"I didn't mean that—"

"No, I know I fucked that all up, but it doesn't mean we can't begin again."

"There's too much between us and we're fools if we believe otherwise."

"You don't even want to try?"

I want things to go back to the way they were before he returned to Chincoteague. As much as I hated the state of my life, it was predictable. I didn't worry about running into him. There was no constant state of unease like what's happening now. I'm going to end up with an ulcer at this rate.

"To what end?" I toss back.

"Not the end, Tea, a new beginning. Yes, we have history and it's messy. A long time ago we made stupid choices, but I'd like to start over." Derek gets to his feet, extending his hand to me. "I'm Derek Hartz. I once was a good guy who was a really loyal friend and I'm an ass who learned from the mistake of hurting someone I loved. And you are?"

I could take his hand. It's right there. I could place my palm to his, shake, and start over. He's not the same, and neither am I. Time has changed us both and there's nothing saying we can't be Derek and Teagan again but grown up.

But by doing that, I'm agreeing to a new start.

His eyes hold mine and I pray he doesn't see the storm that's brewing inside of me.

I open my mouth when I see the sadness fill his gaze. "Teagan Berkeley," I say, taking his peace offering. "It sounds like maybe you're not such an ass after all. I mean, you did try to keep me from being murdered."

Derek laughs and shakes my hand. "Maybe I'm not, but I know I'll do my best to make sure there's no maybe in it the next time."

I really hope so because I don't think I could endure losing him again.

chapter nineteen

Teagan

present

"It looks like he's not coming," Derek says after another thirty minutes.

"Maybe he got a look at you and thought you were my date."

I'm officially dateless and now feel lame. I didn't tell Derek because I was hoping that he would've left so I could've snuck out without him ever knowing. Since that didn't happen, I've been stuck here.

Not that I should complain, since what's-his-face wasn't really someone I was that excited to spend my night with. I could barely even remember his name. The last hour I've laughed, joked, and smiled with Derek.

It's a little like old times, only with some eggshells under our feet.

He's asked about my painting. I've asked about the animals and his family. A lot of commiserating about single parenting. There's something really…nice about the night.

"Then I've done my job." He laughs.

"Of what? Scaring off the first date I've had in ten years."

"Ten years?"

Great. I let him know how pathetic I am. Truth is, it's been longer than that. I haven't gone on a date since Chastity was born. It's never felt like the right time. Which is an excuse, I know this, but it worked for me. Not dating wasn't about Derek as much as it was about the ability to handle one more rejection.

I didn't love Keith or want to spend my life with him, but I wanted him to care for our daughter. Instead he walked away from her without a single afterthought.

"I've been busy." I shrug and drain the rest of my vodka and cranberry.

"Doing? You just finished telling me how mundane and disappointing you feel your life is."

I really need to stop drinking. I seem to have loose lips around him thanks to the vodka.

"My point is that if you scared him off, you owe me."

"Oh, do I?" His grin makes my stomach drop.

I really wish my body would stop doing that.

If I could ignore how cute he is when he smiles, it would make this whole moving on and dating thing a lot easier.

"You do."

"Okay, then."

My eyes narrow because that was almost too easy. "Why do I think I walked into a trap?"

"You didn't. If I ruined your date, I do owe you. We're a sad pair, the two of us. I'm a widower with a teenager who thinks I'm the worst parent alive. You're sexless for over ten years with a teenager who has to deal with mine. I think we both are pretty pathetic."

"I didn't say I was sexless." I shrug as he stares at me wide-eyed. "Please, don't look so shocked." It's not like I sleep around, but the one guy that I hooked up with a few years ago was really fun, and I needed some damn fun.

He cracks his neck, trying to hide his discomfort, and then raises his drink. "Here we were, thinking we had our shit together and it turns out we're a mess."

"No, I knew I was a mess," I admit. "I never said otherwise."

"I'll drink to that," Derek says and lifts the glass to his lips, draining the liquid and then motioning for the bartender. "I need four shots. Two each."

Oh, this is such a bad idea. "Shots? No."

He rolls his eyes and amends his request. "Make that four shots, two vodka with lemon and sugar and then two tequila."

I'm already two vodka-and-cranberry deep, which wouldn't seem so bad, but I don't drink much. I'm already feeling lightheaded and a little less in control. I should probably leave. The smart thing to do is to walk away before I do something I regret. Then there's part of me that's having fun and doesn't want to go.

Derek is laughing...with me.

I hoped for this so many times. The two of us, just hanging out. I've dreamed of us doing a lot more, but this is perfect, and I don't have a lot of perfect in my life.

"I think you're making a mistake. I can't really hold my liquor."

He leans close, his voice soft and deep. "Neither can

I, but I could use a night where life doesn't suck, can't you?"

I nod. "Well, at least I won't be the only source of gossip anymore."

Derek chuckles. "Here's what I propose. Whoever's story is the most pathetic, the other has to take a shot."

"Oh, game on."

He's had six months of complete shit. I've had thirteen years.

"My wife was killed."

"You went right for the jugular there," I mumble. "Fine. I've spent the last thirteen years above an antique store making minimum wage."

Derek shakes his head. "Weak. Drink."

"You said pathetic. It's not pathetic that your wife died…"

"No, but it's the saddest. You having a place to live, no matter how small it is, isn't pathetic, it's actually admirable."

Please, he's reaching here. "It's pathetic and you didn't say sad. If we were trying for sad, then I would've chosen differently."

"My game. My rules. Your story sucked in comparison."

He's still a cheater when it comes to games. Bastard.

"I'm not doing this because I agree," I explain because he'll use this excuse again. "I'm drinking because it's easier to do than argue with you for the next hour."

"Whatever you need to tell yourself. My story beat yours, so drink."

I grab the lemon, pour the sugar on it, hating that I lost the first round. He watches me with his brow raised, definitely not letting me out of it. I pick up the vodka, toss it back, grip the lemon in my teeth, and bite down. I haven't done lemon drops in so long I forgot how much they can burn.

My body shivers from the alcohol flooding my bloodstream. "You're going down," I warn him. "You used your one sad bit on the first one."

"I've got thirteen years of stories, Tea, are you so sure?"

I glare at him. "I guess we're about to find out. My turn." I want to go for the kill about Keith, but I feel like I need to play this smart. "I gave birth to Chastity with the nurse as my coach after you broke up our friendship over the phone."

At that time, I had no one I wanted by my side. My mother and I had been fighting that day and Derek's call sent me into labor. I didn't want to talk to anyone except him and he had made it clear that our friendship was over. The desire to be independent won out over being reasonable.

His face falls. "You were alone?"

"Well, I had Nurse Rose."

"But you didn't have someone who loved you there?"

"No."

The hurt and guilt on his face cause my chest to hurt. It's clear that the two of us are still not over things.

"I'm sorry."

I nod. "And that wasn't even my best story."

"You haven't heard mine yet." Derek's eyes fill with mirth. "You tried, I'll give you that, but…"

"You can't beat giving birth alone after you were heartbroken," I huff while crossing my arms over my chest.

"Are you sure about that?"

"Yes."

There's no way anything other than the fact that his wife was killed could beat it. The seriousness has completely evaporated and been replaced with the playfulness we've had most of the evening.

"Well, prepare to be outdone…I haven't had sex for seven years."

I gasp. "What?"

"Seven. Long. Fucking. Years."

"You…haven't had sex…for seven years?"

"Nope."

"But you were married!"

Derek nods with purpose. "I'm aware."

"Did you enter the priesthood or something?"

He laughs. "Not even close."

I want to feel bad for him and drink, but I really hate losing. I don't even know what to say to him.

"Okay, does your equipment not—"

"No!" he says quickly and nudges me. "My dick works just fine."

Great. Now I'm picturing his dick. He had to say it.

"All right then." I look at my drink, trying to understand why the hell he and Meghan didn't have sex for seven years. That's a really long time.

"Go ahead and ask…" Derek pushes.

Don't have to ask me twice.

"Why the hell didn't you have sex with your wife in seven years?"

He grabs his beer and drains it. "Because she and I were basically separated. We were roommates, trying to make things normal for Everly, but they weren't working. So, it was…hard."

"Or not," I joke.

"Or not." Derek laughs. "So, clearly you need to drink because…I win."

My eyes narrow and I want to give him this win because, Dear God. Then I remember how much my story is really worse than his. He could've left. He could've found someone else or whatever, but he chose to stay with Meghan.

"Nice try, buddy, but you didn't have to push a baby out of your vagina alone." I push the shot toward him. "While your lack of sex is pretty sad, it's not depressing enough to win, therefore"—my voice has a hint of mockery to it—"you're drinking."

Derek leans back in the chair, swirling the shot glass in his hand. "You don't think being married and not allowed to have sex isn't the sadder story here?"

"You were with Meghan when Everly was born, right?"

He deadpans. "Right."

I laugh without humor. "Imagine that entire scene but no one there to share it with. Imagine the pain and no one to hold your hand but some stranger who can't remember your name correctly."

"Why didn't you call your mother?"

This is the question she asks me anytime I bring it up. The answer is stupid, but it's the truth. "I didn't want anyone to see me that way."

"What way?"

I allow the hurt to fill my eyes because the word is…pathetic at best. "Broken."

He reaches his hand out to touch mine, but he pulls it back.

Instead of saying something, which I see he wants to, he grabs his shot and tosses it back. "Fuck."

I giggle as he shudders from the burn. "You should've asked for a chaser."

"Chasers are for pussies."

I burst out laughing. "Which you haven't had in seven years, my friend. So I guess you going without one tonight is par for the course."

He moves in, his lips against my ear. "Those in sexless houses shouldn't throw stones."

There's something I'd like to throw and it isn't a stone. Like myself…at him…which will not happen.

"Okay, you go. We're one and one."

I can't wait to hear this one. Again, I've got ammunition for days. "I've gotta think…"

There's a few things I could go with, like the fact that Keith makes millions of dollars and I make minimum wage. Or how my car barely works and I can't afford to fix it so I bribe our local mechanic with free gifts from the store whenever he's in the dog house.

Now I'm a country song. God help me.

"You're about to forfeit if you don't spit it out." I need to keep this going or my mind is going to get me in trouble.

Thinking is bad because right now, I'm thinking about how cute he looks as he's in his head. How his hair is darker than I remember and his lips just a bit fuller.

I wonder if he sees the little things in me too. Does he wish we could go back in time and tell each other everything?

My head turns toward him as he stares at his drink. "Hmmm…"

I return to my line of thinking as I wish I had the courage to ask him.

Do you?

Do you think about me? Do you think about how we could've been? Do you wish it was all different? Do you see how my heart is still broken? Do you see that I never stopped loving you?

"What?" Derek's eyes are on mine and my heart races.

Please tell me I didn't say any of that out loud.

"What?"

"What did you say?"

"I didn't say anything," I stammer.

"I heard you."

"Then why are you asking?" I toss back.

I can't believe I said it aloud. I have to get out of here. My feet hit the ground and I grab the last shot, tossing it back. "You win."

There's no way I can ever look at him again. I'm mortified. As quickly as my drunk legs will take me, I get outside the bar. The cold air hits me in the face, sobering me a bit.

"I'm so stupid," I whisper to the wind.

"Teagan." Derek's hand is on my arm.

"Please, you don't have to say anything."

"I think I do."

"No, I've been drinking and we were just...it was stupid and I...just let me go and tomorrow we can pretend that this didn't happen."

Derek's eyes are soft and pleading. "Ask me..."

"Ask you what?"

His hands are on my arms, holding me to him, and I'm taken back in time. We stood like this so many times.

Anytime life got overwhelming and we needed someone to ground us. Anytime we needed a friend who wouldn't judge the other for speaking the truth. I could be me, awkward, embarrassed, or anything else, and Derek would be there.

"Ask me, Tea."

I know if I speak that the answer will break my already shredded heart. For so long I've wanted to utter these words, and now he's here, holding me, touching me, and I'm drunk enough to let myself be free if I can find the courage.

But I'm not fearless. "I can't."

And then, before I can breathe or speak, his lips touch mine and I'm gone. My mouth moves against his and I steal his air. I need it to fill me, give me everything I've missed for so long.

He's the piece of me that's been lost. He's the love that I've been desperate for. Kissing him is nothing like I imagined. I thought it would be soft and sweet, but there's nothing gentle about him. He pushes me, kisses me as though it's the only thing he can do.

My fingers wrap around his neck, holding him close, not feeling an ounce of cold…it's all fire.

He consumes me, burns me with each lick of his tongue, turning my bones to ash.

All too soon, he pulls back, his blue eyes filled with passion. The way he looks at me causes my stomach to clench.

I open my mouth to say something—anything. There have to be words to make me wake up from this dream. This is…reckless. Here on the streets of our hometown and half-drunk isn't the way this should've happened.

His hand pushes against my cheek, cupping it so I have to see him. "Ask me." I hear the words as a tear rolls down my cheek.

And with those words, the dream is over and I awaken. "I really have to go."

And just like that, I walk away.

chapter twenty

Teagan

present

My head is pounding and I feel like I ate a jar of cotton. It's like the Sahara in my mouth.

Somehow, I get myself out of bed and pop two Tylenol and chug water. Today is going to suck. It's a Saturday and I have to work downstairs, although thankfully it's off-season and slow, which means I might be able to nap.

Chastity's door is still closed and I'm beyond grateful. She's way too smart to see through any possible lies I could come up with about what happened last night.

I sit in the kitchen with a death grip on my coffee, head on the table because it's so heavy, and try to stop replaying that damn kiss.

The kiss that I've wanted for so long and yet, I stopped it.

I really am an idiot.

Or am I smart for putting an end to it? Our first kiss should've been because we had some big epiphany of our relationship, not because we were drunk and flirty. It feels like a huge letdown and yet it wasn't. It was...everything.

I sit back up and groan.

The store buzzer rings, alerting me someone is here.

I can't people today, but if someone is at that door it means it's either Nina or my mother. I pray for Nina because I might lose my shit on anyone else.

"Hey," I say as I open the door.

Nina smiles and then when she actually looks at me it shifts. "You look like shit."

"Thanks."

"I'm just saying, after a first date most people don't look like they rolled out of bed after lying in the barn. Oh! Or maybe you did get freaky in the barn? Yes? Sexy time on the hay…that would itch though."

I sigh and lean against the wall. "No sexy time on any hay."

"Sad," Nina says wistfully. "So, why after your date do you look like a hot mess?"

"If I went on a first date maybe I wouldn't look like this."

She turns her head to the side and purses her lips. "I'm pretty sure we forced you to put makeup on to go on such a thing."

"You did, but he bailed on me last minute."

"No!" she yells and when I wince she apologizes. "So you got drunk alone in the bar?"

I close my eyes and silently wish I could end this conversation. Nina and I share most things, but I don't know that I should tell her what happened with Derek. Although we kissed in the damn street, so for all I know someone took a video of it. Wouldn't that be ironic.

"Let's go downstairs," I suggest.

"Because?"

I point to Chastity's door. "Because we should work."

"*Ohh*," she says very unconvincingly. "Right. Work. We should get going."

"You really need to work on your acting skills."

She shrugs and heads down the stairs. "You know I'm not equipped with the gift of sarcasm and snark like you and Chastity."

"You're a mess."

She laughs. "Have you seen yourself, sweetheart? I wouldn't be calling anyone else a mess."

We get into the store and I flop on the sofa.

"Spill," Nina says after a minute.

"That about killed you to wait, didn't it?"

"You know it did. Now, spill."

I release a heavy sigh and decide to tell her everything. If nothing else, maybe she can help me figure out what any of it means. "Your perfect match from the online site of creepers texted me while I was at the bar waiting, with some bullshit excuse of work—an hour *after* he was supposed to be there—however, Derek was at the bar. He somehow seemed to know I was on a date and wanted to make sure I didn't get murdered."

Her grin spreads even wider. "So you ended up on a date with your best-friend-who-you've-been-in-love-with-for-your-whole-life! Oh, my God, you're living an actual rom-com movie right now! This is amazing. Tell me more."

"I'm not living anything but a pretty pathetic life."

Nina scoffs. "You've loved that man since you were in high school, even if you didn't know it then, and he's back, and you're trying to act like that's pathetic?"

"What's pathetic is thinking it was anything more than just us being drunk!"

"*More*? What more happened, Tea?"

Ugh. Me and my big mouth. "He kissed me."

"He kissed you!" she screams, and I grab the sides of my head. "Oh my God!"

"Nina! Voices."

She huffs and waves her hand at me. "I don't care that I'm yelling because he kissed you! Did you kiss him back?"

I sure as hell did. The feel of his lips on mine was more than I ever had the ability to conjure up, though. I had no idea the way his hand would feel on my back, holding me against his solid chest.

The truth was, I never wanted to open my eyes. I would've stayed fused to his mouth if I could, but when he spoke, when he told me to ask him my questions, it broke the spell.

I couldn't ask. I didn't want to know.

"It was a mistake."

"So that's a yes."

"Nina." I sigh. "It was stupid and—"

"And it was a long time coming, my friend. You and Derek Hartz have been in love with each other longer than either of you idiots would admit. This is your time."

So what if that first part is true? It still doesn't mean it's our time. "Our kids hate each other, Nina. This isn't time for anything."

"Kids fight and don't like each other. That doesn't change the feelings and love you and Derek have for each other. You're just talking crazy."

This conversation is what's crazy. I love her, but Jesus. She can't possibly believe this is real. "He doesn't love me. He doesn't even know me!" I tell her.

We know the Teagan and Derek of a million years ago. I am nothing like the girl I used to be. He clearly isn't who I knew either. He fell in love with someone else, married her, raised a kid, and all those life experiences changed him at his core.

"You're an idiot."

"So I've been told."

"There have never been two people who have cared about and known each other more than you and Derek."

"A long-ass time ago, yes. Now? No."

"Then get to know him."

I lift my head to the ceiling. "It was a kiss. It wasn't anything more than that."

If she buys that I'll be impressed. It was so much more than a kiss.

"Well." Nina gets up and smiles. "It shouldn't be a big deal to start looking for a new match."

"A what?"

"A new date, since it wasn't anything more than that. There's no reason you can't get your ass back in the saddle."

She can't be serious. I'm not going on another blind date. The last setup did not go well and I have no desire to try again. "Not happening."

"Because? Hmm? Could it be a man you happen to have given your heart to who has returned to claim it?"

She's ridiculous. "It's not because of the kiss with Derek if that's what you're thinking!" I yell at her and point. "That kiss meant nothing!"

A loud thump hits the door from the apartment and both of our heads turn. Shit. I pray to God Chastity didn't hear me. Nina's eyes are wide as she looks at me. "Do you think she—?"

"I don't know."

A heartbeat passes between us and the door handle rattles.

My voice is a whisper. "Don't say anything."

"I've got this."

I have zero faith. Nina's the world's worst liar. Chastity will see through her like glass.

"Anyway," I say loudly, trying to refocus Nina. My daughter is smart—I need to keep talking about the same issue but leave out the kiss and I'll just…improvise if she asks. "I think I'm going to stay single."

Nina nods. "I see."

"I'm serious. I can read the signs that right now isn't the right time."

Chastity enters the room. "Hey."

"Hey."

"Hi, honey," Nina says a little too brightly. "Did you sleep well?"

"Sure. I would've liked to sleep in later but you two were yelling and I was worried Grandma was here and Mom finally snapped."

"Funny," I huff.

"She knew you had a date last night. Which I'm waiting for details on…"

I once really liked my kid. Now, not so much. "Why would you think telling Grandma any information was a good idea?"

I focus on the first until I can feel her out more on what she heard.

"She's very persuasive when she wants information."

"In other words, she bought you."

"She promised I could have Mr. Stinkers—inside."

Unreal. I asked my mother two months ago and she was against it.

"You're kidding me, right?"

Chastity smiles. "Nope."

I'm too hungover to care right now. "I give up."

"So, what were you guys yelling about?"

I'm not sure if she's baiting me. "My failure of a date last night."

"Failure?"

"Yes. Failure."

"Was he ugly?"

Did you hear me say something about a kiss and you're trapping me? Gah. This kid is too damn good at mind games sometimes.

"I wouldn't know. He didn't show up."

"Aunt Nina?"

Oh, sure, go for the weak one.

Nina clasps her hands, giving away that she's nervous. "Yes, honey?"

"Next time, I get to pick the guy...not you."

Nina laughs. "You'll have to convince your mother of that. I doubt she'll be dating anytime soon."

"Not if you two are picking the guys."

Chastity shrugs. "I'll find you someone, Mom. Just wait."

I close my eyes and shake my head. "Let's get to work...and not on my love life."

Lord knows I've done enough damage to my own life in the last twenty-four hours.

chapter twenty-one

Teagan

present

"Hello?" I answer the number I don't recognize. I'm praying my daughter didn't list my phone number on that dating site.

"Good morning."

"Who is this?"

"I'm crushed that you didn't recognize my voice," a deep male voice says with a chuckle.

"Derek?"

"Don't act so surprised, I do have your number, and since we're friends, I figured it was time I called."

I haven't heard from him in the last week. I've done my best to not talk about him, think about him, or look for him at every turn. I hoped that after the last thirteen years of doing just that, I would be a pro. However, I've yet to master this skill. He keeps starring in my dreams, and I find myself daydreaming about his lips.

"Sorry, you took me by surprise. Not to be rude, but why are you calling me?"

"Chastity asked me to."

Okay, but why didn't she call me? That initial fear that something has happened to her hits me. "Is she okay?"

"She's fine. I should've led with that. She's at the house after working with my dad at the clinic. They got a little sidetracked with the animals and then my mother refused to let her leave without eating."

"Okay..." I say, confused. "What is she doing now?"

"She's doing her homework. Are you okay with me dropping her off or do you want to come get her?"

"I'm sorry, did you say she's doing her homework—at your house?"

Since when does she hang out where Everly is?

"Yeah, it's a long story."

I'm sure it is. "I can come get her. I have to run out and I can grab her on my way back."

Tonight, Chastity and I will have some mother-daughter time. I baked a cake that I plan to eat for dinner. Cake has eggs and eggs are healthy.

"Sounds good. What time are you thinking?"

Yeah, sounds great...I won't be able to avoid him face-to-face.

"An hour? Is that okay?"

I'm not sure why I'm asking him if that's okay, she's my daughter.

"I'm guessing that's fine, she and Everly are talking now."

"Umm...*what*?" I ask with a hint of panic and a lot of confusion in my voice.

As of last night, Everly was being referred to as Satan's mistress. I don't think the two of them suddenly became best friends.

"Yeah, I had the same reaction. Apparently, the school is trying to force them to be friends."

"How so?"

"They were paired together on a writing assignment about social media."

That's really not the smartest idea. Chastity likes working with a partner as much as I like the idea of seeing Keith's face. She always ends up doing the entire thing on her own, getting the other person an A, and complaining about incompetence in the education system.

While I normally find her frustration funny, I have a feeling this time it won't be entertaining.

"I'll call her teacher," I say, already planning how to get her out of this.

"Why?"

"Because they hate each other." Is he seriously not thinking this could be bad?

Derek clears his throat. "Do you remember how we became friends?"

He can't possibly think this is the same. First, it's girls. Girls are…mean. Derek and I didn't hate each other and plot an untimely demise of the other. These two *hate* each other. The last few weeks it hasn't gotten better. Everly has almost doubled her efforts, and Chastity has been on a rampage about ways to make her sick without it showing on a toxicology report.

"You can't force this. The school shouldn't either."

"I know it's not ideal but Everly will be supervised."

My first instinct is to bite back at him that they're supervised at school, and yet that hasn't stopped his daughter's behavior. "I'm not comfortable with this, Derek."

"I understand that you're not, but this could be a good thing."

"What about this is good?"

He sighs. "I don't know, but I think we need to let them work this out. If we intervene it'll be worse for Chastity. It'll look like her mother had to stop her from having to be around a bully. Trust me, I spent a good part of my life dealing with the end she's on."

He's right. If I call the school and get her paired with someone else, Chastity will suffer. This parenting thing is really freaking hard. I owe my mother a cake too.

Well, maybe one with some laxatives.

"Fine. But you should know, Chastity shares everything with me and if I find out that while under your supervision she was tortured, I assure you that I will retaliate."

It's an idle threat, but still.

"Against a thirteen-year-old?"

"No, against her father, who won't have to worry about another seven-year drought because he'll be missing a certain appendage."

Derek chuckles. "Noted. See you soon, Tea."

Great. "See you soon."

There are a few errands I need to do before I get Chastity. We need supplies for our girls' night in. Plus, now that I know she's being forced to work with Everly, I'm going to need to sweeten her up because I can't even imagine the mood she'll be in.

I grab my purse and head to the grocery store, where Mrs. McCutchrey is changing the decorations on her storefront. She does this each month and it's the big excitement on the off months in this beach town. Who knows what theme she might pick?

It sounds pathetic even in my head.

"Hi, Mrs. McCutchrey," I say with a smile.

She's the nicest woman in this town. While others have gossiped about my life choices, she's never said anything. In fact, when Chastity was born, she made her a blanket and brought me a meal each Friday for the first six months.

She will always hold a very special place in my heart. Plus, Chastity loves her and she makes the best macaroni and cheese in town.

"Oh, Teagan, hi, honey."

"How is the decorating going?"

She grins. "Just fine. I'm going for a Parisian theme this time. I'm hoping Ed finally takes the hint and whisks me away."

Their marriage is one that everyone envies. He dotes on her and she takes exceptional care of him. Each day around eleven, she leaves the store to cook him a hot lunch. If he's working late, she brings dinner and joins him until he's finished. I asked her once why they do that, and she explained that there's nothing more important than sharing meals together, which is why she brought me one each week.

Of all the people in the world who should've had kids, it's them, but they never did. However, I don't think they were lacking in love. They've sort of adopted the misfit kids in this town and made them theirs.

"I'm sure he knows. You talk about it each year."

She nods. "And yet, the man doesn't listen."

"Do any of them?"

"Not one. How is Chastity? I haven't seen her in a few weeks."

That's strange. She always comes and visits with Mrs. McCutchrey. "She's okay, it might be because she's been working with Dr. Hartz."

Her eyes brighten. "Yes, I heard that. Such a shame that the older Dr. Hartz hasn't been feeling well."

"It's a good thing he has his son." I smile.

She watches me with a knowing eye and then turns back to stringing the lights. "You and Derek were always such a joy to watch. Have you two reconnected?"

While she doesn't gossip, she does meddle. I told her when I was really sad and sleep deprived after Chastity was born about my fight with Derek. She held me, let me cry myself to sleep, and then stayed all night taking care of Chastity.

The next day, she touched my cheek, kissed my nose, and told me love worked in mysterious ways and some people get lost on the journey.

I still don't know if she was talking about me or him.

"We have."

"Oh? That's wonderful. I hadn't heard..."

I tilt my head to the side and grin. "That's interesting, since you usually know before the people involved figure it out."

She laughs and waves her hand at me. "Now, that's just silly. How did it go? Are you friends again?"

I don't really know where we stand since the night at the bar. I haven't seen him.

Before the kiss, though, it was great. I smiled—truly smiled. I wanted things to stay that easy between us, but hurt isn't something that I can just *release* because he offers me pretty words.

"We're...working it out."

She climbs down. "Maybe it shouldn't be work?"

"Isn't it you who told me every relationship that matters takes effort?"

Mrs. McCutchrey laughs once and nods. "I'm sure I said something like that, but we were discussing your mother at the time, dear."

"Now, that is work."

"Yes, but she loves you, just as I suspect the young Dr. Hartz does. You know"—she heads to the register—"I like to think I have a sixth sense about men."

I love her but she's nuts right now. "You do?"

"I do. I think you'll be surprised."

That's already happened, but I can't tell her that. I need to figure out how to deal with seeing him first.

"I'll let you get back to your display. That's a surprise I'm looking forward to."

"All right, honey. I'll be sure to stop by the store this week and we can catch up."

In other words, she plans to grill me.

Another person to add to my list of people to hide from. Although, she's probably the one I could never actually avoid. She'd find me.

"I will."

I bag up my supplies of cereal, milk, eggs, chips, whipped cream, and the cookies that I really shouldn't be eating, but don't care. Tonight, calories don't count. It's all about me and Chas hanging out. She's been looking forward to it all week and so have I.

Hence the chocolate cake that's waiting for me at home.

Once I'm all checked out, I wave to Mrs. McCutchrey and head out before she can accost me. I've gotten really good at avoidance of late.

The drive over to the Hartzes is weird. I can't remember the last time I was here. Not since before Derek's wedding, I think. When I pull up, memories of my childhood flood me. This house was always so warm and inviting.

It was the house where the door was always open to any person or animal that needed someone. I loved Mrs. Hartz very much. Even knowing that I wasn't the best person as a teenager, she never made me feel unworthy.

I've missed her cookies and wisdom.

"Teagan Berkeley, you get in here," Mrs. Hartz yells from the door.

I smile, and get out of the car. "Sorry."

"What were you doing out there?"

"Remembering."

Her eyes soften and her lips pull into a sad smile. "I remember too, honey. But look at you...you raised a wonderful, smart girl."

"The only thing I seem to have done right," I say as a half joke.

"Now," she chides. "I've known you a long time and you've never fished for compliments before."

Busted. "Forgive me?"

"Nothing to forgive. Us mothers are always trying to figure out if we've screwed up or finally done something right. I still feel like I'm behind the curve, and my son is grown and raising his own...teenager."

"How is Everly?" It's easier asking about her to Mrs. Hartz, and I don't know why. Maybe it's because there's a lot of Meghan in Everly and that scares me. I wonder if she hates me because her mother did or because she hates everyone.

Mrs. Hartz sighs. "She's going through a lot, but...it's

been hard for her, and Derek is beside himself on what to do. I don't like the way she's acting and I've made my thoughts clear on that. Being angry and hurt doesn't give anyone the right to treat another person poorly."

I try not to smile because I remember the rest of that saying all too well. "It's the measure of a person's character to behave, even when we feel the worst about our situation."

She touches my arm and nods. "That's right."

Those words were what snapped me out of my poor life choices. One day when I was waiting for Derek to be done with his dad, I was talking to Mrs. Hartz about things I was feeling. She was so different from my mom. Her nature was calm, understanding, and she never judged me. I didn't want to be the person who kicked others when I was down. I wanted my character to show that even if I was low, I would help lift another instead of bringing them down to my level.

Mrs. Hartz doesn't know how many times I've uttered those words to myself. When Keith was dragging me through the mud, I tried to be *my* best self because that was all I could control.

"Teagan." Derek says my name from behind his mother.

My heart skips as I see him for the first time since we kissed. His stubble is almost a beard and he looks tired, but irresistible at the same time.

"I'll let you two say hello," Mrs. Hartz says with a smile. "Let me go make sure there's no bloodshed."

I look to them both.

"Mom." He sighs.

"I'm sure they're fine. I was kidding."

It may have been a joke but could be a possibility.

"If you want to just get Chas, I'll head out."

"Nonsense, Teagan, you come in and have a snack."

I smile as I look to Derek. She forgets we're not seventeen. "I think she can have wine, Ma."

"Yes, wine, of course. It just feels like old times with you two together again. I've missed you, sweet girl." The warmth in her voice could bring tears to my eyes. I always loved her. She treated me like I was precious and not because I was an object in her life.

"I would love to stay, but—"

"Five minutes, Tea," Derek says as a plea. "Just five minutes."

"Five minutes."

He smiles and holds the screen open, forcing me to walk through. "I like you when you agree."

One day I'll be able to say no to this man. I would really like that day to be now but clearly not. "Yeah, don't get used to it."

At least I can talk tough.

chapter twenty-two

Derek

present

"What do you see here?" I ask Chastity as we examine the cat that she's now able to bring in the house. Mr. Stinkers has been acting strange for the last week from what she says.

After Teagan came over the other day, Chastity has been here, helping more. Yesterday she explained her cat needed an exam and asked if she could work extra hours to cover it. I told her that wasn't necessary, but she insisted.

"Is that a lump?"

Well, we could call it that, but it's a bit more complicated. "I wouldn't call it a lump. More of a bump...where something or more than one something is growing."

She looks at me with horror. "Oh my God! Is he going to die?"

"No, no." I laugh. "He isn't a *he*. He is a she and *she* is expecting."

"He's pregnant?"

"Technically, she's pregnant, but yes."

"Oh, no! Mr. Stinkers is actually Mrs. Stinkers." Her face is priceless. "My mother is going to kill me!"

Chastity has made no secret of the lack of affection Teagan has for the cat.

"I'm happy to talk to your mother if you want, to help mitigate the situation."

She shakes her head. "It's fine. I've been handling my mother for a long time now. She'll go off the deep end, calm down, see the cute little kittens—after the gore that will stain her carpets—and then throw me and the cats out on the street. It'll work out."

Sounds like Teagan.

I chuckle and nod. "I'm glad to see you've got it all worked out. If you need a place to stay, you're welcome here."

She goes back to petting Mr.—Mrs. Stinkers and sighs. "At least we won't be homeless with new babies, right? We can live here or in a barn or maybe the abandoned lighthouse."

I love when people talk to their pets. I was the same way at her age. My dog was my entire world and I did everything I could to make him know he was loved. It also helped that growing up with my father as a veterinarian sealed the deal. There was no shortage of animals to care for.

"You really love her, huh?"

She nods. "I found her on the beach. Mom used to take me there whenever she wanted to breathe—whatever that meant. She'd let me run up and down the shore and I found him—her—under a little box."

"Well, she's very lucky."

"Let's hope when I tell my mother she's going to be a grandma she doesn't kill us both."

I burst out laughing. "Maybe you shouldn't tell her in those words."

Chastity's mischievous smile grows. "Oh, but where would the fun in that be?"

In this very moment I see how much she's like her mother. "Well, leave me out of it. I don't need your mother pissed at me."

"Have you spoken to my mom lately?" Chastity asks as she picks up the cat.

In my head, I've called her a million times. In my head, I've confessed my heart to her and explained how much that kiss meant. However, in reality, I haven't done any of that.

Mostly because she walked away from me and I don't want to push. I'm the one who deserted her and I have to earn that trust back.

"Not since the other night when she was here, why?"

"Just wondering."

I don't think kids just wonder anything. "Okay."

"I know she mentioned you were at the bar the night of her big date."

"Yeah," I say, turning my back to her, as though I need to clean my instruments. "Did she mention the guy calling her since he never showed up?" *Did she mention me?*

I've been following Teagan's lead, but my patience is wearing thin. Our kiss that night changed me in some way. I felt alive again and—wanted. Meghan sure as hell didn't want anything to do with me.

It was never easy for me to admit the state of our marriage. We had come to the agreement that we would live together but live separate lives because whether we liked it or not, we didn't love each other. Meghan resented me and, in some way, I hated her for taking Teagan out of my life. It was the choice I made, rationally I knew that, but my heart didn't care.

Then there was this deep desire to find a way to salvage our marriage. Maybe if we tried harder, loved stronger, we could get back to what made us fall in love. It was a lie, no amount of work could repair the damage. For Everly's sake, neither of us wanted to divorce, so we agreed to stay together until she was off to college. Looking back, I think Everly would've been fine. It would've been hard for her, but no harder than the coldness she felt in that house. Yet I couldn't do it.

Thanks to my parents, I still felt the need to be faithful to Meghan. I tried to date once, and I couldn't bring myself to actually cheat on her. Plus, I didn't know how to explain it. How do you tell a potential lover that you're still married but aren't? You're just…in limbo.

That's all over, though. Meghan is gone and there's a fresh type of guilt because now, I'm free. I can date and no one would bat an eye. I could see if this thing between Teagan and me is real or just a fantasy we've both been living in.

"Well, Mom said that she won't ever talk to that guy again, but she seemed to have had a good time with you."

"Good, it was nice seeing her."

"You guys were best friends?"

I nod and turn back to her. "We were."

"So did you know my father?"

Shit. I have no clue what Teagan has said or not said about Keith. "I'm not sure we should talk about this."

She gives a sad smile. "I know who he is. I mean, he's on television each week during football season. Mom has never lied to me about him, but she doesn't really talk about him either. So I don't know anything about him."

I look at this girl and wonder what the hell he could've been thinking. She's a good kid who didn't do anything wrong. How Keith can walk around knowing a part of himself is out there and not attempt to see her is baffling.

"I knew Keith," I say carefully. I don't want to bad-mouth him even though I think he deserves it.

"It's crazy, right?" She kisses the top of the cat's head. "I live in the same town as my grandparents and they go out of their way to avoid me. They sort of duck and hide on the other side of the street if they catch sight of me. Then, a few years ago they bought a house for the winter in the South or something. It's easier to avoid Mom and me in the winter."

I laugh once, trying to picture it. "I can't imagine them avoiding either of you very well."

She shakes her head. "Mom is the best with it. She made it a game."

"A game?"

Why does that not surprise me?

"She tries to make us run into them and see how fast they get away. It's really funny."

"I imagine it is, but it's also pretty shitty."

Chastity is a thirteen-year-old girl, not the bubonic plague. Trying to avoid her is ridiculous.

"Yeah, but it is what it is. A part of me is glad they're not in my life because if I turned out like them or their son that would be the worst thing possible."

"That's very mature of you."

"I guess since I've never had them in my life, I don't know what I'm missing. My mom has made sure that I've always known I was wanted by her."

I look at her, imagining what her life has been and what Teagan's gone through to provide for her. She's sacrificed everything. I've thought of her so much over the last few years, wondering what Chastity might be like. I should've been her fun uncle. I wouldn't have replaced Keith as her father, but I could've been a positive male figure in her life.

The regret fills me.

"She and I stopped talking before you were born, but I can tell you she never wavered on wanting you."

She smiles with a bit of sadness. "I hate that her life has been so difficult. My sperm donor got to do everything and she's struggled. It's why I'm so protective of her and why when Everly..." She bites her lip.

"When Everly attacked her, you stood up for her." I finish her sentence with pride ringing in my voice. She should defend her mother.

"Yes, but I still should've never brought her mother into it. That was really horrible."

Chastity is wise for her age.

"Well, hopefully the two of you can find a way to get along."

Her lips form into a thin line. "Hopefully." She turns, putting the cat in the carrier. "Do you think we can work with the goat again? I think he could use some attention."

It's clear she wants to end the conversation, and I'd like the kid to stick around. Not that her mother and I may amount to anything, but because I really like her. There're not many kids who want to spend their spare time mucking up stalls and taking care of animals.

I was that kid because people...they were work.

"Sure thing. Let's see if we can give him a bit of fun."

* * *

I've been at my parents' house for longer than I'd planned. I love my mother, don't get me wrong, but if she could realize I'm not sixteen anymore, it would make life easier.

Today was the last straw.

She opened my bedroom door, at six in the morning, and started to clean up. She flipped the light on, grabbed the laundry—which I'm perfectly capable of doing my damn self—and then left without a word.

When I called her out on it, she said I was under her roof and she will run her home like she sees fit.

Normally my mother is a pretty straightforward person, but I have a feeling this was her way of telling me it's time to find other accommodations.

In her sweet, didn't-want-to-hurt-my-feelings kind of way.

So, I'm going house hunting, and I'm going to guilt Teagan into coming along so I can force her to spend time with me.

This is what my life has become.

I push open the door to the store and I hear her voice from the back. "Just look around and I'll be with you shortly!"

That's not going to work for me. I head to the area where I think her voice came from. This store was always like a maze but it's gotten worse. Furniture is used as a way to make aisles, and there's no rhyme or reason to the merchandise piled all around. Lamps sit on top of the chairs and there are paintings on the floor but plates hung on the walls. I used to hate coming here to meet her. I swore there was a dead body in one of the chests that she couldn't get open.

God help whoever bought that.

"Tea?"

"Derek?" she calls out with a hint of panic. "What are you doing here?"

I smile to myself. "Shopping."

"Here?" A laugh fills the air. "Not likely."

"What are you doing?"

"Just looking at something."

I lean over but I can't see anything but the top of her head behind a table and chairs. "Okay. I have to talk to you, could you stand up?"

"I'm good, go ahead and talk…"

It would make things a little easier if she would look at me. "I can wait."

"Really, it's fine. What's up?"

"It's more of a question…"

"Yes?"

This is ridiculous. "Teagan, I'm talking to the top of a table, please get up."

She groans. "I'd rather not."

"Why?"

"Because. That's why."

"Really, Tea?" I squat down, ready to battle her and let her know she's out of her mind, but when I see her, I almost fall to the floor laughing. Teagan has managed to get her hair stuck to the underside of the table. "Because why again?"

"I hate you. You had to look?"

"Of course I did."

"This is mortifying."

"How, pray tell, did you manage to do this?"

She glares at me. "I was checking something written under here and then somehow I turned and my hair got stuck. Can you help me?"

I ponder that for a minute. Right now, she's literally trapped. She can't run, unless she wants to be scalped, and would need to hear me out.

"Of course."

She releases a sigh of relief. "Thank you."

"After we talk."

"Derek." Teagan's voice is low.

"Teagan."

"You're going to help me once you get what you want?"

I shrug. "No, you don't have to agree to what I want, but you have to listen."

"When I get out of this," she warns, "I'm going to kill you."

"All the more reason to keep you trapped." That was definitely the wrong thing to say. I'm pretty sure she's ready to lose her hair at this point. I better make it quick. "My point is, I need your help, if you're not homicidal by the end of this."

"Help with what?"

"I need to move out of my parents' house and I'm supposed to meet the Realtor in an hour. I was hoping you could come."

Her eyes narrow a bit. "That's what you wanted to talk about?"

"Yeah."

"Not…"

"Not what? Is there something else you'd like to discuss?"

Like the kiss that has kept me up every night. The way her lips felt with mine. How long I've wondered what it would be like and now it's all I can think about.

"No. House hunting sounds fine—great even. So, you want me to go look for a place for you and Everly?"

"Yeah."

"But regardless of my answer, you'll release me?"

Like I'd leave her here? How the hell would that go over in terms of ever seeing if that one kiss was a fluke or real? It wouldn't. And I have to know.

"Well, that depends, now, doesn't it?"

"On?"

"On your answer." I smile, and she groans.

I didn't say I wouldn't have fun with it, though.

chapter twenty-three

Teagan

seventeen years old

"This is a hammer," Derek says with a smirk.

"I know what a hammer is."

"Well, I don't know what you know. Do you know how to use it?"

I know I'd like to hit him in the head with it, but that would probably be frowned upon when you're working on rebuilding a barn that was burned down.

"Yes. I do."

Derek challenged me to do something for someone else without anything to gain. I know Mr. Mitchell needs his barn back after the storm took part of it down so he can care for the horses he helps, which is why we're here. I called all the football guys and organized the whole thing.

There are about twenty kids, but the best part was that when the town caught wind of what we were planning, the adults lined up to help as well. Then, Mr. Harvey donated lumber and others helped out financially.

I can't explain the joy I feel inside knowing we may actually build this thing today.

It was nothing compared to the look on Mr. Mitchell's face, though. He had tears in his eyes and kept shaking his head in disbelief.

"Okay, killer, let's see what you've got." Derek takes two steps back with hands raised.

I really question our friendship some days.

I take the nail, lining it up, and pull the hammer back. *Please don't let me hit my finger.*

"Today, Tea."

I turn and stick my tongue out at him before going back and hitting the nail.

Well, attempting to, because instead of it going into the wood frame, it falls to the floor.

"Crap."

He laughs. "You have to hold it until you hit it. The nail doesn't stay there because it knows it's about to get hammered."

"I knew that."

He raises one brow. "Really?"

"Yes, really. I didn't want to hit my finger."

Derek takes the nail between his finger and thumb. "Then worry about hitting mine."

My eyes widen because there's no way I'm going to hammer his hand. It was bad enough worrying about hurting myself. "You're nuts."

"No, I trust you."

Now he's really crazy.

Our friendship has saved me in so many ways. I don't worry anymore about Kelly and Lori, who have told me that my being friends with the animal-whispering nerd has officially left me out of the cool crowd. I told them that was perfectly fine with me and then reminded them that all of us have secrets.

I am not weak. I'm strong and have power as well.

Derek gave me that back.

Not by doing anything magical either, just by being my friend. While he may trust me, I'm not about to smash his finger.

I drop the hammer to my side. "I trust you too, but I don't trust myself with blunt objects."

"It's not going to nail itself, Tea. If you don't do it, I'll be forced to stand here all day."

He leans against the wood just to prove his point.

"Stop being an idiot."

"Stop being a chicken."

"Fine," I huff. "You asked for it. When your finger needs to be amputated and you can't work with animals, don't say I didn't warn you."

He rolls his eyes. "Don't hit my finger and we won't have that problem."

"And will you forgive me if I hit you?"

"Depends."

"On?"

Derek's smile grows. "On whether you hit it or not."

chapter twenty-four

Teagan

present

My father has always griped about shopping with my mother and I never understood why. She's never in a hurry, she likes to window-shop a lot, and overall, she's just relaxed. Dad isn't that way. He likes to get the task done so he can move onto what he really wants to do—like fishing or football.

House shopping with Derek has given me a whole new understanding for my father's pain.

First, the agent that is driving us around is an idiot. She's gotten lost twice, and this town is not that big. Then, Derek's being the most ridiculous person ever. Each freaking house he finds something else, something that doesn't even matter, as a reason to move on to seeing the next listing.

"What was wrong with that one?" I ask as we leave the fifth showing.

"Too...beachy."

The agent clears her throat. "I can find something less beachy if you'd like."

"Thank you." He grins as though he's won a prize.

"We live on an island! The whole damn thing is a beach."

"Yeah." He sighs. "But it was old beachy."

I didn't know there was such a thing. "So you want more of a new beach feel?"

"I want it to feel like home."

"It won't be a home if you never pick it."

He chuckles once but covers it with a cough.

"We have four more homes lined up that we can look at," the agent informs us.

"Great. Teagan and I are ready for more."

Yeah, so ready…

I groan. "I should've cut my hair off when I was under that table."

"But then we wouldn't have this fun day together." The first house we'd looked at was perfect. It was a few blocks off the beach but had amazing views. There were some upgrades he could do that would've been simple enough. I couldn't believe how spacious it felt considering the square footage. I would've bought it, but he walked out after three minutes.

"Oh." I laugh without humor. "This is fun?"

"I'm enjoying myself."

"I'm glad one of us is," I mutter to myself.

Each house we visit, I try to picture Derek and Everly, and then, somewhere about five minutes into the vision, I show up with groceries or a painting in my hands. Then, Chastity comes out of the front door, smiling with that humongous pregnant cat of hers, and we're all happy. As though I'm not looking for a house for him, but for us — which I'm not.

It's a dumb fantasy that keeps coming back.

"I'm begging you to just let me walk home."

"Here, look at this one." He ignores the comment and takes the listing paperwork the agent handed him from the front seat. Of course, I'm stuck back here with him because her office is literally her passenger seat.

Derek shakes his head. "Let's see this one next. Teagan is getting hungry and it's close to the store. We'll get you a Snickers since you're clearly in a mood."

I wonder why that could be.

"You better get two."

"Only if you're nice."

"Then I guess I'll be hungry," I retort. I lost the ability to be nice three houses ago.

We pull up to a brick home, and he won't even get out of the car. "I don't like it."

I might kill him. "You haven't even seen it yet!"

He shrugs. "I don't want to see it."

"I think you're trying to torture me. I think this is all some ruse so that you can drive me crazy or force me to hang out with you."

"Is it working?"

I glare at him.

"I'll take that as a yes. So, if it is a ruse, I'm winning. If we're looking for a house, which I assure you, we are, I'm still winning. Honestly, today is perfect."

Instead of responding, I bang my head on the seat in front of me. This is my version of hell. I'm trapped in a car with a man I still have feelings for, looking at houses, and imagining myself in the house with him.

We drive to the other side where the tourists really never go. It's definitely the location I would prefer to live

in. I like the privacy this section of the island offers. It's
not about the wild horses or how big of a house you can
build.

It's true beach homes.

What people could afford to build and where they
could live a comfortable life.

"So, about that kiss…"

My head shoots to his to find him sitting there with a
smirk.

"Now is not the time," I say quietly.

"Why not? I'm sure you've been nuking it in your head
for over a week now. I think the car, where you can't escape, is the perfect time."

Oh my god. I'm seriously debating throwing myself
from a moving vehicle to avoid this. "Seriously, not now."

We don't know this agent and who she might gossip to
in town. And anyway, we were doing just fine pretending
nothing ever happened.

"Well, if you don't want to talk, that's fine."

I breathe a sigh of relief. At least he's being reasonable.

Talking about that kiss is bad. Talking about it makes it
real and I'm just fine letting it be a dream. He has no idea
what dating when you have a kid is like and I'm not ready
to be hurt again.

"I'll talk." *Oh, for the love of God.* "I liked that kiss. In
fact, I've thought about it a lot and I think *you* liked that
kiss."

"I'd like you to stop saying *kiss*," I say between gritted
teeth.

"Which leads me to wonder why you liked the kiss so
much and why you stopped the kiss."

There's something wrong with me, that's why. It's the

only thing I can come up with. He was married, had a kid, I had a kid, and our lives—and we—are nothing like we were before. We've grown up, we aren't the same starry-eyed kids with big hopes and dreams. We're both battle worn, tired, and have responsibilities that come first. I can't jump into a relationship—or go around kissing him—when I don't trust my heart not to make more of things. That's why I stopped it. None of that is going to come out of my mouth, though.

"I'm wondering if I could survive a quick exit."

"If you liked it and I liked it, what could that mean?"

"That you're trying to make me crazy?" I suggest.

"It means that we should kiss again."

That stops me. "I'm sorry, what?"

"You should kiss me again." Derek watches me, his eyes showing no signs of humor.

"You're kidding me."

"Do I look like I'm kidding?"

No, he doesn't. He's dead serious. He thinks we should kiss again and that now is the appropriate time to bring it up. Do I want to kiss him again? Yes. Yes, I do. Do I think it's a good idea? Not at all.

His daughter is still reeling from her mother's death. We don't know each other as adults, well, not really. I'm not in a financial or emotional state for a relationship, and our kids hate each other. It's not…it's just not the right time for us.

I'd do well to remember that and shut this down.

"You should be. You should be joking about this instead of looking at my mouth like that." I glance out the window, avoiding all eye contact, as we make a right onto Sycamore Street.

When I turn back to him, the heat in his eyes causes my heart to sputter. His gaze caresses my face and then is back on my lips.

"Like I want you too? Like I think about it all the time? Like it's been a long time coming? Or like it never happened and we pretend there's nothing we're both feeling?"

My throat is tight, but I manage to rasp the words out. "Yes. Like that."

Derek grins. "Well, I asked a series of questions and I'm happy to pick which one I'd like that answer to go with."

Before I can respond, the Realtor clears her throat and the discomfort in her voice would be comical if Derek hadn't just made me half crazy. "Here we are."

"Thank God," I say and get out of the car as quickly as I can. Then I realize we're on Destiny Lane. How fitting? The one street in this town named after something other than trees, nature, or numbers.

I walk up to the front, ready to be done with this day, when I come to a full stop. I can't move. I can't think because I'm staring at the most perfect house. I don't know if it's the house or the conversation we had that has me so unsettled, but that's the weird part, I'm not unsettled, I'm grounded.

All I keep thinking is…this is *the* house.

This is where I would live. This is a home.

I stand here, my eyes taking in the two-story home with the coziest front porch. It's a light blue color with thick siding that makes the house look a little bigger. There's an addition to the right that's completely made of windows, and a two-car garage off the driveway with more than enough room for a proper workshop or Chastity to experiment with her weird science stuff. It's…perfect.

I don't even need to look inside because no matter what condition it is in, I would fix it. It's the home I've dreamed of without even knowing.

I can see myself in that sunroom, painting while looking out at the oak tree that's swaying in the slight breeze. Chastity would sit on the porch, reading a book or even on that tree swing while she daydreams.

Derek stands next to me, both of us looking straight ahead.

"This is the house," he says.

My eyes snap to his. "What?"

"This is it. It's the one. I'm going to buy it."

No, this is *my* house. This is the house I need to live in. I need to talk him out of it and then sell my body to be able to buy it. "But you haven't even gone inside."

He turns to me. "I don't need to."

"Derek. Be rational! You can't know this is the house and that this wouldn't cost you a fortune to fix. You can't live here."

"Why not?"

Because I'm going to someday.

I feel like he's pulling my heart from my chest. How can this house be causing me so much discomfort? It's a house. It's just a fucking house.

But it's more.

"Because." That's all I can get out.

He turns to the Realtor. "This is the house. I'd like to make an offer."

"But, Dr. Hartz, you don't even—" The Realtor tries to speak, but Derek turns to me.

"Tea?" His gaze is intent. "Do you need to go inside?"

"No."

"Why?" he asks with a knowing smile.

This can't be real. "Because I know."

Derek slowly nods his head and grins. "As do I."

How can he know this house is right? How can he possibly feel what I'm feeling when I see this home? It doesn't make sense, but then again, nothing has ever been anything but strange with us.

He turns to the Realtor again. "We need a few minutes."

She doesn't say anything, but I know she's left us. He takes my hand, pulling me closer. We walk the pathway, up to the porch. My fingers touch the pillars and glide along the banister. There's a swing at the end, facing a huge old oak tree that stands beside the house.

We sit down, my hand still in his.

My eyes meet his and he smiles. "Sometimes I feel like I can still see in your heart and head. There are times when it feels so natural."

"And times when it doesn't…"

"Yeah, but the times I can"—Derek sighs—"it's like coming home."

It's this house, that's what's making him say these things. It has to be, because the way he's looking at me it's as though he's seeing into my soul.

I don't want to cry, but I can't stop the tear that forms. No matter how I'm trying to deny what I want, it's there. Derek may have been absent from my life, but never from my heart. "It scares me."

He watches me, seeming to grapple with something before he answers. "Me too."

"I can't handle it if you were to cut me off again. Not if I let you in this time."

Derek's thumb grazes the top of my hand. "I can't walk away from you again, Tea. I don't think I have it in me."

There are no guarantees he can give me and I would be stupid to think otherwise. "You say that now, but we're not exactly in the best position to make promises."

We have things that are against us becoming close again. Everly and Chastity being the biggest.

"I'm not making promises, but I'm not going to spend the rest of my life waiting. I can't just sit around and hope that things come to me. I did enough of that in my past. I felt something the other night. It was there the first time I saw you again. I feel it now, sitting here, looking at houses with you. If you think there's nothing between us—you're lying to yourself."

Avoidance is a beautiful thing until it's taken away. There are no veils of lies I can hide behind right now. He's forcing me to be honest with myself and I would've much preferred not to. I don't want to go back and feel all that hurt again. I've done what I can to move on from it and while we may be some version of friends, my heart is still made of glass with a crack in it. One bump or careless touch and it'll shatter.

"Why this house, Derek?" I ask, feeling raw and vulnerable.

"Because it's right. I know you see it. I want to stop second-guessing and fighting back something that's clearly perfect for me."

I shake my head because I'm not sure we're talking about the house. All of this is making my emotions a jumbled mess. He's saying everything that I've wanted, and yet the fear is crippling me from taking a chance. Anytime that I've allowed myself this sliver of hope, I've had it torn away. The hurt of losing, failing, and being alone has handcuffed me in some ways.

Derek is the key.

But what if he's the wrong one? What if this house is another symbol of the dream instead of the reality?

And then I wonder…what if all of this is the one dream that will come true? Am I brave enough to take the risk?

"That's the thing, sometimes we have to second-guess because our gut can be wrong." I put as much strength as I have into my voice.

"Stop worrying, Teagan. Trust me. Trust what we feel."

"It's not that simple!" I move away from him, needing the space to think straight.

"Why? What's complicated? We both have feelings for each other. We owe it to ourselves to see what it means."

"And what about our kids?"

"What about them?"

I shake my head. "Do you really think Everly will want you to date or explore your feelings so soon after her mother's death? Or what about the fact that of all the people you could choose, you're choosing the mother of the girl she hates? Then, there's my daughter…"

Chastity has never asked for anything from me. She's always appreciated the sacrifices I make. I've never once been made to feel like a bad mother in her eyes. It doesn't matter what my mother or I feel about my life, to Chas, I'm a hero. I've given her a roof, happiness, friendship, love, and always made sure she was cared for.

To force her to have to be around Everly feels like it would be a slap in her face.

"I know there are obstacles."

I laugh. "There are boulders in front of the trail that neither one of us can push."

"Then we stand in front of the boulder until we're both strong enough to move it together. I'm asking for a date, Teagan, not forever."

But somewhere deep in my heart, I know that Derek has always owned my forever.

"One date. One date and you don't buy this house."

His smile could brighten the sky if it were dull. "One date, and I'm putting an offer in today."

One date and then we can go back to just friends.

chapter twenty-five

Derek

present

"Where are you going?" Everly asks.

"Out."

She was supposed to be with her friends tonight and it was the perfect chance to leave the house without facing a million questions, but that didn't happen.

"I see that, but where?"

"Where people are."

Everly huffs. "Dad."

"I'm going out with a few friends from high school." It's not a lie…completely. I'm going out with Teagan on a date and there could be other people we went to school with there. You never know.

She rolls her eyes. "Let me guess, Teagan Berkeley?"

"She'll be there."

"Mom hated her," she states with disgust. "You know that, right?"

"Your mother was upset, and I'm part of the reason, but Teagan did nothing to deserve that anger."

There was no making Meghan happy because she didn't really want to be. The saddest part was that I would've done anything she wanted if she would've let it go. I did love Meghan. But I shattered her heart and it never healed.

"Mom hated her. She told me how you were friends and you were in love with Teagan and were going to leave us."

I hold back the rage that starts to build. I hate that Meghan would ever tell Everly this. Everly is a kid. She should've never been aware of the issues Meghan and I had, but when it came to Teagan, she apparently felt no need to filter.

Meghan was so damn sure I was going to leave the first chance I got, I guess she wanted to poison Everly just in case. It didn't matter that I stayed, even when our marriage was nothing but a façade.

"I didn't leave, and I didn't want to. I'm not going to discuss this with you, though. I lost a friend years ago and now that we're back in touch, I'm not going to lose her again."

"I hate her."

"You don't know her."

Everly crosses her arms. "I don't care. I know Mom did and that's enough for me."

I nod once. "Well, you can have your feelings and I have mine."

Arguing with her isn't going to change anything, and right now, Teagan and I are friends. My feelings for her are stronger and hers are as well, but Everly doesn't need that information.

Which is what I think Teagan's entire point was. For now, we need to see what this is and if we're willing to navigate it.

"Don't do this, Daddy," Everly begs as I get to the door.

I turn and see a scared and sad little girl. Not the tough one who doesn't care about anything. "Do what?"

"Date her."

I walk toward her, gathering her in my arms before kissing the top of her head. "You know that I've been alone for a long time, right?"

It's time we discuss what we know to be our past.

"Yes. But you loved Mom! I know you did!"

"I did. I loved her. I loved her very much."

She shakes her head, tears forming. "Then you can't do this. If you loved her, Daddy, you can't date Teagan!"

I sigh, rubbing my hand down my face. "When you love someone, really love someone, you want their happiness above all else." I look up at her, watching the tears fall. "I wanted your mother to be happy. I thought that maybe somewhere deep inside, I would've made her happy, but I couldn't. I hurt her a very long time ago, and I don't think she ever forgave me."

Everly wipes her eyes. "Because of her."

"No, Everly, not because of Teagan." I catch an errant tear on her cheek. "It was because I was never brave enough to tell anyone the truth. I don't want to make those same mistakes again. I like Teagan and I don't want to be unhappy anymore."

She nods, fighting to stop another round of crying. "I know. I don't want you to be either."

I wish she knew that even as unhappy as I was, I still didn't want this to be how my story with her mother ended.

"I miss your mother. I know that may not make sense

to you since we weren't happy, but I do miss her. She was funny and beautiful. She lit up a room when she walked in and God knows I never wanted anything to happen to her."

Everly's tears fall. "I just keep waiting for her to come back."

"I know."

"I keep thinking it didn't happen, but I know it did." Everly's lip quivers.

"I wish none of it happened and your mother was still alive."

She sniffs and wipes her eyes. "I don't want you to replace her."

"That's not what I'm doing," I tell her. "I'm not replacing your mother, there is no replacement for her."

Everly takes a step back. "Then you won't date Teagan?"

"No, that's not what I'm saying."

Her sadness is gone and it's now replaced with anger. I understand on some level how she feels. I can't imagine my father dating if he ever lost my mother, but then again, their marriage is nothing like mine was.

While I may have just lost Meghan, she hasn't been mine for a long time.

There is nothing wrong with what I'm doing right now.

"You've never cared about what I want anyway, why should you start now?" she says and then rushes out of the room, slamming the door behind her.

I sit on the bed, wondering if this is wrong. Should I do what she asks and cancel? Am I being a bad parent because I want to move on with my life or because after all this time, I feel again?

There's a soft knock on the door, and I don't have to ask who it is. "Come in, Mom."

"Sorry, honey, I overheard Everly."

"What am I supposed to do?"

She sits on the bed beside me. "What do you want to do?"

I look at her because I honestly don't remember the last time anyone asked me that. "I don't know."

"Don't you?"

"No. Yes. I don't…"

"You don't know who you are anymore, Derek." Mom waits for me to respond, but I can't. "It's not a bad thing, we all go through this. Lord knows I did after you left for college. When we lose something or someone who defines a part of us, we have to redefine ourselves."

My mother doesn't know the truth about my marriage. I'm sure she assumed a lot and probably knows more than I'd like to believe, but I've never told her the truth.

"I wish it was that simple."

She smiles softly. "Nothing is simple. But when someone makes you feel better in this world, they're a chance worth taking."

"You mean Teagan?"

"Sweetheart, you and Teagan have always been like two planets orbiting one another. When you told us you were getting married, do you know I thought it was to her?"

"You never…"

"Of course I never said anything, and when you stopped talking to her, I assumed it was because Meghan had the same concerns."

I will never underestimate my mother again. "Yes."

"She was probably right to be doubtful, but it was sad for Teagan, don't you think?" And me. It was sad for everyone all around. "I would hate to see you hurt her again because of Meghan. The words you heard tonight from Everly weren't hers. They were her mother's. We both know it and now you get to decide if you're going to allow someone else to dictate who you love or whether you're finally going to listen to your heart."

chapter twenty-six

Teagan

present

I'm parked outside the restaurant where we're supposed to meet. My nerves are out of control. Thank God Nina came over and picked out my clothes because I was completely lost.

What the hell do you wear to a date with a man you've loved your whole adult life?

Nothing looked right. I was trying too hard, not trying hard enough, or just plain frumpy.

Now, I'm here, in a deep purple dress and my hair curled in long waves—sitting in the car—like a chicken shit.

This is crazy. This is completely stupid and crazy. Derek can't possibly want to date me, not really. He wants to figure out some weird thing in our past and see if it's true. He must be just…going through some move-back-to-small-town-life crisis.

I start the car and then a knock causes me to jump. "Jesus."

Derek is at the window, with a smile on his face. "Going somewhere?"

I close my eyes and let my head fall to the steering wheel. "God, I hate my life."

"Were you running away?"

"Not very well."

He chuckles and then opens the door. "No, but I give you a C for effort."

"Just a C?" I ask as I turn my head to the side to catch a glimpse of him.

"I'm being generous too."

Lucky me. "How long were you watching me?"

I have a feeling this is going to be the worst part. If he just happened upon me I won't have to die from mortification, but if he was somehow skulking in the shadows and saw me sitting here for fifteen minutes, I'll never live it down.

"Oh, since you pulled up."

"Of course."

"What were you doing? Convincing yourself it's totally cool to bail on your date? I know you didn't like being on the receiving end of it."

"I wasn't going to bail like he did. I planned to have a better reason," I huff.

"How magnanimous of you."

He leans over me, turning the engine off, and taking my keys.

"Hey!"

"We're not eating in the car and really, you've lost the element of surprise."

I glare at him as he grins. "Fine."

"Just the way I like my dates to start off…"

I laugh and shake my head. "You haven't been on a date in over thirteen years."

Derek wraps his arm around my shoulder, pulling me to him. "Yes, and look how great this one is already going."

We enter the restaurant and get to our table. I haven't been to Pasta Palace since I was in high school. It's a few towns over, which we thought was a good idea so we lessen the chances of running into anyone. Privacy is a commodity we don't have an abundance of.

"You look great," he says as we look over the menus.

"Thanks. You look good too."

And he does. Derek has always been good-looking, but man, has he aged well. There's a sexiness about him that I don't remember when we were younger. He grew into himself. His body was a little disproportionate and he wasn't quite sure what looked good or not. There is zero of that now.

Derek commands the space around him, forcing it to conform around him, making his presence felt everywhere.

It's sexy.

Very sexy.

The waiter appears, takes our drink order, and informs us of the specials.

"Everyone knows you only order off the pasta section here," I whisper conspiratorially. I would hate to see him end up with food poisoning.

"I didn't know that."

"Oh," I say with dramatics. "It's a thing. Last month, Nina ended up violently ill after she thought maybe the chicken was safe."

"And you suggested here because?"

"Because we live on the island and our choices are limited."

It's not like we're basking in options. In the winter, it's slim pickings. We get what we get and eat in if we don't like it.

"I forget sometimes what it's like living here."

"Yeah, South Carolina was a bit different, huh?"

"Much."

"Do you miss it?"

Derek shrugs. "Not all of it. I miss my house and my practice."

"It must've been hard to leave."

"My dad needed me. He's not as healthy as he'd like to believe and, honestly, I needed to be around family. I'm so out of my league with Everly, and my mother seems to connect with her. We were alone down there. I worked crazy hours, and leaving Everly home with the neighbor for hours wasn't fair."

"We do what we have to as single parents."

He nods. "I didn't have to stay there. I could've come back the day Meghan died. I worked because I needed to stay busy. I immersed myself in my practice so that I could avoid the questions and people who wanted to know how I was feeling. How do you tell people you're upset but then there's relief too?"

I wish I could answer that for him, but I don't think he really wants that. He's been holding this in, and for some reason, he trusts me enough to let it go. "I'm sorry."

"That's the thing, I'm not…at least not for me. I'm sorry for Everly. I'm sorry for Meghan's parents, who are still devastated and can barely look at Everly now. I'm sorry that she had to go so soon because she didn't deserve to die. But…"

"But?"

"I'm not sorry for me. And that is the most horrible fucking thing I can ever say."

It feels wrong to offer words of comfort to him, but it also feels wrong to chastise him. Instead of doing either, I reach my hand across the table and hold his hand. I offer him no judgment, just friendship.

"You know, I was dreading moving back here. I fought against it so hard because I knew. I knew you'd be here and because…"

"…because?"

Our eyes meet and I don't need him to finish the statement, I already know. As much as I'd like to be angry, I get it. I would've spent the rest of my life avoiding him too if I had the option. There's a lot of things we've had to deal with and we're not done yet.

"Because it'd be easier than seeing you and having you hate me."

I shake my head. "I didn't hate you, Derek. I didn't understand. I was hurt, and angry, but I never hated you. I loved you too much to hate you."

The waiter clears his throat and we both lean back with a polite smile. My heart is beating against my chest and I grab the wine, thankful for the distraction. That was a pretty intense first ten minutes of a date.

We both order the pasta with a grin shared between us. After the waiter leaves, Derek and I sit in comfortable silence. There's so much to unbox from our previous conversation, I think we both need a second to process.

"Did Chastity know you were coming out?"

"She did. I don't keep much from her and I thought if she was going to hear about our date, it was better coming from me."

"Again, another display of how inept I am at dealing with my own kid."

God, I can only imagine what that means. "I take it Everly knows?"

"She does."

"And she took it well, I see."

He laughs. "It's hard. She knew that you and Meghan didn't get along."

"Well, that's not entirely true." I didn't have a problem with his wife. And really, his wife had nothing on me. I didn't write that damn journal entry. I never once made any kind of advance toward Derek. They were married, and no matter how broken I was over it, I didn't do anything to warrant her hatred. "I thought I got along with Meghan, she didn't like me for something *you* did."

"I'm sorry. I shouldn't have said that. It's not really first-date discussion."

"I don't think you and I could have an authentic first date," I say with a smile. I don't want my first, and probably only, date with Derek to be a bad thing. "We might as well call it what it is when it comes to us—weird."

I want to be able to remember tonight with affection. This has been something I've dreamed of and now it's here. The last thing I want is us spending it bickering or talking about heavy shit.

"How can you still do that?"

"Do what?"

"Change topics so fast. It was always something I wished I could do."

"It's a gift," I say and then take a sip of my wine.

I've never really tried to dwell on things that don't matter. I like to handle it and move on, except where Derek is concerned. He's always been my weakness.

"Okay, well, how did Chastity take it?"

"The truth?" I ask.

"Always."

Chastity is a great kid. She never has given me pushback and usually is very supportive when it comes to things regarding me living a life, but this time not so much. "I want to preface this by saying it's not you."

"It's my daughter."

I nod. "She loves you. She thinks you're really funny, clearly she doesn't know your humor is lacking, and she's learning a lot by working with you. I think she's just afraid that you and I could mess that up."

She also said she'll cut all my hair off in my sleep if I ever think she's going to live under the same roof as Everly. Sad thing is, I don't doubt her.

"I would never stop allowing her to work with me. Chastity is great with the animals and a huge help," he says earnestly.

"Other than she came back telling me her male cat is actually a pregnant female."

"Yeah, there's that, but she's been reading a lot about what to expect—"

"Oh, I heard all about it. I didn't realize they even have photos to help guide her through."

Derek laughs and shrugs. "I thought she should be prepared."

"How noble of you."

"I'd be happy to keep Mrs. Stinkers when she's closer to her due date."

I roll my eyes. I didn't want a cat to begin with, now to find out we may end up with a litter of kittens and the cat. Freaking kid. She's lucky I love her so much.

"You can keep her longer. Think of it as a gift from me…like a mascot for the office."

Derek shakes his head with a smile. "You're too kind, but I think your daughter really needs a cat. It's imperative for kids to have pets."

We grew up so differently. He had so many animals, mostly because his father was fixing them, whereas I had none. I feel pretty okay with the fact that I didn't have anything else to take care of. My weekends were for cheerleading and stupid boys.

Maybe I should get her two cats…

"You might have a point."

He leans back with that shit-eating grin that looks sexy on him. "I usually do."

The rest of the evening is very sweet. We have a great dinner—well, an edible one—and we talk about the past. A lot of old memories where we did stupid things and thankfully didn't get caught. It took my mother almost two years to figure out I snuck out to meet Derek on the beach most nights.

It was our thing, though.

The time when the rest of the world faded away and we were just two friends on a beach.

"Tell me more about your painting," he says as we finish another glass of wine.

"What about it?"

"Why aren't you selling them?"

I sigh. "I don't want to share them. They're just for me."

It's not that I don't think they're good, because I do, but then I think every painter thinks that. If I didn't love them, I wouldn't create them. Those paintings are my art, my soul, my truths all laid out for someone to see. Giving that to another to judge is…terrifying. I'm not that brave. I'm still trying to figure out what the story I'm painting really is. Is it my sadness? Or is it the hope of what I think the world could look like on the shore?

"I think they're beautiful."

My heart swells with pride from his compliment. Nina and Chastity always tell me they love them but there's something different about it coming from him. "Thank you."

"I'm not just saying it," he insists.

"I didn't think you were."

"It's the perspective of the painting. It really shows so much and the colors are vivid but not so in-your-face that you don't know where to look. I felt like you were showing me something that I've seen so many times, but never really understood. You have an amazing talent, Teagan, and you should share it with the world."

"I don't think you understand. I've failed at pretty much everything in my life. I don't need one more thing to not be good enough at. For now, it's an outlet that I love."

He shakes his head. "You aren't failing at anything. You've done an amazing job with your life, and your paintings are another thing that you should be proud of."

I place my hand on his and he stops talking. The two of us look down at where we're joined. His other hand covers mine and my breathing slows. It's like everything in the room around us fades. We're the only thing in this moment that exists.

I've seen it in movies and listened to Nina describe it in books and thought it was lame, but here it is, happening to me.

Derek has always made things come into perspective for me. He was the grounding force in my life when I had him. That's why it hurt so damn much to lose him.

But he's here now. He's touching me, holding me steady, and keeping me from floating away. When he speaks of my art, somehow understanding what it is even when I don't, it's indescribable.

It's like drifting but being tethered, bringing me back in when I go too far. He pushes me outside of the bubble I've put myself in, and it's scary and yet I'm not scared. How can this still be us? How can all this time have passed, but he is still the man who understands me at my core? After the years we've been apart our connection should've been broken, but it hasn't.

Both of us continue to look at each other, questions, answers, and more questions passing between us.

"Do you want to take a walk?" he asks, pulling his hand back and breaking the spell we were under.

I nod without saying a word.

Derek stands, his hand extended to help me up. My fingers touch his palm, and that calm rushes over me again and I realize I was such a fool to think I could do one date and not come out unscathed.

chapter twenty-seven

Teagan

present

I should've known this is where he'd want to go.

We pull up to the far end of the beach where we would meet all the time. In every way, this is our spot. The place where two kids found someone who would forever be a part of the other.

"You wanted to walk here instead of the town we were just in?" I ask as I exit my car.

"Was there any other option?"

I shake my head. "No. This is probably exactly the best place."

Derek walks over with a blanket and takes my hand in his. "Come on."

We make our way to the shore, set up a cozy spot, and sit. Twenty years ago, I would've sat in front of him, his arms around my middle, my head resting on his chest as I stared out at the sea, but now, we're beside each other.

"Do you remember the night you told me you were pregnant?"

I release a half laugh because it wasn't funny. I was more afraid of him than of my parents. Disappointing him was the last thing I wanted to do. Not to mention, I was horrified it happened.

"I don't know that I could forget. I threw up four times before I saw you."

"Well, you were pregnant."

"It was nerves."

He shifts so our shoulders are touching. "I felt so many things that day, it was really the first time I started to wonder if what I felt for you was more than friendship."

"That was the day?"

"I was so pissed because I kept thinking it shouldn't be Keith. He didn't deserve to have that piece of you. I was beyond angry and couldn't wrap my head around why. Which pissed me off further."

I laugh. "Sounds like you."

He wasn't the only one pissed. I had the same emotions because I didn't want to have a baby with Keith. I didn't even want to be with him, but I was young and stupid. My feelings for Derek were growing by that point, and I knew he was who I loved, I just didn't know how to express that.

Then I found out I was pregnant and it felt like I'd missed that chance.

"Yeah, but then…"

"Then you had Meghan."

As angry or hurt as I was, I never told him how I felt. It wasn't like he knew I was in love with him, but God, I couldn't handle it.

I don't know that it makes any of this any easier, but it's the truth.

"I really didn't know what I was feeling."

"You don't have to explain, Derek. We were kids, you were confused, I was pregnant, and it all fell apart. I will tell you, there is nothing close to the level of heartbreak I felt when I watched you marry her."

I've never felt that level of emotional pain. Knowing he was going to pick her with me standing there. Watching them profess their love when all I wanted was for him to love me the way I loved him. It was excruciating. I wanted to be happy for him, God I tried, but I couldn't.

There was the man I wanted to marry, marrying someone else.

I couldn't do or say anything.

I was trapped, watching it, pretending my tears weren't because my heart was being torn from my body.

When we stopped talking, it was different because he'd already hurt me once. I guess that makes me a fool, but...

He shakes his head. "I didn't know."

"I know you didn't. But even if you did, would it have changed anything?"

Derek's mouth forms into a thin line. "I want to say yes, but I really don't know. I loved Meghan and I was so hell-bent on proving I loved her, then we got married."

"And she was pregnant."

He nods with a laugh. "Yeah, there was that. Were you angry?"

I shake my head. "I couldn't be. You were doing the right thing by marrying her, where Keith was doing the opposite. Besides"—I smile and nudge him—"Derek Hartz is a good man who would always be the kind of man who married the girl he loved and knocked up."

"Great. That's what you think of me."

"It was never a bad thing. I just was afraid that things were going to change even more than my life was already spiraling out of my control. I had hoped and prayed that I could have you at least as a friend. I would find a way, I knew I would, but I needed you."

And he left me anyway.

"Do you think, in some way, it was what we needed?"

"Is there really a right answer to that?"

He shakes his head. "No. Probably not."

"On one hand, we were so young and I was…not ready for a real relationship, being pregnant when I felt like my life had imploded, so who knows if we would've made it? On the other hand, I would've liked to have tried."

Derek leans his arms behind him, looking up at the sky. "I think I had to lose you."

I wait for him to elaborate and when he doesn't, I decide to push. "You what?"

"I know it sounds crazy, but you were…you. You were Teagan, my Teagan. Even when you were with Keith, I knew we weren't really like that. I had this ridiculous delusion as to what our lives would be and I was so fucked in the head that when that vision was shattered because you wouldn't leave him, I rebelled. I knew that you would never love me, at least that's what I convinced myself of. By the time I got my head out of my ass, it was too late. I was married with a baby on the way. I had done permanent damage and continued to destroy everything." He sits back up and his voice is a little broken. "I didn't deserve you then. I'm not sure that I do now either, but I know that I would like to try."

Now it's my turn to stay silent. All of this feels like too

much. Tonight was meant to be a date and now we're deep into talking about the past and what we could have in the future. I never expected that there even could be a future.

I've spent so much of the last decade telling myself this would never happen. None of it. I would never see Derek again, talk to him, and then I stopped allowing him to enter my mind. I focused on being the best mom I could for Chastity. Everything I've done has been for her.

Now, I'm at this bizarre crossroads and there are so many more potholes and construction signs up. There's Chastity, my family, his family, Everly, the fact that our past is murky, and I don't need murky.

I need clear.

I need to feel secure because for so long, I haven't been.

"What are you thinking about?" he asks.

"Us. What any of this means and if we're still stupid kids trying to fulfill some destiny we defined."

There's no point in lying, and it's better if we get this stuff out now so I can move on with my life and stop driving myself crazy.

"Me too."

I tilt my head toward him. "Well, that's not all that comforting."

Derek sighs and sits forward. "What can I say? We're both a little gun-shy and for good reason. I broke your heart when I stopped talking to you, and you were always between Meghan and me even after I did that. It wasn't your fault, but in some ways, I've been in a relationship with you for years."

"Why did you stay? Why didn't you find a way to talk to me?"

His head drops and I know this is probably the last

thing he wants to talk about. "I loved her, in my own way. She gave me Everly, and for that, I wanted to try. After a while, it was just what I thought I needed to do. She worked a lot, so did I, and we became…roommates. Also, God, this is going to sound bad," Derek warns. "I knew if I saw you again, I'd struggle with the idea of staying with Meghan and forgoing all I was doing for Everly. If you were single, that would've been all I needed to know and I would've left my wife."

My heart stops and everything around me turns hazy. All of my life I've wanted to hear that from him, and it's bittersweet in every way.

"I don't know whether to laugh or cry."

The breath escapes his nose and he leans back in the sand again. "I would go with both because it's pretty pathetic and also a little romantic."

I don't know what he finds to be romantic about spending years married to someone who he wasn't really a husband to because he was too chicken, but I'll let him have this one.

"Did you buy the house?" I ask, switching topics to something safer.

He laughs. "I told you I was going to put an offer in."

"Are you trying to torment me?"

"Not in the least."

That's what he's doing by loving that damn house. "Why do you want it then?"

Derek turns toward me, his expression is serious, and I feel like this is one of those moments I should pay attention to. "Because you like it."

"That doesn't make sense! Clearly, you want to torture me by making me know that you now own *my* house."

"That's where you're wrong, Tea. It makes perfect sense. If you felt that way, standing there, then there's a reason. I don't have to know what it is or why. Whenever it comes to you, it's been right. Look at tonight, you can't tell me you don't feel it."

The moonlight shines down on his face, showing me his eyes. There is so much emotion in them, I can't focus on one. "I don't know what you feel. I don't know what I feel," I confess.

"When I do this…" He lifts his hand, pressing it to my cheek. "What do you feel?"

Everything.

"Warm."

I feel his heat, the warmth that emanates from him, thawing my heart from the years I've kept it frozen. A fire inside of me that was just dwindling embers is kindling back up into a flame.

Then I remember that heat can burn you, scar you, and leave you exposed and raw.

"And what about this?" Derek leans in and I don't move a muscle. His mouth inches closer and I don't know what to do. If I let him kiss me now, there's no drinks to blame it on, I'm stone-cold sober. However, his lips don't touch mine, they press against my cheek. "What do you feel there?"

I release a shaky breath as I try to slow my racing heart. "Nervous."

"Do you know what I feel when I touch you, Teagan?"

My head moves side to side.

"I feel content. I feel like everything makes sense in a world where none of this should."

"It doesn't make sense."

His lips inch closer and I know that he is going to kiss me, not on the cheek, not on the nose, but he's going to kiss me, own me, claim me as his and I don't think I have the wherewithal to stop him.

"We make sense." His voice is soft, as if he doesn't want to disrupt the moment. "What do you want to feel, Teagan?"

My pulse is racing and every muscle in my body is pulled toward him.

I look up in his eyes as he waits. "Tell me something real," I say with fear and hope.

Derek moves so our lips are a breath apart. "I'm really going to kiss you."

chapter twenty-eight

Derek

present

The first time I kissed Teagan Berkeley we had been drinking, and even in the slight alcohol fog in the moment, everything felt right.

She felt right.

We are right.

This time, my entire life makes sense. It's as if the pieces of me that were floating, searching for their rightful spot have just…connected.

Our mouths move together and I pull her in my arms. For so long I've felt such jarring emotions when it came to her. It was too intense and made no sense, but this is why. Because I didn't know that having her would calm everything.

I hold her cheeks, needing to keep our lips fused. She's the air, the ocean, and I would drown in her if I could.

She moans into my mouth and I push her to her back, cradling her as we go. Her fingers slide through my hair, gripping the strands as though she has to keep me here. I don't plan on stopping anytime soon.

I kiss her for the years I couldn't. I kiss her for the time that's passed and I didn't get to touch her. I kiss her as a promise and an apology because I hurt her. My heart, which has been dead inside, is beating and she's who gave it back.

Maybe it was never mine to begin with and it's always been Teagan's.

"Derek." She says my name in the softest tone.

"I'm here."

Teagan's eyes are filled with desire as she stares up at me. "This is real, right? This isn't a dream."

I shake my head. "It's real."

"Real." She says the word as if it's the first time.

Her fingertips graze my face and I watch her watching me. "I've wanted this for so long."

"You're not the only one."

"This is going to be complicated," Teagan warns.

I'm not sure if she's telling me or reminding herself. However, I don't care what we have to do to make this work. There is no way I can walk away. Not when everything in my life is finally fitting.

When I lost Meghan, I didn't know what it meant. I thought it was a punishment of some sort. I believed I deserved to be alone now because it was how she must've felt.

Then, when I had to come back here, I again thought it was another way to have to be reminded of the man I couldn't be for Meghan. I had no idea if Teagan was married or happy. Surely she had to be. She's beautiful, funny, smart, and I never would've been able to handle watching her with another man.

"I can do complicated," I assure her.

"We can't tell anyone."

I smile. "I can keep a secret."

Teagan laughs and then runs her thumb across my lips. "I'm going to need to go slow."

"Are you trying to give me an out?" I ask as I lean back, pulling her up with me.

"I'm just giving you the reality."

My finger slides under her chin and I lift it so our eyes meet. "I don't need fast. I don't need to tell people—right now," I say because I won't be able to lie for very long. "I've waited a very long time for you, even when I didn't know that's what I was doing. We can go as slow as you need. We can tell as many or as few people as we want. The only thing you can't do is tell me this is all we get."

Time is fleeting. It doesn't care that the reasons she may have are valid, because when it runs out, you can never get it back. I won't live like that again. I know what I want. I see my life in front of me and every aspect has Teagan in it.

I'm buying that house because one day, she'll live in it. I don't know when, but it will happen. I don't care if every room in that house has to be renovated, I know that it's where Teagan and I will be.

Her eyes are warm and her smile soft. I lean in, pressing my lips to hers.

Because I can and because I need her.

chapter twenty-nine

Teagan

present

Kissing him like this is everything. It's coming up for air. It's drowning. It's feeling as though I have everything I want, but not really knowing if it's real. Derek's hands cup my cheek, his thumbs brushing against the skin in soft caresses, and I melt.

I give myself permission to just feel and catalog the senses. I inhale the sea air, allowing the slight sting of the salt to flow through me. My fingers run though his soft hair, the strands feeling as though they were meant for this exact moment.

He licks against my lips and I open to him. I'm his right now. I am taking and giving because resisting him is the last thing I want to do.

"Teagan." His deep voice rasps over my name, and I vow never to forget the way he sounds. How full of need his words are.

Derek's fingers drift down my arms and then snake

around my back, pulling me tighter against his chest as the kiss goes on.

Time seems to stop or maybe it disappears completely because this moment is perfection.

Every time that I imagined this, I was so far off. I couldn't have known that it would *feel* this good. There's not anyone who would have been able to articulate how one kiss could make my world flip upside down, but that's what he's always been for me.

A game changer.

"Tell me you feel this," he says against my lips.

"I feel it all."

Derek pulls back, the moonlight behind him, which should make it impossible to see him, and yet it's as though the sun is around us both. I can see the desire in his eyes. I can taste the want that pulses between us and the apprehension that we're both trying to make sense of.

I want him, but God, if it doesn't terrify me.

Giving in to this has a potential for disaster.

"If I had known…"

I touch his face. "You would've what?"

"I would've come for you. I would've not been such a fucking pussy and told you everything. I would've been at your door each day until you let me in and forgave me."

"You wouldn't have had to work that hard. I don't know that I could've resisted you," I confess.

He smiles with a soft shake of his head. "I think we both know you wouldn't have been that forgiving."

"Maybe not," I admit as I rub the beginning of his five o'clock shadow. "I might have made it difficult for you, but I think we would've been right here after a few days."

"You have no idea what I'm feeling."

"Tell me."

Derek takes my hands in his, our fingers intertwining, and he steps back. "First, there's regret for the fact that we didn't have this sooner. All this time that we've wasted. Years of anger that has built up. I have fear because I don't know if you'll ever truly forgive me, just as I'm not sure I forgive myself." I start to open my mouth to say something but he continues. "More than anything, I want you, Teagan. I always have. I want to lay you down on this blanket and make up for all the time we've lost. I want to worship you, claim you, make you remember nothing else but me. I feel a need for you that is unparallel to anything I've ever felt before."

As though neither of us could take another second, we both crash together. Our hands are on each other, holding the other closer. My chest is so tight to his there's no space. I want to absorb myself in him and become one.

His words ignite a part of me that I thought might be lost forever—to be wanted.

I've longed for someone to see me as more, and he does.

Derek sees the woman I could be. I worry that if I allow the part of myself I keep locked away to come to the surface, the vulnerability will be too much.

His fingers tangle in my hair, gripping the strands and guiding my head the way he wants me. I let him lead, needing for him to keep kissing me.

I slide my hands up his chest, loving the low, deep, filled-with-lust sound that emanates from his throat.

God, this is going to end with us naked if we don't stop it.

"Derek." I breathe his name, not sure if I'm asking for more or warning him it's too much.

And that's the thing. It's both.

He must take it as the second, though, because he gives me two soft kisses and then rests his chin on top of my head, struggling to catch his breath.

We stand here, with the sea at his back as I cling to him, unsure whether if I let him go, this will all disappear.

Derek seems to mirror my thoughts because he looks down at me and shakes his head. "Is this real?"

"I really hope so."

"I do too, Tea."

The thing is, I don't know what any of it means. "I feel as though we're moving too fast, but at the same time we've been waiting for this forever."

He smirks. "You've dreamed of this?"

Oh, please. Like I'm going to admit that. "And you haven't?"

"I most definitely have." Derek's warm hands glide up my arms, sending a delicious shiver down my spine.

All of this is too fast. There is a lot to consider and things that we need to talk about before I go any further. Even though there's nothing I'd like more than to strip him down and see if the rest of my fantasies are even close.

"Derek, this is…this is a lot." I take a step back. Maybe a little space will help us.

"Hey, what's wrong?"

"Nothing's wrong. It's all so…much. I've been waiting so long for this." I pause, trying to find the right words. "Chance. This possibility of us, and I don't want to dive into something that neither of us are really ready for."

"What makes you think I'm not ready?"

He hasn't said or done anything to say he's not, but I can't help worrying that he hasn't really comprehended what being a single parent is. Everly isn't going to be an easy kid either based on what is going on now. Then there's my kid, my own issues, his family, and we have different goals.

"I don't know if you aren't ready, but are you? Do you have a clue about what we're doing?"

He reaches his hand out, taking mine. "I'm ready for us, Teagan, and as for what we're doing...I don't have a clue what it is but I know that I want whatever this is. I know you make me feel alive and that I have no intention of this being our last date."

And I have no hopes of resisting him.

"I don't want that either."

"Okay, then don't pull away."

I wish it were that simple. "I'm a mess, Derek. I'm not proud of it, but it's the truth. I'm scared of being hurt. I'm scared of what it means for my daughter, because if this goes badly, animals and working with you is her solace." The words come fast and I can't stop them. "My life has been this series of bad choices and then unhappiness. I don't want *us* to be that. I've been waiting and hoping for you for so damn long and now you're here and...God, that could go away. Then what? What happens if you realize I'm the mess you don't want to deal with? Because that could happen."

"Not a chance."

"Yeah, you say that now but..."

"But nothing, Teagan. Look, I don't know what the hell the future holds any more than you do. You're not the only one with a mess, okay? I got a pretty fucking big one too. Here's the thing, do you want to walk away right now from what this could be?"

"No." There is no hesitation.

"Then all I ask is if you get scared and you need us to slow down, you tell me."

Could this man be more perfect? I don't think he could.

"Okay, but you have to promise me something."

Derek releases a breath, almost as though he wasn't sure I would give him that. "Anything."

"If my mess starts to become too much, you'll tell me before, so I can clean more of it up."

His fingers tighten in mine and he pulls me to him. My chest is now pressed back against his. "Deal. Now, I'm going to kiss you until you tell me to stop, okay?"

I smile, my heart feeling just a little more hopeful and the desire I thought had diminished is back in full force. "Absolutely okay."

And he wastes no time doing exactly as he promised.

chapter thirty

Teagan

present

"Are you telling me that your date was better than you thought?" Nina asks with a smirk.

I had to go over every single detail with her. She asked the weirdest things, but then again, it's Nina and she lives in a fantasy-relationship land.

"It was."

"And you guys are going to go out again?"

There's no point in denying it. "Yes."

She screams and starts to jump up and down. "I knew it! I knew this would happen! Gah! It's like the book I just finished. This girl, who loved this guy, was so angry that he left because his job called him away—"

"Nina," I say, trying to stop her before she ruins the book and I never get to read it.

"—It was so sad too because she thought he left because of the job but it turned out it was because his father didn't like her, but that's not the point. It was because the hero really wanted to protect her from the evil father who had plans to ruin her." She begins to ramble more, with her hands going as she explains the entire plot.

"Nina."

"Oh! The best part though was when he told her that he came back because he couldn't live without her. It was so sweet. They were these star-crossed lovers and he finally stood up to his daddy and told him where to stick it. Then, they were in love and everything was great. Of course the book ended with a wedding where the father was there, supportive finally."

"Yes, finally."

"You should read it."

I groan and drop my head. "That entire thing sounds great, but it's nothing like Derek and me."

"No? You mean that the father isn't like his ex-wife and he didn't come back?"

"Sure, it's like the book, now that you put it that way."

The phone rings and we both smile, knowing it's Mrs. Dickman and that we have a surprise for her. "You want to get it or should I?" I ask.

"You're the manager and should be the one…"

I smile and grab the phone. "Island Antiques, this is Teagan."

"Teagan, dear, it's Mrs. Dickman…I wanted to inquire about the chairs."

I don't know if it's Derek's returning and me wanting to bring things back to where they might have belonged all along, but I've been scouring the antique world for Mrs. Dickman's chairs this last week. I've called every antique store that I could find in the state of Virginia. Then, when I exhausted that, I went to Maryland, Delaware, New Jersey, and finally, when I got to Connecticut, I had a break.

"Actually, I'm glad you called, I do have some news."

Her gasp is loud and I can't help but smile.

"You do?"

"I do. I was able to locate one chair."

"Oh! Teagan!" I can almost hear the tears through her voice. "You found one?"

"I did. My mother is heading up there in the next few days and is going to grab it. I'm hoping we find more. The other store owners I contacted are all on the hunt as well."

She sniffles once. "You have no idea how much this means. Thank you."

"It's not all of them, but piece by piece we'll find them."

"That's how life works, my sweet girl. Piece by piece we find what we're missing and sometimes we become whole again."

How right she is. "We'll keep trying."

"Thank you." Her voice is shaking and then she disconnects the line.

Nina has tears rolling down her face. I swear, this girl is such a sap, but then again, I'm tearing up too. Mrs. Dickman has been waiting for so long and I almost hate myself for not understanding more how much she's missed what she's lost.

"You've made her very happy." Nina wipes under her eyes.

"God, we're a bunch of babies."

She laughs. "It's romance, Tea. It's a beautiful part of her story that you've given her back. To us, they were stupid chairs, but to her, they represented the love she had for her late husband."

I nod, knowing exactly what she means. "I want to cry."

Nina wraps her arms around me and she pulls me close. "I always knew you had it in you. We just needed Derek to come back to remind you that you do believe in love."

"Oh, dear God. I wouldn't go that far."

She slaps my arm. "Stop it. Now, tell me about the kiss."

I smirk. "Which one?"

Nina squeals again. "I knew it! Did you do more? *Please* tell me you had sex because that would be exactly like the book I read before this one."

"Umm, no." I laugh. "We are taking things really slow."

"Oh, Jesus."

"What?"

"Slow? You two have been at the pace of the tortoise on a freaking marathon. He's still only on mile marker two after fifteen years of running."

Now that's some good imagery there. To some extent, she's right. We have gone at the slowest pace ever, but in some ways we haven't. Neither of us knew our feelings until it was too late. The history we share isn't exactly a smooth one either. I think slow is smart. I need smart because I've done an awful lot of stupid.

"I'm not saying we'll be running a marathon with the tortoise pace, but I need to make sure I don't jump in headfirst and end up with a concussion."

She sighs and leans against the counter. "You're not getting any younger, you know."

"Neither are you."

Nina's eyes narrow. "We're not talking about me. We're talking about you and the man that you've loved your whole dang life being right in front of your face."

"And if it's right," I say with as much conviction in

my voice as I can muster, "then tomorrow, he'll still be in front of my face."

I can see her displeasure, but that's the way it is. We're going slow and it's not just because I'm scared, which I am, but because it's not just about me or him. It's also about two other people—our daughters.

"You should be naked in his bed right now. The two of you should be locked in a room somewhere, working off the last decade of sexual frustration."

"Well, we're not."

Although I do agree that I have a decade's-plus worth of sexual frustration that made it really freaking hard to pull away last night. But he was so sweet and understanding.

We kissed…a lot. We kissed as though we were two teenagers who just found out how fun kissing was. He walked me to my car, kissed me again, told me he would call me, and then he watched me drive off.

I wanted to turn back around, to feel his lips on mine again, but I somehow held myself back.

"You're thinking about him naked, aren't you?" Nina accuses me with a grin across her face.

"No."

"Liar."

"Fine, I am, but only because you brought it up."

She laughs. "Whatever you need to help you sleep at night. So when are you seeing him again?"

The twenty questions with her are killing me. "I don't know."

"How about now?" Derek's voice fills the space and I jump.

"How the—?" I say because the damn door didn't

chime. My cheeks burn and I can only imagine how red they are.

"How long was I here and what did I hear?"

Oh, this is so bad. My heart is racing and my mind is searching for something to say. Nothing can make this better if he heard me admit to thinking of him naked. I will never live this down.

"That would be good information to know now, yes."

His smile is full of mischief. "Tea, now where would the fun of overhearing a conversation you definitely didn't want me to hear be if I told you?"

"Well, I think the fun part would be telling me so I know how long I have to hide."

He walks closer and shrugs. "I guess we have different ideas of fun. Although"—he turns his head toward Nina—"I like her suggestions of being naked."

I cover my face in my hands and pray the good Lord takes me now.

"Naked is the new dating," Nina says.

"Really? Well, it's a good thing Teagan and I are dating."

"Nina's insane."

"She's onto something," he tosses back.

"She's also about to be fired."

Nina bursts out laughing. "Your mama likes me more than you, my friend. I think if she could, she'd make me manager just to torture you."

Now, that I don't doubt.

Nina walks over, kisses Derek on the cheek, and pats his chest. "You were always my favorite…after Romeo."

"You were always mine too…after Teagan."

Damn him for being so sweet.

"I'll be in the back, organizing the new plates. Then I'll call around to a few more stores to see if we can find those lost chairs. You know, give you *time*, just in case." She turns and winks at me.

There are no new plates, and I don't know what she thinks Derek and I need time for while we're in the store, but I appreciate her giving us a minute. He moves closer, hand resting on my hip, and smiles. "Hi."

"Hi."

I try to keep the grin off my face but the way he's looking at me makes it impossible. He's so damn cute and he's here. On what was probably a busy day, because there are more animals than people in this town, and he came by…to see me.

"You look very pretty."

Now he's lying. "I definitely do not." I'm in a pair of old jeans, my hair is up in a messy bun—that I can't pull off—and my T-shirt with a plaid shirt over it doesn't scream sexy. It's more like, I look like I don't have enough money for new clothes but I'm trying for country chic.

"You do."

"You're going blind in your old age."

His hand tightens, eyes glance around the store, and then to my lips. He's going to kiss me.

"Stop talking," he demands and then his lips are on mine, hand sliding around my back, keeping me to his chest.

Kissing is definitely not overrated.

We don't rush as we take each other in. It's only been a few hours but I missed him. How crazy is that? I missed the way he smells, how his hand feels on my skin, and the way he says my name.

It's stupid.

It's ridiculous.

It's magical.

"Now, don't ever call me old again," he warns and kisses my forehead.

I don't care what any woman says, when a man kisses our foreheads, we melt. Just a little. If he ever learns how much I like it, I'm pretty sure he'll win every argument.

"If you kiss me each time I do," I say playfully, "I might call you old more."

He laughs while shaking his head and then steps back. "Can I steal you away for a bit?"

"I have a lot of work to do...my mother is due back today too."

"She's off shopping for used goods?"

We used to laugh at it as kids. Buying old things with the hope of turning around and selling them is a gamble, but she's good at it. This store has thrived over the last forty years.

"She went to a few estate sales this week down in Virginia Beach, and to visit my cousins."

"Ahh, how is Mark?"

"The same, I'm sure. A little bit stupid and a lot unstable. He's married now," I tell him. I forget that he doesn't know anything that's happened in the last few years. Mark is a former Navy SEAL and scares the crap out of my mother and aunt.

"Is he? I never saw that coming."

No, I didn't either. "Yeah, her name is Charlie and she's amazing. She kicks his ass, which makes us all smile."

"Well, he tortured you as a kid," Derek reminds me.

"Yeah, all of my cousins did."

"They were fun."

"Sure, that's the word we'll go with," I scoff. They were mean and tormented me because they could. Derek would join in too, because apparently it was...fun.

"I need a half hour, surely you can spare that?"

I really want to go, but I can't leave Nina in case my mother returns early, which she's known to do.

"I don't know..."

"Oh, for heaven's sake, just go," Nina says as she comes around the aisle. So much for privacy. "I'll handle your mother, don't worry. Go!"

I gnaw on my lip, not sure if I should. I feel like this is the opposite of slow, but then I remember what Nina said and it's true. We're not a new relationship, and even with the time that's passed, he still seems to know me. Not the things in my life that he wasn't there for, but me at my core.

Derek extends his hand and I place mine in it because you only live once and I'm ready to begin the life I dreamed of.

* * *

"You brought me here?" I say as I look up at the house I love. The one I know, deep in my heart, should be mine.

I hoped when I saw it today that I wouldn't have the same reaction because when he buys it, I'll be sad. Sure, there might be another one—a better one—down the line, but this one is...home.

My home.

"I did."

"Why?" I ask with a bit of wistfulness.

"For lunch," he says, as though it makes perfect sense.

"You thought this was a great spot?"

Derek grabs the cooler out of the back of the car. "I did."

"And how is that?"

"You wanted us to be secretive, well, no one but us and the Realtor know about this house. You wanted slow, and lunch is about the slowest of dates there is. Then you said this would be complicated, but"—he shrugs—"I uncomplicated it."

This man is a mess, but he's a cute one. "How did you uncomplicate it?"

"I brought lunch to the place we could be alone and secretive."

"You thought of it all, huh?"

"I did." He beams with pride.

"You know you don't own the house, so we're kind of trespassing."

Derek smirks with his brow raised. "Ye of little faith, I talked to the previous owner, who has accepted my offer, and he told me I would be doing him a favor by looking after the house while he's in Florida."

"You got the house?"

"He accepted the offer this morning."

I knew he would—Derek always gets what he wants—but I did hope just a little bit that he didn't. Which makes me a terrible person. Derek has endured a tragic loss and he needs stability. I'm being stupid, but I decide to give myself two seconds to be stupid and then let it go.

One.

Two.

And I'm done. "I'm really happy for you. Have you seen the inside yet?"

"I thought maybe we could do that together."

"I can't believe you bought the house without going in."

He shrugs. "I'm a rebel."

"Or an idiot, but sure."

"I'm going to pretend you think I'm fabulous."

"Whatever you need to make you feel better."

Derek takes my hand, kisses the top, and grins. "I just need this."

I start to smile and then I look away, feeling the heat on my cheeks. He makes me smile, even when I don't want to.

He unlocks the door, extending his arms so I can go first, and I stop. Oh. My. God.

I can't turn my eyes to look at him, but I feel him beside me, doing the same thing, taking it all in. What in the hell did we just walk into? There are no words to describe the scene I'm looking at.

This house…is…

"Wow," Derek says.

"Yeah, wow."

"I guess…" He trails off, looking to the right, and my eyes follow.

"The owners were…" I can't even speak because my head can't comprehend what I'm looking at.

This beautiful, picturesque house that I dreamed of each night since I've seen it, is filled to the brim with dolls. There has to be thousands of them. They line the staircase going up, and the wall as if they're the baseboards. Dolls are on shelves, on top of cabinets, and…they're everywhere.

I can't look in one place because my eyes are overwhelmed.

"Does Everly like dolls?" I ask, trying to contain my laughter. "Because…I'm pretty sure you'll never find them all."

Derek's gaze meets mine and he bursts out laughing. "This is some scary shit."

"No wonder he took your bid!"

We both continue on with the loudest laughs I've ever heard. "I've never seen anything like this," he says as he gasps for air.

"I can't stay in here." I snort and hold my arms around my belly. "They're all staring at me and I think one just talked!"

I haven't laughed like this in ages. The muscles in my stomach hurt and we both make it outside unscathed.

"Let's head to the back."

"Yes, where it's safe."

I stifle another fit of giggles and we make our way onto the deck.

It's truly beautiful and secluded back here. There are tall trees that create a barrier and give so much privacy that you'd forget you even have neighbors. It's a bigger lot than what this town normally has too, which helps. The shed is off to the left and the deck is covered and has a great little eating area.

"At least they kept the outside cleared of…dolls."

"Well, I'm sure they're still watching us."

He shudders. "I'm going to have nightmares."

"You and me both! That was insane. You bought the creepy house full of dolls that no one else wanted." I start laughing again.

He joins in. "You wanted the house too!"

"True. But I didn't buy it."

"Yes, but you wanted to."

"I would've at least looked inside."

Derek runs his hand down his face. "I was so sure this house would be magical."

"Oh, there's magic in there all right. Hmmm." I tap my finger on my chin. "Maybe we should call you Ken from now on!"

The two of us are laughing so hard that tears are falling. "Then I'll call you Barbie."

"Hell no, this is your house, creepy dolls and all." I wipe my tears and try to stop the giggling.

"You laugh now, but one day you will be living here too!"

Well, that sobers the moment.

We both stop laughing.

I stare at him, unsure if he knows what he said. Derek looks down at me, his Adam's apple bobbing as he swallows. He moves closer, our breathing is accelerated, and I'm unsure of what to do.

I could ask him what he meant or pretend it didn't happen.

However, I'm not sure I can unhear what he said and I don't know that I can pretend otherwise.

"What?" I ask, my voice is barely a whisper.

"Don't look so surprised, Teagan." Derek's hand lifts and he takes a strand of my hair and then tucks it behind my ear. "I told you, I'm not going anywhere and I don't have any doubts that I'm here with you for a reason. I can wait until you know it, but what we're doing here, isn't ending."

My heart is pounding so loud, I can't hear anything else. I want to believe what he's saying more than anything, but this is really not slow and this is a million times beyond complicated.

"Please don't make me promises like that," I say with fear and apprehension. "I don't think I could handle the loss again."

He wraps his arm around my back, forcing me to put my hands on his chest. "Then hold on and don't let go this time."

"You're the one who let me go the last time."

The regret fills his eyes. "And I won't ever make that mistake again."

I lean up, kissing him because I need to seal it. I want that promise to be unbroken. I can feel my insecurities bubbling up, telling me that this isn't how life works out for me, but I fight against it. If I can just hold on to this, then maybe it'll be okay—we'll be okay. It's different this time for us. We're not kids and we both are being honest. I told him I would tell him if I wanted to run, but this time, it's not *away* that I want to go.

Our lips move together, hands gripping one another as I'm desperate to do as he says—hold on.

His tongue slides into my mouth and we both give each other everything. I moan when his hand makes it way down to my ass, pulling me against him, feeling his erection against my leg.

This kiss is different than the others. We're not tentative with each other. This isn't both of us holding a piece of ourselves for safekeeping. I'm letting go of all the past right here. I'm giving him more than just words. I'm giving him me.

Derek's hands are everywhere. I feel his warmth through my shirt and I want more. I know I said we should go slow but I can't stop myself. I need more. Each touch, each second our mouths are connected, the further my desire deepens.

He's the man I've always wanted. He's starred in more dreams than I can count, and against all odds, he's here now in my arms.

I feel his hand slide to my chest, just barely brushing my breast, and I can't stop the noise that escapes me. When he does it again, I gasp and break the kiss.

"Tell me to stop and I will," he promises.

"Don't stop."

"You're so beautiful, you've always been." He kisses me again, this time squeezing my breast and rubbing where my nipple is under my bra.

His touch, is everything. It's been so long since anyone has been with me this way, and having it be Derek right now means so much more.

My fingers move down his chest, needing to explore him. He groans when my hands get to his stomach, feeling the ridges of the six-pack that hides underneath his shirt. Derek kisses me harder, moving me back until I'm wedged in between him and the post of the deck.

I feel like this is a dream. There's no way that he's kissing me. I have to be asleep or daydreaming, yet I don't want to wake up.

I close my eyes, needing to hold on longer.

His mouth moves to my neck and my fingers slide through his hair. He has really great hair. Hell, everything about him is great.

"Derek," I whisper.

His head lifts, eyes filled with yearning, and both of us are struggling for breath. "Tell me something real," he says.

I can taste him on my lips and his cologne is all around us. "I really don't want to wake up from this dream."

"You're not dreaming."

My hand touches his face. "Tell me something real then."

Derek's lips touch mine in the sweetest of kisses. It's almost as though he's woken up from the dream himself. "I really want you, Teagan. But not like this. Not here, not yet, but I want all of you, and that's the most real thing in the world. Now, let's have our lunch date."

"And you say I switch topics easily," I joke.

He releases a heavy sigh. "If we keep talking about all the things I want to happen between us, the word *slow* isn't going to apply to our relationship. So, let's eat and follow your rules"—his smile grows and mischief dances in his eyes—"for now."

chapter thirty-one

Teagan

present

"Are you still dating Dr. Hartz?" Chastity asks as we sit at my parents' table.

I've done a pretty good job the last week keeping things under wraps. We had our date, spent pretty much each night on the phone talking about all the things we've missed, and met once on the beach just because.

"Dr. Hartz?" My mother says while her fork drops, clanging against the plate. "You're dating Derek?"

"I've been on one date." I leave out the other things because, technically, it's one date.

"Right, but I heard you guys on the phone again, and Everly said she heard her father telling his parents that it's going well."

I used to love my daughter. I really did.

"Can we talk about this later?"

My mother's head turns to me. "Why can't you talk now?"

Because I don't want you to hear this, duh. "It's between Chastity and me."

"And you don't want me to hear this."

That was freaky. I wonder if she can hear all my thoughts. Maybe that's why she hates me so much. She knows I've killed her a hundred ways...with my mind.

"No, Mom, that's not it—completely. I think my daughter"—I say with a pointed stare—"and I need to have this conversation in private."

"Would you like your father and me to step out?"

"Huh?" my father asks, oblivious to the conversation.

I have always envied that about him. He can tune my mother and me out like no one else. We'd have full-blown arguments and he wouldn't move a muscle. He'd sit in his chair, ignoring us both.

"Just eat, Dad."

"Okay."

Chastity giggles once and then looks back to me. "All I wanted to know was if you guys were dating still."

"What does it matter?"

"You're my mother...I'm curious."

She's baiting us both and I know that as soon as my mother is on the hook, I'll be reeled right in. Damn kid knows all my weaknesses.

"You know, I'm not sure what it is right now since we're just enjoying being friends again." And making out a lot. "So, once I have something to report, you will all be the first to know."

Chastity gives me a sarcastic smile. "Great."

Then something she said before hits me. "Wait. You and Everly talk?"

"Well, it would be hard to do the social media project if we didn't."

Yes, but they're talking about more than the project. "I

didn't know that Dr. Hartz and I were part of your presentation."

She crosses her arms and leans back. "It's kind of hard not to talk about the fact that our parents are dating."

I raise my brow and then take a bite of my cake.

"Well," Mom draws the attention back to her. "I'll say that if you *are* dating, which it sounds like you are, it's encouraging that you're not going to die alone in that store. Besides, he's a doctor and was always a good man."

"I'm glad you approve, Mom."

"I wouldn't go that far…"

Yes, why would we ever want to actually go that far? Approval is aberrant to her. "My point is, we're going slow and taking our time."

Chastity snorts. "That's not what Everly said."

"What does that mean?"

As much as I'd like to avoid this discussion right now, it's clear Chastity is intent on keeping it going.

She slams her hand down on the table. "It means that I went from being made fun of for the way I looked, dressed, that my father didn't want me and my mother was supposedly a whore, to now being the girl whose mom is going after a man who just lost his wife!" The anger in her eyes roots me to my chair. "I hate this town! I've always hated it, but you always made it better. Now, you're making it worse!"

I sit here, unsure of what just happened.

"What are they saying?"

"Oh, nothing other than my slut mother has to go after a man whose wife died not even six months ago. That you couldn't help yourself because no one in this town who knows you would want to date you so you went after a guy who hasn't seen you in years."

"Now that's just absurd!" My mother huffs. "These girls are being ridiculous. No one says that."

"No, Mom, that's what many people in this town say." I turn to Chastity. "I'm sorry that you feel this way, but I'm not going to live my life based on what other people say."

"Not even if you're ruining my life?"

I fight back the urge to roll my eyes because she's thirteen and everything is the end of the world at that age. "I'm living my life, Chas, not ruining yours."

"Yes you are!" Chastity gets to her feet and rushes out of the room.

My mother touches my hand. "She'll calm down, Teagan."

My heart breaks because I'm hurting the one person who matters most. The thing that I was most afraid of is coming to fruition. My relationship with Derek is ruining the closeness I have with Chastity, and that can't ever happen.

I won't allow any man—or any person, for that matter—to be the source of her pain. And it's clear that is exactly what's happening.

"I have to end this." I choke on the words as my chest tightens.

"End it? Because your daughter doesn't want you to date someone?"

I look up and nod. "She's my world, Mom. She needs to know I have her back even when no one else does. I'm not going to be the cause of her anguish."

I never want to hurt her.

"You're going to walk away from a man that you've had feelings for because his daughter is making things difficult for Chastity? Of course she is. She's angry, hurting, and mourning the loss of her mother. That doesn't mean she has the right to dictate how her father lives his life. I know you think I don't love you." She shakes her head a bit. "I know I'm not the mother you wish I could be. There are many mistakes I've made, but neither of those kids know what it's like to raise a child. If you make this choice, no matter what the reason, what does it accomplish?"

I don't know, but I can't let her think I don't care. "I need to talk to her."

My mom nods with her lips in a thin line. "Talk to Derek too. I would bet he's not willing to walk away from you over two kids in middle school."

Maybe not, but that doesn't mean it's not the right choice.

I rush out the door and find Chastity sitting on the step. "Hey."

"Hey," she says with zero enthusiasm.

"Why didn't you tell me?"

She and I sat on this very step many times when she was an infant. It was my way out of that house where I felt like I was suffocating. Now, it seems she's found the same purpose for it.

"I didn't think it bothered me until today."

"That she was making fun of you?"

Chastity shrugs. "I like Dr. Hartz and you dating him, but *God* she makes it hard for me. It's bad enough that I have to be around Everly at school and whenever she is at the clinic, but having her talk about you like that...I hate it."

"I'm sorry. I really am. I didn't know."

"She's such a horrible person. She's always nasty and talking about people. I think she finds joy in other people being miserable. And then, she's just as big of a bitch to her 'friends,'" she says, making the air quotes with her fingers. "I don't get it. It makes me happy that I don't have all those stupid people around me. It makes no sense."

I nod, knowing all too well how she feels. The thing is, I don't think she really cares about Everly and her friends. It's more like Everly and integrating her into our lives.

"It doesn't, but that isn't what you're upset about, is it?"

"Mom." Chasity shifts so we're eye to eye. "If you marry him, I would have to live with her."

"Back up, Chas."

"No, I'm serious. You think I'm dumb and that I don't know, but I've heard you talk about him before. You cried once to Aunt Nina about a guy named Derek."

So much for thinking I was quiet about that. "He was my best friend when I was in high school." Maybe telling her will help her understand. "We were the most unlikely friends. He was sort of nerdy but not the smart kind and I was…"

"Yes, we know, you were the queen."

I laugh because she loves to make fun of it. "I was."

"Lame."

"It is."

"So, you became friends and he…"

"We were just that. He was always there for me and when I got pregnant with you, he was who got me through it all." Not the tape or blackmail because that came after she was born. But through the whole pregnancy, Derek was there. He came to visit me each weekend, helped take care of me when I was trying to keep afloat, and then held me as I cried when Keith treated me so poorly.

She chews on her bottom lip, which is her tell that she's mulling it over. "Why have I never heard of him then?"

"Because, he got married to Everly's mom and she apparently didn't like me."

Chastity gasps in mock horror. "Who knew? One person didn't love you!"

I slap her arm. "Watch it."

"I'm kidding."

"I've waited a very long time to find someone who held a candle to Derek."

"Even after he left you?" she asks. "You still thought he was great after he cut you out of his life?"

This is the part that's hard to explain. Yes, Derek chose someone else over me, but then isn't that the way it should've been? His wife asked him to make a choice for their family, which he did.

I don't know that my life would be any better had he been in it. But there's not a doubt in my mind that he would've been a huge part of Chastity's life and given her something I can't…a man to look up to.

"Derek made his choice and I've made choices too. I've longed for someone to make me feel the way he does. With him, I'm not the homecoming queen, the naive young girl who got pregnant, the woman who works at her parents' antique store, or the loser. I'm Teagan. I see myself in his eyes, and I always have."

"I don't understand why, of all the people in the world, it has to be her father. Can't you find anyone else who will see how awesome you are?"

I smile at her compliment. Then the words come out so easily it has to be true. "It will only ever be him."

Chasity looks away, shaking her head. "I won't ask you what I planned to."

"You wanted me to end things?"

She nods.

"I'm glad you won't because I don't ever want to disappoint you. But walking away from him might have just killed me."

As much as I would like to believe for her I could, I don't know that I'd have been strong enough to do it. Derek is the man that I want. He's who I've been waiting for. We both have spent so much time apart, and if he had never returned, I would have survived just fine. Now though, I know what it's like to be in his arms, kiss him, and have him here again.

I know what comfort he brings when I'm having a bad day and I can call him. I know what silly lunch dates and text messages are. I've gotten the opportunity to experience what we were too stupid to look for before.

"Just don't ask me to be nice to her if this works out."

I smile, wrap my arm around her shoulder, and pull her close. "I wouldn't dream of it."

* * *

Tonight is going to be another real date for us. Only this time, we're staying in. Chastity is sleeping over at a friend's house and Derek is on his way here.

I'm nervous.

We won't be in public and I have no one to rush home for. I would be anxious about him seeing my home, but I saw the house of dolls and he can't say a damn thing now. I plan to use that any chance I get.

I hear the car door shut and I rush to greet him.

When I open it my heart begins to race. He looks so good when he's not even trying. He's wearing a pair of jeans that fit him in all the right places, his polo shirt is tight enough for me to see the muscles in his arms. God, he's freaking hot.

"Hi," I say with a smile.

"Well, this is nice."

"What?"

He takes a step forward, and kisses me. "You meeting me at the door."

"I like that you like me meeting you. Come in."

We head up the stairs to the tiny apartment that I both love and hate. It's small, which I hate, but I've busted my ass to make this place look the best possible. We may be poor, but we fake being rich very well.

"This place is so you, Tea. Seriously, it's exactly like I pictured it."

I look around at the cool gray-colored slate floor and the rich-looking ivory curtains that go from the ceiling to the floor to make it appear bigger. Everything in this place is secondhand, but Chas and I spent time repurposing the furniture. The kitchen table was an old barn door that I sanded down and then added legs to. It cost me ten dollars total. The chairs, dressers, end tables, are all thrift store that I painted or upholstered where I could.

I'm proud of this place.

"I'm going to take that as a good thing."

He wraps his arms around my waist. "It is."

"Good." My fingers play with the collar of his shirt. "I missed you."

"I saw you yesterday."

"Yes, but that was just to pick up Everly."

Which was very interesting to say the least. The girls had to work on their project, since it's due next week and apparently, they have to do it here. They're doing something with the power of social media and using the antique store as the subject. It makes no sense to me, but according to Chastity, people of my age group don't get it.

I guess they're taking photos of something and posting it on three sites to see which has the greater impact.

They seemed to be getting along, and I stayed out of the way as much as I could.

"I know you said she behaved, but did she really?"

It's clear Everly doesn't particularly like me, which is her choice. I can't imagine I would like anyone my father dated if my mother died.

"She was fine. I stay out of her way when I can, since I know she hates me."

He sighs and releases me. "I don't know what to do with her." Derek's back is to me, but I can hear the confliction in his voice. It's so hard sometimes with kids. When they're little, it's almost as though you can convince them you've got it all figured out. Now, not so much.

"She'll get over it—or not—but it'll be what it is."

I know Chastity wants me to be happy and will accept what our relationship will become. We have a bond and even though the idea of having Everly in her life is her equivalent of hell, she'll do it for me.

"I don't want it to be what it is, baby." My heart races at the term of endearment. It's the first time he's called me anything other than Teagan or Tea. "I want it to be better. I want her to accept you."

"She doesn't know me, Derek. She can't like me if she doesn't see that I'm not all the things she has made up in her mind."

He runs his hand down his face. "I don't know how to fix this."

I smile and walk up to him. He looks so upset by all of this and it warms my heart. I love that he cares so much and wants this to work. I know I want the same. Everly getting to know me isn't on him—it's on me. "When she comes over tomorrow, I won't hide. I'll talk to her in a way that won't seem like I'm trying. Let me fix whatever is broken between the two of us."

Derek nods and then lifts his hand to my face. "I don't know what I did in this life to deserve you. It's only been a few weeks and I can't fathom how I lived without you."

My eyes well up with tears because I feel the same. "I've missed you too."

He brings his mouth to mine, kissing me slowly. Each beat of my heart feels like it's for him. I don't know how it ever worked before. Just by being near me, he's fixed all the things that were broken.

Derek is the balm to my wounds. He's the air that fills my lungs in a way I didn't know I was missing. It's as though, everything I felt is being validated. I never really *knew* before if we were right together. But I hoped.

My fingers slide through his hair, holding his mouth to

mine, hoping that I convey all I feel within my heart to him. He has to feel all that I am, right? My body can't possibly contain all of the love I feel for him.

His mouth grows hungrier and I'm now gripping his neck. I need more. I want everything from him. My fingers drift to his shoulders and then around his back, pulling him closer.

Derek's hands move to my ass, and then hook under my thighs, lifting me up. I wrap my legs around his waist and hold on. He moves us so my back is to the wall. I can feel everything and yet not enough.

"We should stop," he says against my mouth.

But I don't want to stop.

"No," I whisper and then bring our mouths back together.

He kisses me with so much passion I could explode.

"Tea." He says my name and then his lips are on my neck. "Tell me what you want."

"You. I want you."

His eyes meet mine. "I'm yours."

Those two words seem to settle my entire world. He is mine and I want to be his. I want to touch him, taste him, love him the way I've always hoped. Our lives have been wasted time and I'm done living that way.

"Will you let me down?" I ask tenderly.

I see the confusion in his eyes, but he doesn't hesitate to release me. When he does, I take his hand in mine and start to walk toward the bedroom.

"Teagan." I appreciate his apprehension, but there's none from me.

I turn to him, letting him see the truth in my eyes. "I've wanted this for so long. I've spent my life wondering, and

I don't have to wonder, Derek. We don't have to wonder. I've loved you in some form or another what feels like my whole life and now, I want you to make love to me."

His chest rises and falls faster and his other hand touches my cheek. "I love you more than I thought I did before."

"Then show me."

chapter thirty-two

Teagan

present

My bravado is impressive considering the nerves that are swirling inside of me. I make it to my bedroom and it feels like I could cry. Not because I'm scared, but because I'm in a bit of disbelief. Derek and I are going to have sex. Real sex. Not in-my-mind sex.

He stands with me. His eyes feel like they're seeing through to my thoughts. "Tell me something—"

I put my hand to his mouth. "Don't say it, please."

"Why?"

"Because tonight, what we're going to do is real. I don't have to tell you because I want us to stop talking." I press my hand to his heart. "I want us to stop thinking. I think it's time to start feeling."

"Then tell me what you feel." His voice is low and husky.

The two of us are in uncharted water, the shoreline is ahead, but we don't know the way.

"That tonight is going to change everything."

Derek's fingers brush my cheek. "No, baby, it changed the first time my lips touched yours."

"I think it was before that."

His hands slide down my neck, then my arms, before he lifts my hand to his mouth. "I've loved you for a long time, Teagan. You've been the part of me that's been missing."

"You have no idea how much I want to believe what you say," I admit. "I do, but it scares me because I feel the same."

"Then, I'll just have to do as you said." His lips move closer to mine. "And show you."

Derek's mouth is on mine a moment later. I can do nothing but hold on to him, letting myself go and feel it all.

Each time I kiss him, I find another part of myself that was lost. I can't imagine what I'm going to feel when he's inside of me.

His hands are at the hem of my shirt and he breaks the kiss long enough to pull it over my head. I do the same to his, and try so hard not to have my mouth hanging open, but he's perfect. Every inch of him is better than I could've ever expected. His chest is wide and the muscles tense from my touch.

Derek doesn't move until our eyes meet. Then he lifts his hand, touches the strap on my bra, and pulls it down before doing the same to the other. I don't know if he's waiting for me to stop him, but I decide to show him that's not happening.

I reach behind and unhook my bra, letting it fall to the floor.

"You're so beautiful," he tells me.

I've never truly felt beautiful until now. It's silly because since I was a kid I've listened to people tell me how I was pretty or how they wished they had my hair and eyes. They were just words though. It meant nothing because I didn't believe it.

My whole life I've never felt good enough. I've struggled with things turning out the way they have, but right now, it's as though it all makes sense.

Those struggles have made me who I am. They've formed this woman, standing in front of Derek, the man I still love and wonder if this is what it's all led to.

I want to argue that I'm not beautiful, but for some reason, it feels wrong. They're not empty words and he means them. "I don't think I've ever believed that until right now."

"That you're beautiful?" I nod. "You, are the most beautiful woman I've ever known, Teagan Berkeley. Don't ever doubt that."

I don't when he looks at me.

We're two broken souls, searching for something real and have found each other.

"Kiss me," I request.

He does, taking my mind off all the heavy and allowing me to just feel again. I lose myself to him as we explore each other. His hands slide up my stomach to my breasts and he rubs my nipple between his thumb and forefinger, driving me crazy. My head falls back when his tongue touches it and then he takes me into his mouth.

My hands are in his hair, keeping him there as he drives me crazy. It feels so incredible—and right.

He comes back to my mouth, kissing me, drinking in my moans, and I move my hands to his belt.

Derek walks me back until my legs hit the bed. "Lie down, Teagan."

I scoot back, and he undoes his belt, but not his pants. Then his fingers hook in my pants, as he pulls them off. I'm completely naked before him. There's a part of me that wants to cover myself. It's been so damn long since I've done this, and I pray it really is like riding a bike because I'd like this to be perfect for us.

"I need to taste you."

He doesn't wait for a response, his mouth is against my calf, slowly moving his way up. God, this is happening. My heart is beating so fast I'm sure he can hear it. I close my eyes and focus on trying to not hyperventilate.

When his tongue swipes against my clit, I lose it. My fingers are gripping the comforter so tight I can feel my nails through the fabric. His tongue slides around and then flicks in the best way. I want him to stop or maybe never stop, I can't even think.

"Derek." I say his name, asking for something that I don't know. "Please, yes, God!"

He continues to push me harder, sucking on me and then flicking again and I'm so damn close, but he backs off right before I can reach the crest.

Then, he inserts his finger, swirling it around while sucking—hard—on my clit and I explode.

I writhe, calling his name out over and over as he keeps going, milking every ounce of pleasure from my body. I lie here, spent, but desperate for more.

He climbs up my body, kissing his way to my neck. "You're fucking perfect."

"No," I say, half laughing. "You are."

"I need to be inside of you, Tea."

My fingers touch his face. "I need that too."

He's divested himself of his pants and I reach down between us, taking his dick in my hand, pumping and relishing in how his teeth clench.

"Does this feel good?" I ask.

"Are you serious?"

"I need to know what you like." I move a little faster, keeping a steady rhythm as if he was inside of me now.

"Anything with you I have a feeling I'm going to like."

That's a good answer.

"There's a condom in the top drawer," I tell him and he moves lightning fast.

He has the wrapper opened and he's rolling it on before I can sit up.

This is the moment of truth. He lines himself up with my entrance and stares down at me. I wait for him to move, but he's completely still.

"What's wrong?" I ask with nerves building.

"Nothing is wrong, it's just...right."

My hands grip his arms and I squeeze a little. "It's because it's us."

"You and I have waited a long time for tonight. Let's not wait another moment. I'm going to show you how much I love you."

My vision fills with tears and then he enters me. The joy I feel in this instant is too much. A tear falls as we both stare at each other. My heart is so full there's no way he can't see the way I feel written on my face. I love him.

I love him and he loves me.

It's not words. It's real. It's right here in this bed and it's ours.

* * *

"Last date?" Derek asks.

"You really want to ask that as one of your five questions?" I ask as we lie here, wrapped up in the sheets. My hand is on his chest, chin resting there as I look up at him.

We haven't said much about what just happened. I feel like we're both still in a little bit of denial, but comfortable denial at least.

His fingers slide up and down my bare back and his other arm is behind his head—while in my freaking bed. This is surreal.

"I get five and you have to answer them."

"Okay, it's your waste of a question," I say with a grin. "I don't really remember. It's not like I had a lot of time to date so I just sort of stopped."

"No men?"

I smile up at him. "That's another question."

"That's a follow-up to the real one."

He's still a cheater. "Fine, we each get one follow-up. If you're asking about sex, I wasn't a nun, but it's been a really long time."

His hand stops but then a small smile creeps across his face. "Okay."

"Okay?"

"Is that your question?"

"Is that yours?"

We both chuckle a little. "I said okay because there's a part of me that likes knowing there were no other men. I don't know why, but it's almost as though we were both waiting for the other."

"I feel that way too. Okay." I sigh. "My turn. When did you realize you were really and truly in love with me?"

He starts to play with a strand of my hair and his body tenses a little. There's no more anger and disappointment that I feel toward what happened—it's curiosity driving me now.

"When you told me you were pregnant was the first indication. Then, it was really clear after I married Meghan. I looked at her, loved her in some way, but it was nothing like what I felt for you. And I felt so guilty, because Meghan and I had fought before we got engaged about my feelings for you."

"You did?"

He smiles and nods. "She knew. I think she always knew even when we didn't. Which is why when she found the confirmation in my journal it set her off. I'd never seen someone so hurt."

I try to imagine being a new wife and finding my husband's journal where he wrote about loving someone else. I would've been broken. "She loved you the way…"

"The way I loved you."

"God, that's…sad."

"I couldn't leave her. I felt this intense sense of moral responsibility to fix things. I tried. God, I fucking tried. Cutting you out was hard, but watching her grow to hate me ate at me. I worked as much as I could because she seemed happier when I wasn't around."

What a horrible way to live. "I wanted you to be happy, it makes me incredibly sad that you weren't."

"I wasn't always unhappy. There were good times before the journal appeared. And afterward, she tried to get over it. But she couldn't. And eventually she and I settled into a routine where we became a version of friends, mostly for Everly's sake, but she also loved me."

"Do you miss her?" I ask the question and instantly wish I could take it back. There's no right answer to that and I don't want him to be uncomfortable. "You don't have to answer that."

"No, I do, I promised myself when we started this that no matter what, I will tell you the truth and we'll work through it."

My finger moves making patterns on his chest as I wait.

"Yes, I do miss her. We may not have been married like most couples and our relationship was more like room-mates, but she was my wife for thirteen years. She was my friend, the mother of my child, and had she not died, we'd still be living the life we settled into." His eyes move back to mine and then he shakes his head slightly. "That said, I'm happy to be out of the relationship we had. But I wish that it wasn't her death that brought you to me."

"I wish it wasn't that either."

I never wanted Meghan to die. I didn't understand what happened with all of us, but the last thing I would've wished was for something to happen to her.

We both fall quiet, and then he clears his throat. "My question. Since we're onto the heavy stuff and I was plan-ning to ask about orgasms and positions, I figure we'll shift to trial and error with those." I giggle and roll my eyes. "Why did Keith give up all of his rights and, follow-up to that, why the hell would you let him?"

Jesus, I don't want to answer this. I wish I had built in a veto option to this game. But this is Derek. Derek won't judge me. He never has. Nina is the only person who knows. I was too mortified to tell another soul.

I sit up, pulling the sheet around me, clutching it like it might save me if this goes a different way. I don't know that anyone will want to be with someone who has a sex tape looming out there.

My stomach is in knots and I open my mouth but shut it.

"Hey," he says at my distress. "What is it? Why do you look like you're going to be sick?"

I don't want to look in his eyes, but he has been honest with me and I need to do the same. "It's bad."

"Okay. I'm not going anywhere."

He might after this.

"After Chastity was born, Keith insisted on a paternity test, which was ridiculous, considering he was the only man I'd ever been with, but he didn't believe me. By that point, I knew he was probably screwing around on me, but I didn't care or maybe I did, I don't know. Anyway, I granted the test immediately and that's when the floor dropped out and I found out what lengths he would go to in order to get his way."

"What did he do?" he asks through gritted teeth.

"It wasn't just him, Derek. I was stupid. I trusted him when we were together. I wanted him to...I don't know...fill the hole in my heart. I thought that maybe Keith could love me until you were ready to. I was in college and we were drinking and I did dumb things during that time. I let him..." My stomach heaves and I want to throw up. Instead, tears form at my mortification. I've always been ashamed of trusting him, but saying it to someone I love, makes self-hatred so much worse. "I let him tape us."

"Tape you?"

I look up, begging him to understand without having to say the words. "Yes, when we were…"

"A sex tape?"

I nod as the bile climbs up my throat.

"And he what?"

"He threatened to expose it. To leak the tape and ensure my daughter had to live in that shadow."

Derek's eyes close and he releases a heavy breath through his nose. "He threatened you?"

"He gave me a choice. I either let him sign his rights away or he would ensure that my life was the one that was altered."

A tear falls down my face. I'm so ashamed. I knew better and yet I didn't say anything when he said he wanted to do it. Men often come out of sex tapes as the hero in some way—it's women who bear the fallout. I was young and if I didn't live in this town where everyone's memories fade but scandal never does, I could've told him to fuck off. However, I do live here, and in order to make sure Chastity never had to deal with it, I let him off the hook.

I protected her, myself, my family, and any future I might've had. Not only would Keith never love our daughter, but he would also have made it so the town she was surrounded by whispered more than they do now.

In the distance, I hear my phone ring, but I can't move to answer. I wait for Derek to respond, because I'm dying inside.

"Who else knows?" he asks.

I see it now, I'm going to lose Derek too because who wants to be with *that* girl? He has a daughter to think about too. How fitting this is. I always knew this tape would be the end of me, and now I'm going to watch it play out.

"Only Nina."

"And Keith?"

"Yes, and I don't know who he told. But I don't think he's told anyone, it's been thirteen years and I've never done anything to provoke him."

He pinches the bridge of his nose.

All the happiness I had with him fades away. My walls start to come back up, needing to protect myself so that I don't break.

"I'm…"

The house phone rings and the fear I had shifts. No one but Chastity and my mother have this number. It's our phone for emergencies. "I have to get that." I leap out of the bed and reach for the phone. "Chas?"

"No, it's your mother."

I sigh and wish I had checked the stupid number.

"Is everything okay?"

"You need to come to the house, someone is here."

I look to Derek, who is staring at me with a look I can't decipher whether it's confusion or anger. I turn back to the wall, not wanting to deal with any of this.

"Who is it?"

She clears her throat. "Keith."

chapter thirty-three

Teagan

present

"You don't have to go," I tell Derek for the fifth time.

He's been silent on the drive since I told him Keith was at my mother's house. I have no idea what to think or why the hell he's there. Part of our agreement was that he gave me all copies of the tape and I would never contact him and he would leave me alone as well. I wanted to ensure he was gone and I would never have to worry about this exact scenario.

"So you've said."

He's being cold and it hurts. Not to mention I'm a fucking mess. For all I know Keith is going to try to take Chastity or he released the fucking tape. I don't know anything and I feel like I'm ready to explode.

Between telling Derek and this…I'm at the edge. I don't need his attitude.

"You don't have to do this. I've done just fine by myself."

He shakes his head. "I'm going."

Great. I really could use someone who is pissed off to
deal with Keith for the first time in thirteen years—not.

I release a heavy sigh. "Look, I understand you're upset
with me, but it took everything inside of me to tell you
about the stupid tape. I'm sorry that you're so disgusted
with me that you can't look at me, but if this is how it's
going to be, I would've rather come alone."

He doesn't say anything, he jerks the car into the park-
ing lot of Mrs. McCutchrey's store. "You think I'm angry
with you?"

"You haven't said a word the entire time. I'm clearly
upset about reliving my past and now I have to actually
see him. You're being cold and distant, which is everything you're not. What the hell am I supposed to think?"

"That I'm on the verge of fucking killing him! That's
what you should think. You should know that the idea of
that son of a bitch threatening you would lead me to de-
bate homicide and whether I could endure conjugal visits
instead of having you every day and whether Everly could
survive it. That's what you should think. You should
know that I've always loved you and wanted to protect
you and right now"—his voice shakes—"I hate myself for
failing you when you needed me."

The hurt I was feeling dissipates. He isn't angry at me,
he's angry at Keith. There's no disgust, just rage at the person who used a situation to get what he wanted. I don't
know that I could love this man any more than I do right
now.

"Well, I suggest against those options." I say it as a joke,
but there's nothing in his eyes that says he sees anything
funny about this.

"He threatened you, Teagan! He took away all your

power because he didn't want to part with what? His precious money?"

"I guess."

"He's a coward."

"Yes. He is."

He takes my hands in his. "I'm sorry. I'm sorry I wasn't here. I'm sorry I didn't tell you years ago how I felt and then maybe you wouldn't have dealt with him the way you did. I would've protected you or I don't know…been there! Keith should be castrated for what he did. He gave up his kid and for what? Freedom? And then he comes after you because he's that much of an asshole? I swear to God, Teagan, I'm going to beat the fuck out of him. And then, I want to punch myself! I'm fucking sorry that I acted like a dick and you thought it was you. It's not you, baby."

It's the first time I've felt like what I did wasn't so horrible.

"You didn't do anything," I try to reassure him.

"No. And that's the problem."

I've spent so much time hating myself for the things I didn't do when it came to Derek and it seems he's done the same.

"If we're going to work…" I say tenderly.

"We are going to work. There is no *if* in this."

I smile. "Okay, well, in order to make this work, we have to start really forgiving ourselves for the past. We did what we did, and it sucks that we didn't have time together, but we have the future. Keith, Meghan, all the things we should've done, have to not be things you and I dwell on."

He nods, releases my hand, and then turns to look out

the window. "Do you have any idea why he could be here now?"

The nerves are back and my stomach is in knots. "I don't and that's what worries me."

"Are his parents here?"

"They fly south for the winter."

He shakes his head.

"I don't get it."

Keith hasn't so much as stepped foot in this town since Chastity was born. His parents go see him. If he did visit, I never heard of it and that would be some pretty stealthy movement. Not to mention, he's a hero here, so everyone would've been talking about the perfect football star returning.

"I don't either, but there's only one way to find out."

He wraps his fingers around mine and we head to the house.

We don't say anything, but there's no more anger swirling around us. We're quiet, almost as though we're both preparing for all the possibilities. I have no idea what Keith could want. All I know is he has a lot of money and that means he has power. For all I know he woke up today and decided that he wants Chastity.

He could fight me.

He could use the tape to get what he wants. Yes, he signed his rights away, but I have no idea if he can get them back. All of these things going through my mind make me want to scream.

When we get to the door, I feel sick. Derek and I stare at the knocker and I finally bring words to my worst fear. "If he tries to take her…"

"He can't."

"We don't know that."

The only thing keeping me from losing it is the constant pressure from his hand. He hasn't let go and I don't know how I'd do this if he weren't with me.

"He's too selfish, Teagan, and if for some reason he does try to take Chastity, no one will allow it."

God, I hope so. Chastity is my life. She's everything good in this world and if he were to try to take her from me, I would die.

"Okay. Let's go get this over with."

My body is trembling as I turn the handle. He's here. It's been so long. I don't think I can do this.

"I can't." I stop and look up at Derek. I'm weak and stupid, but more than that, I'm scared. I don't want to face him. My parents don't know anything about the tape and I will never recover from seeing the shame they'll show.

He shakes his head and cups my face. "You are stronger than any person I've ever known. He's the one who should be afraid."

"They don't know, Derek."

"Who?"

"My parents. They don't know anything about the details of the custody agreement. They think I forced Keith to give up rights because I wanted her to myself. My mother has constantly reminded me how different my life could've been if I weren't so headstrong. They have no idea of the real reason."

Derek rests his forehead against mine. "I keep trying to forgive myself for letting you do this alone and then I find out something else. This is another example of how strong you are, Tea. You can do this and we'll make sure we shield them from that coming out as much as we can, okay?"

God, I hope so. "Okay."

He opens the door, and we walk through.

So many times I've envisioned what would happen when I saw Keith again. Would I slap him? Cry? Knee him in the balls? In all my visions, I never thought I would simply stand here, unable to speak as he sat on the couch in my parents' house. The same couch that we used to fool around on.

"Teagan." Keith gets to his feet and walks over. "I...hi." He looks over to Derek and laughs through his nose. "Hartz."

"Keith," Derek says through gritted teeth.

These are the times when I wish karma came around to kick people in the face. I've seen Keith on television after a game, but not in a few years. We've avoided football Sunday in our house, opting for DIY Network or something less—Keith. Time has been kind to him. He's tall, broad shoulders, and he isn't even balding.

Why are the fates so unkind? Couldn't he at least have a crooked nose or something?

He grins at me as though he can read my mind. "I didn't know you two were still close, but I'm not surprised, you and Teagan always had a special bond," he says, as though it's a compliment, but it's not. Keith hated Derek. He was always finding some way to cut him down to me and anyone else. As much as Meghan hated me, I assume Keith felt the same toward Derek.

"Yes, we did." He wraps his arm around me, holding my hip. "It's good to see you, Keith. What brings you around here?"

My father sits in the room, watching this transpire, and I see the distrust in his eyes. My father is a stoic man, but when it comes to Chastity, he's not able to hold back. He is the one person in this town who despises Keith. To Daddy, he's the worst kind of man. To leave me and Chastity is abhorrent to him, not just because he's my father, but also because he is a father.

"Yes, Keith, what brings you here after all this time?" Daddy asks from the chair.

Mom comes in the room and freezes. The room is cold with all the testosterone and hatred flowing in the air. She looks to me and I'm still, trying to keep a hold on my emotions. I still have yet to find my voice. What is it about this man that makes me like this?

She clears her throat. "Yes, Keith, you haven't been here in so long, I'm curious what made you come now?"

My mother's eyes soften when they meet mine and I could hug her.

Keith faces my father. "My father passed away two days ago in Florida. I had to come to the house ahead of my mother, and I thought if I was back in town it would be best to see Teagan."

I step out of Derek's hold and find the courage I know I have to say something. "I'm sorry to hear about your father, but there's no need to see me. I'm just fine."

He turns back toward me. "It's been a long time."

"Yes, I'm aware of exactly how long." I turn to my dad, wanting to get him and my mother out of the room. "Daddy…"

Now that I've spoken, I feel like the words won't be an issue. I'm not the same girl I once was and Keith doesn't belong here.

Dad gets to his feet and walks over to my mother. "Meredith, let's give them some time to talk."

I nod once to my mother, hoping she knows I'm okay.

Once they're out of the room I stand with my arms over my chest. "Why are you here?"

"I told you."

"Yeah, that's fine, but according to you, I was to consider you dead. You look alive and in my parents' living room, so what do you want?"

Keith shakes his head with a smirk. "I don't want anything. I didn't want to see you on the street. I figured you would rather this."

"I would rather not see you ever again, but thank you for considering me for the first time ever."

He takes a step closer and I feel Derek move at the same time. "So are the two of you together and raising our daughter like a happy little family?"

"You don't have a daughter," I remind him.

His eyes flash to mine. "You know she messages me on Instagram?"

My stomach drops. "What?"

"I get messages from her or someone claiming they're her and in the last few weeks, they've been more frequent."

The words I thought I had are gone. Chastity is messaging him? Why? She has never had any interest in him. She's always said she didn't want to know someone who never cared for her.

"I'm going to assume by the look on your face you didn't know. Don't worry, I don't respond."

I push the air from my chest and shake my head. "Like that's better? She is reaching out and you ignore her? How cruel can you be?"

"I'm doing what we agreed on and I don't actually know it's her."

Bullshit. He knows. He had to in some way or he wouldn't have brought it up.

"No, you're here, that's not what we agreed on. You must want something because you always want something." Derek's hand rests on my shoulder as my anger grows.

"I'm here for my father's funeral, not for any other reason. I figured you might want to be aware, and that regarding our kid, maybe you could…"

"What? Keep her away?"

"Yes, actually," he says with a hint of amusement.

He's disgusting. More so than I ever thought. "How can you live with yourself? You had a daughter. One that apparently wants to know you and you come here to make sure that what? I protect you from her?"

I ball my fist and wonder if he would press charges if I punch him. Stupid asshole. He didn't want her and I understand that, but he will never understand what his rejection probably does to her. To reach out to a man who knows you exist and be shunned must break her. Then, she goes to school and is ostracized even more.

My heart is breaking for her. All I want to do is go get her, wrap my arms around my little girl, and love her enough for all of eternity.

"I'm not her father, and I don't need any issues with the press either, Teagan. I'm doing my best to clean up my image and some illegitimate child from college would ruin that. I've worked hard to keep this all behind me."

I gasp.

What a fucking asshole.

"Keith, maybe it's best you leave," Derek suggests.

My throat is tight but I manage to speak through gritted teeth. "Yes, maybe you should go back to hell too, I'm sure the demons miss their leader." I stand tall, refusing to cower to him.

Keith grips the bridge of his nose. "You are the same as you always were."

I laugh. "No, I'm much worse. I'm stronger and no longer think you are anything more than a piece of shit and a coward. I'll keep Chastity from you, that's her name in case you forgot. My beautiful, smart, funny girl that despite half of her parentage has turned out to be the best thing in the world."

"Good. I appreciate it."

"Oh," I step closer. "I'm not doing this for you, I'm doing it for her because I never want to give you the opportunity to hurt her. Now, get the fuck out of here."

chapter thirty-four

Derek

present

Teagan has been quiet since seeing Keith last night. I stayed at her house with her, mostly because I didn't want to leave. Our first night together should've gone differently. I would've held Teagan for hours, told her how I felt, shown her that my heart was hers.

Instead, her fucking ex that I thought would never be an issue appeared.

"You don't have to babysit me," she says as she stirs her coffee, which she's been staring at for five minutes.

"I didn't realize I was."

"I'm saying that I'm fine. Last night was…weird, but I'm okay."

I don't believe her, but sure. "I'm here because Keith wasn't the only thing that happened last night."

She stops stirring and looks up. "No, it wasn't." Her voice is soft. "It was…everything."

I reach my hand out to her and she does the same.

Sex with Teagan was everything. It was fucking incredible and worth the wait. I want to tell her how I feel and the things I hope she'll come around to. I don't want to scare her off. I think she's had enough in the last twenty-four hours and Teagan overanalyzes everything. I can't imagine what her head is doing right now.

"The good thing is that Keith will be out of this town in a few days and then I can breathe again."

"What about the fact that Chastity's reaching out to him?"

She sighs. "Yeah, that I don't know what to do about. If I tell her that I know, she'll be upset and think I snooped on her. On the other hand, she and I...we talk about everything. I *thought* we didn't keep secrets."

Their relationship is unlike anything I've ever seen. They're friends to some extent more than mother/daughter. Teagan talks to Chastity about us and I'm trying to get Everly to just talk at all.

"What are you going to tell her about him being here?"

Teagan shrugs while her head falls back. "That he's here and she should avoid him. I feel like as many times as I imagined how this would go, this went way off course. What if she goes to see him? What if she completely ignores my wishes and then he treats her like shit?"

I'm completely out of my element right now. I don't know what to tell her because I can't comprehend what she may feel like. "Chastity trusts you."

"I don't know. I really don't. She's messaging him for fuck's sake! Why? The man has never once tried to be a part of her life."

"Maybe because it can't be easy knowing he's out there and not talking to her?"

I'm just winging it here. I know that it would bug me.

"She and I have the relationship we do because of his absence. We've been friends to some extent, relying on each other, and I swear to God, Derek, if him being here takes that away from us…"

I see the worry in her eyes. It brings me to my knees because I would give anything to take it from her. "I really fucking hate him for this. I hate that you're worried and he's anywhere near you and Chastity."

"Yeah, me too."

"What time is Chastity due home?" I'm not sure what the rules are of me being around when she gets here.

"She knows you were sleeping over." Teagan smiles.

"So she knows you and I…"

"She knows that you're the first man to ever be here overnight, so, yeah, I'm sure she's assuming we had sex."

I groan. "I have to work with her today."

"Were you planning to talk to her about what we do?"

"What the…?"

Teagan grins. "I'm kidding. It'll be fine, she'll be home soon, you can have that awkward, *I just slept with your mother* moment and then you two can go back to your weird animal stories."

I roll my eyes. "They're not weird."

"Yeah, the fact that you two talk about changes in poop of the stupid cat, who I still hate, is weird."

For the first time since her mother's call interrupted us, I see my Teagan. The girl who smiles, makes fun of me, who can radiate the world by being around because she's who she is. Her laugh is infectious and I hate that he stole any of that from her.

"It's important when it comes to the health of an animal."

She shudders. "It's strange."

I lean over the table. "I think you like strange."

Her smile grows as she inches closer to me. "Do you?"

"I do."

"And what if it's not strange I like?"

"Hmm…" Our lips are a breath apart. "What do you like?"

She closes the distance. "You."

"Good answer because I like you."

I make the final push and press my lips to hers. I've wanted to kiss her since we got here last night. But minutes after we got into bed she was asleep on my chest, her hair over my arm, looking so peaceful as I held her. I did kiss her forehead, but that was because I couldn't stop myself. I want her like that every night. I want to wake up with her next to me. I want to come home from work and see her in that house, making dinner or painting. Any way that I can have her, I will take.

"Gross." Chastity's voice cuts through and I quickly move back in my seat. "Can you guys not make out when I'm home."

Teagan shrugs. "When you pay the rent, you can determine the rules."

"No, Mom, I work with him and…gross."

"I happen to think kissing is a very natural thing. Derek, kiss me."

"Hi, Chastity," I say, hoping to stop their conversation and get out of this.

"Hi, Dr. Hartz."

"Derek, please call me Derek," I tell her again.

She's pretty much refused to, and I don't know why.

"Fine, Derek. Good morning."

"Good morning." I smile. I can't remember the last time

that Everly said that to me. Maybe if the two of them could get along, she could convince my daughter I don't suck.

Teagan gets up, grabbing the plate of eggs and bacon she didn't eat, and I grab it. "I'll eat that."

She laughs. "You're still the same, always hungry and willing to eat anything."

"And you still eat like a bird."

Chastity sits at the table. "See, Mom, we should get a bird."

I grin. "You should."

"Why? So the stupid cat can eat it or worse, I'd end up with a pregnant bird."

"I bet you're more of a dog person," I say conspiratorially.

"Oh! Yes, a dog." Chastity beams.

Teagan turns and glares at me. "I know what you're doing and I'm not getting an animal. I live in this tiny-ass apartment where I can barely fit the human crap, no way are we getting a dog."

"Don't let her fool you, Dr. Har—errr-Derek, she has a million excuses and none of them involve space."

"I love animals, thank you very much," Teagan defends. "Outside."

"It's fine, Chastity and I will make you an animal lover," I inform her.

Chastity lifts her hand in a fist bump. I, of course, return the bump and Teagan is fighting a smile while trying to appear pissed.

"You." She points at me. "Out. My daughter and I need to talk about alliances and whatnot."

"Sounds good." I walk over to her, not sure if I kiss her or do we hug?

So, I wait…praying she takes mercy on me and leads. Teagan looks at me with a grin and then finally she wraps her arms around me and kisses my cheek. "I'll call you later."

"Still gross," Chastity says.

I walk over to her and give her the fist bump sign. "See you later to help with the horses?"

She lifts her fist, tapping mine, and nods. "Definitely."

As I walk out of the apartment I can't help but smile. Moving back to Chincoteague has been the best thing to happen in a long time.

* * *

My phone rings from a number I don't know. "Hello?"

"Hi, Dr. Derek, it's Chastity. Listen, I'm not going to be able to make it today. I have to work on my project before it's due. So, Everly and I are swamped and are going to be a while."

I dropped Everly off at Teagan's earlier today and I guess they got tied up. "Okay, I totally understand, school comes first."

"Thanks."

I hang up and text Teagan.

Me: Things okay over at your house?

Teagan: Girls have been doing their social media thing, no screaming so I take that as a good sign. They said they need to work on it and then take other photos for this account thing.

I knew that's what they were doing. This was an excuse to talk to her today.

Me: I want to see you.

This is really the point. It's been twenty-four hours and I fucking miss her. My entire body yearns for her.

Teagan: You just saw me when you dropped off Everly.

Me: Not the same. I couldn't even kiss you, touch you, be near you other than the few seconds we had.

Everly was not having it. She stood at Teagan's door, waiting until I left to go inside. It's hard because Chastity isn't the issue, it's my kid. She's still upset about her mother and then she's got these delusions about Teagan. I worry how she'd react if I did get Teagan to agree to move into that house with us.

It won't go over well, but I'm also not willing to wait until Everly is ready, considering I don't think she ever will be.

Teagan: I miss you too. I'm going to drive Everly home and maybe you can sneak out for a kiss?

Me: Maybe we can go to that old make-out spot and I can get frisky?

Teagan: I'm not sure because last I remember, you didn't do the make-out spot.

I smile. All the kids went there and I never did. If I wanted to make out with a girl, it wasn't going to be sur-rounded by ten other kids. But if that's the only way I could've kissed Teagan, I would've been there with bells on.

Me: Maybe I didn't have the right girl.

Teagan: And you do now?

Me: Damn right I do.

Teagan: I might just let you touch my boob for that one.

Teagan makes me feel like a teenage boy. I'm standing here, smiling as I look at the phone like I'm the luckiest bastard alive, and I am.

I put it down and head into the clinic. My father is putzing around, opening cabinets and looking in the wrong places.

"You okay, Dad?"

"Huh? Who's there?"

Shit. He's out of it. His eyes are glazed over and his hands are shaking. "It's me—Derek. I asked if you're okay?"

"Yeah, I can't find my thing."

"What thing?"

"The thing that I use for the cats when they have their babies."

My father has had two pretty bad episodes in the last year. Once, my mother found him down by the beach where he had no recollection of the night. It was like he was in a trance. Then, two months ago, he woke up frantic. He couldn't remember who my mother was and thought she was an intruder.

I'd never heard my mother so distraught. That's when I knew I had to come home. My father can't be working if he can't remember who he is.

"I'll help you look, Pop."

He nods. "Did you know there's a bunch of horses in the stalls?"

"We're helping the rescue for a bit."

"Oh." I hate hearing the disappointment in his voice. He's been a great father my entire life. I wanted to be like him, which I guess I've done my best to become. I'd like to think I'm honorable, caring, and I definitely share the same passion for animals, but he's more than that. When I was young, he always made time for me. He was at my baseball games, even though he didn't care for sports. I never had to wonder if he was going to show up for anything that mattered.

I've tried to be that kind of father for Everly, but I'm sure I've fallen short. Too many times I had an emergency that I had to go to as a young veterinarian. I was building a practice and sometimes that meant I had to sacrifice.

I regret that.

"You know, Pop?" I draw his attention as we keep looking for a thing which I have no idea which thing it is. "I could really use your advice."

"Yeah? What about?"

"I like this girl," I confess.

"You and Teagan, huh?"

I stop moving and watch him.

"What? You and that girl have been in love since you were kids, even if you were both too blind to see it."

"You think so?"

He smiles a little. "I never understood why you married Meghan anyway. She wasn't the girl for you, son."

I have no idea if he's fully back with me or he's still confused. "Do you think Teagan is?"

"Only you can answer that."

"Evasive as ever, Pop."

"A man has to make his own choices."

I've made plenty that I wish I'd chosen differently.

"You're a smart man, anyone tell you that?"

My father walks closer, and touches my shoulder. "I married a smart woman."

And there he is, the man who loves my mother more than anything. "Mom is pretty special."

His head shakes as he looks down. "I forget sometimes." His voice is full of shame. "I don't remember things, important things, and I don't want to forget her."

A part of my heart breaks. No one in this world deserves this, but least of all him. He's been the pillar of strength and someone to admire. My mother and father have loved each other more than anything.

I grip his hand, waiting for his eyes to meet mine. "She knows it's not you. Mom loves you and remembers enough for the both of you."

A tear forms in his green eyes, but he wipes it away. "Marry that girl, Derek. Marry the girl who you'd cry over if you forgot her. Marry the girl who even when your brain can't remember, your heart does."

"That's my plan, Pop. I just have to get her on board."

He pats my shoulder and leaves the room.

I look at my messages and there's one from a client who is having issues with her horse. I grab my bag and head out the door, thankful to have something to do other than think.

On the ride over, I drive down Main Street, and see a girl who looks an awful lot like Chastity carrying a book-bag. I pull over, roll the window down, and call out her name. "Chastity?"

She can't hide the shock in her eyes quick enough. "Oh, hi, Dr. Derek."

"Do you need a ride?"

She shakes her head quickly. "No, no, no, I'm just walking."

I'm not buying it. "Where? I thought you were work-ing on the project with Everly?"

"We were. We finished a few minutes ago so I'm going...to the...to the McCutchreys' store. I need to get something."

She really needs to work on her storytelling if she's go-ing to lie. "That's where I'm heading, hop in."

"No, really." She looks around. "It's totally fine."

"Come on, your mother would never forgive me if I let you walk in the cold."

"It's not cold."

I grin. "And you're not telling the truth."

She sighs and her head falls back. She looks so much like her mother right now. "Fine, but you can't tell my mom if I tell you."

I'm thinking that's not a great bargain to make with Chastity, but the last thing I want is for her to end up in trouble. "I can't promise, but if it's not illegal, I won't."

"I'm going to see my father."

That was not the words I was expecting. "Your father?"

"Yes, he's here in town, and I know Mom was adamant

I stay away from him and I know she's right, but I have to see him. I *need* to see him. He's here and I can't…I can't not…I have to…"

I can't imagine the turmoil she's feeling. "Get in," I say as I open the passenger door.

"Please, don't tell her. She left to drive Everly home and I don't know, I just walked out thinking I would get back before her. You can't tell her, Derek. She will never forgive me or understand."

"Forgive you?"

Chastity tucks her hair behind her ear. "I sent him a few messages," she admits. "She'll think I contacted him because she's not a good enough mother, but that's not it. It's because he's famous and people talk about how great he is and I want to know why. How can he be here and not even want to see me? How can he think I'm not good enough?"

"You are better than him, that's how. He's an idiot and it's his loss."

"It doesn't matter. I was going to see him and then come home without anyone knowing."

This girl is brave beyond her years. I hate keeping this secret from Teagan, but at the same time, I feel like Chastity needs someone. I can't imagine doing this alone, and if it were my daughter, I would want her to not be alone. "You were going to your grandfather's funeral to see him?"

Her eyes widen. "You know he's here?"

"Yes, I went with your mother when he showed up in town."

She shakes her head. "I need to see him. I won't make a scene or anything, I just want to…meet him…just once.

I want to say that I looked him in the eyes. Do you understand?"

I release a heavy sigh. "I don't, but then again I don't know what it's like to not have a father. How did you think you'd pull it off?"

She pulls her backpack around. "I was going to change into my black dress and just go. I figured I could blend in?"

"Chastity, everyone in this town knows who you are."

"He doesn't."

"No," I say with resignation. "I guess he doesn't."

I'm not sure what to do, but I can't let this girl who was brave enough to go to a funeral to get a glimpse of her father go alone. I also don't want to betray Teagan, but Chastity's going to do it whether I say to or not.

"You can't go alone."

"I can't tell anyone."

"I was heading to look at a horse, but I have about twenty minutes. Why don't you let your mom know you're with me, we'll stop by the funeral for a *minute*, and then you can help me, deal?"

Her eyes light up and her smile is blinding. "Oh my God, are you serious?"

"Yes, but we are telling your mother after, understand?"

She nods. "Okay, that's totally fine."

I have a feeling it's not, but this is what I think is the right move.

We drive the few blocks to the funeral home and head inside. I can practically feel the nervous energy rolling off of her. She rushes into the bathroom to change, and then stands off to the side of the room, not making eye contact with anyone. It's the very end of the viewing, which is a good thing because it means we have fewer people who will be here and see us.

"Ready?" I ask as we're at the entrance to the room.

"Yes."

I'm glad one of us is.

She grabs my arm, stopping in her tracks as we get about halfway into the room. There stands Keith, looking at the casket, with his head bowed.

"That's him," she whispers.

"Yes. Are you sure you're okay?"

She looks up at me with tears in her eyes. "I don't know, it's so strange."

No one has noticed us and this would be the perfect time to exit. "Let's head back now."

Chastity nods.

When we start to make our way out the door, I hear Keith's voice. "Derek?"

Shit.

I turn to Chastity. "Just play along."

"Keith, I'm here to pay my respects. I'm very sorry for your loss."

His lips are in a flat line and it's clear he doesn't want me here any more than I want to be here. "Thanks. Is this your kid?"

No, she's yours.

"Yes, this is my daughter, Everly."

Chastity looks up at her father and extends her hand. "Hi."

"Hey."

My head is spinning at the fact that he's standing here, and he doesn't even know it's his daughter.

"You play football?" Chastity asks.

"I do, are you a fan?"

She shakes her head. "Not really."

His eyes narrow and I clear my throat. Last thing I need is him to suddenly grow a brain and figure it out. "Well, we have to get to a client..." I say.

"Right. Thanks for stopping by and sorry about the other night. You know how it is with kids, I'm just not built for it. I was trying to do the right thing but with Teagan that's pretty impossible."

No, I don't know how it is, Keith. In fact, I think you're a fucking idiot who needs to have the shit kicked out of him. You're a spineless prick for taking advantage of Teagan, and now for being a horrific excuse for a man by hurting your daughter, whether you ever wanted her or not and if I didn't have my own kid to worry about, I'd be in jail.

I can't say any of that because I'm standing here with Chastity—at a funeral. So, I nod a little, as though I think he's got a point, which I don't. "Well, I would appreciate you staying away from us while you're around."

He looks at Chastity again and then back up to me. "Won't be a problem. I have no desire to see anyone in this town."

chapter thirty-five

Teagan

present

"So," I say with my best half-awkward-half-excited voice. "Are you settling in here?"

Everly scoffs. "You may be dating my dad this week, but we are not going to be friends."

Oh, good, and I thought this might go poorly.

"You're right. You totally don't need friends."

"Nope."

"I get it."

She turns her head to look out the window.

I swear, I owe my mother one hell of an apology. "Your dad said you went out for the cheerleading squad?"

"Yup."

I'm trying here, but Lord am I failing. I'm not sure how to connect with her. Cheerleading was my for-sure in, after that I've got nothing.

Maybe I can draw out some form of emotion and then go off that. At this point I don't have anything to lose.

"Can I ask why you seem angry at me?"

Everly's eyes turn toward me. "You can't have my dad. He's still in love with my mother and he will never love you like he loved her."

I release a heavy sigh. I want Everly to at least be open to liking me. There's a long way to go before that will ever happen but this is a start in the right direction.

"You're right."

"I'm—what?"

Good. I've flustered her a bit. "You're right. He will never love me like he loved her." She opens her mouth and closes it. "Did you think that I thought he would?"

"I don't know what...I mean..."

"I'm not under any delusions that we will ever have what he had with your mom, who I know you think I didn't like, but I did. I really respected her. She was funny, pretty, smart, and I remember she could do that thing with her nose." I smile warmly.

"She thought she was a witch." Everly's voice loses a touch of her edge.

"She would wiggle it all the time when we talked to make your dad lose his train of thought."

Meghan may have hated me, but the feelings weren't mutual. I wasn't her biggest fan, but I will never allow Everly to think I hated her mother. She got the guy. I wasn't strong enough to tell him and that was on me.

"He hated it. He would yell when they were fighting and she'd wiggle it to make him stop."

"I can imagine she would." I chuckle.

Everly's hands unclench and she rests her head back. "I didn't know you knew her like that."

"I was friends with her too, which is why losing them both was so hard for me. I wish I could've at least talked to her again." I say the words and park in front of the house. "I would've liked to have met you, especially."

"Me?" she asks with narrowed eyes.

"Yeah, your mom and I were pregnant at the same time. We talked about our kids being best friends. Which is apparently the opposite of what you and Chastity are."

"Yeah, we're definitely not alike."

"No, she's actually like your dad, which is weird."

Making fun of Derek wasn't my goal, but whatever lane opens, I'm going for. She's not giving one-word answers, and for that, I'm grateful.

"Yeah, and he says you and I would've been friends in school."

"We would've," I say with a smile. "I was really cool, unlike your dad. Who I can assure you was a total dork in high school."

"My mom wasn't."

"No, she wasn't. She was really kind."

In many ways, Meghan was a lot like me. We were both popular, smart, and athletic, but Meghan had the courage to always be nice—at least in college from what I knew. We used to joke with Derek that he was still trying to fit in with the cool kids. I knew the truth though—he was a million times better than I was and I was trying to not let him figure it out. I was always afraid he'd see the truth and walk away.

I haven't thought about that time in my life in so long. It had to have been horrible for her to make him hurt me.

She tucks her hair behind her ear. "I really miss her."

"Of course you do, honey. She was your mom and loved you very much."

She nods.

"I'm sorry that you've lost her."

Everly is a good kid, I don't doubt that. She is overwhelmed with feelings that she doesn't know how to handle. When I look back at the meanest people in school, they were often the ones in the most pain. They cried out because it was easier than sitting in the hurt.

I believe it's the same with Everly.

She lashes out because it's the best way to hide from her grief.

"Me too."

"Well, if you ever want to hear stories or talk about her, I'm here."

Her brown eyes are filled with unshed tears. "Why did you guys stop talking?"

This isn't something I feel right telling her. "Because when we're young, we think with our hearts and forget to hear with our head."

"That doesn't make sense."

I laugh. "When you're older it will. You don't have to feel like I'm trying to take your mom's place. I don't want your dad to forget her. I'm just me, and all we can do is be kind, right?"

Everly's eyes widen. "Mom said that."

I nod with a grin. "I know."

"Can I ask you something?"

"Of course."

"Why do you paint?"

The question brings me up short. I haven't told her that I paint, but it's also not top secret. Her father may have told her or even Chastity.

"I paint because the world I see isn't the one I'm living in. So, I make the canvas into what I hope it could be. It's hard to see things sometimes, and when I have my brush, I'm able to open my heart just a bit."

"What if you don't like the world no matter how you're looking at it?"

So deep for such a young girl. I smile wistfully, wishing that she saw things easily at her age. "Then you get to create what you want or you get to paint it as ugly as it is and accept it."

Everly looks out the window. "I don't really feel like there's much pretty right now."

It's got to be so hard to be her age and feel that way. "You know, you're not that different from Chastity in a lot of ways. I know you don't think so, and when I was your age I would've totally laughed in my face if I were you, but…" I pause, hoping she's still with me. "In a lot of ways, she lost a parent and had very little choice in how things went."

"And now you do?"

"No," I tell her with all the honesty I have. "I don't. I had to drop out of school, raise a kid on my own, and I work for my parents. I want you to see that when you're at the top, there's nowhere to go but down. And the top of middle or high school is really not that great."

It'll probably all fall on deaf ears, but at least I tried.

She nods once, exiting the car and then stops, sticking her head back in. "I wish I knew you didn't completely suck earlier. I would've at least smiled at you—since you were so popular at one time and all."

I'm not sure what exactly that means, but I'm going to pretend it's a compliment. "Thanks…I think."

"You're welcome. See you around."

I wave. "See you around."

* * *

"This is a little weird," Derek says as we make plates for the girls.

"I know."

"But they're working on their project, so we can't really be blamed for this."

Their project is due tomorrow so we suggested we'd all have dinner. It was meant to be a very casual thing, but both girls have made snide comments about this not being a regular thing.

At least Everly said hello this time to me, so there's a small sliver of hope on that front.

They're down in the store, doing whatever it is they need to do for this social media experiment and he and I are being very…domesticated.

Derek comes behind me, wrapping his arm around me as I plate the food. "I could get used to this."

"You could, huh? I'm pretty sure your mother cooks for you daily."

His low chuckle reverberates in my ear. "Yeah, but she's not you."

"And you think I would cook for you?" I ask as I turn around to face him. He's totally walking into a trap, but I'm not about to stop him.

"I would hope so."

"What would you do for me?"

He grins. "I'd definitely do things for you."

"I bet you would, but, if I'm in the kitchen slaving away, I'd like to have specifics."

Derek turns, looking at the door, and then back to me. "First, I'd do a lot of this…" His lips touch mine softly at first and then he deepens the kiss. My fingers tighten around his shirt, loving that this is one of the things.

"Then"—he breathes as he shifts back—"I'd do that, in other places." My stomach clenches as I think about where his mouth would otherwise be as well.

"That's a start."

"I'd—"

"God." Chastity's voice breaks the statement he was about to say and I turn bright red. "You should be happy it was me," she says as she grabs the notepad off the table. "All I've had to hear about for weeks was my stupid mother and her stupid father and how that didn't mean we'd be stupid sisters. Like I'm excited by this idea?"

"Aww, sisters."

She rolls her eyes. "And what did you do to her?"

Derek puts his hands up. "I didn't do anything."

"Today, she's being all nice and it's freaking me out. Pissed off and mean Everly I can handle, but she's asking me about how it's been to be raised by a single parent and if my mom is my friend. It's weird."

I can't help the smile that forms. There was no guarantee she would actually hear what I said and not just mentally flip me off. The two of them share a bond that they don't know. I always notice that, when two people think they're different, it's often because they're so similar they can't accept the other. It's the things that bond us that can also divide us.

Chastity and Everly could be best friends, but they choose to be enemies.

"Maybe she's trying," I suggest.

"Maybe she had a lobotomy or was abducted by aliens last night. Either way, you guys need to stop…touching and stuff."

"Nice to see you too, honey," I say with a smile. "Derek and I were just checking the temperature of the sauce with our mouths."

Derek steps to the side before clearing his throat. "I'm…"

"Oh, don't try to placate her, she's being an ornery teenager. Like we're not going to catch them making out with their boyfriends? Please."

His eyes shoot to mine and then it dawns on me what I said. I said that we were going to. Not me. Not him. But as though we'd be raising them together and catching them. I don't know when that shifted.

When did I start thinking of us as a couple? A real couple.

It's always been me doing it on my own. I've had it all mapped out because I never saw it any differently. Now I'm talking about being a team with him. It's foreign but at the same time, deep in my gut I know that it's what I want.

My world has been turned around and finally, I have hope for more.

"Yeah, I guess we will."

Chastity groans and leaves the room. "I should've moved in with Grandma."

Both of us burst out laughing. "Well, I guess I'm glad she didn't say her father. Thank God none of us had to see him all that much when he was here."

Derek stops laughing and something in his face changes. I'm not sure what, but it was so weird that my stomach drops a little. He turns his face and starts to busy himself.

Why did he turn away when I said something about Keith? He hadn't shown up again after that night at my parents', and from what I've heard he left town yesterday. I'm just grateful my life can go back to normal.

"Derek?" I call his attention.

"Teagan?"

"Why did you turn away?"

He straightens his back and sighs. "I hate thinking about Keith."

"Well, no one really likes to think about him, but you seem...I don't know...weird."

"I hate him and I still hate what he did to you. And that there even is a tape."

My heart sinks. I thought maybe after he knew the whole story, he'd understand. He didn't seem bothered by it after. He was angry, which I get, but not at me. Derek felt a lot of self-hatred for not protecting me—which is stupid.

He couldn't have stopped it. I don't even know that I would've told him.

"I get that, but it's in the past, seriously."

He nods. "Agreed, but I still don't like him."

"Oh, me neither."

"Good, then let's stop talking about him."

"Okay," I say apprehensively. "Dinner is done anyway."

Derek gives me a quick kiss. "I'll head downstairs to get the girls."

This could be so easy if we can get the girls to be civil, which seems to be happening on its own. There are no hurdles to overcome other than merging our lives. I don't think we'll struggle there. Even though years of us being apart has changed things about us, we're still the same.

We just—click.

It's why I think I see the future with him.

There's a knock at the back door that leads down to the store, which means it can either be my mother, Derek is locked out, or it's Nina. I pray for any but the first.

When I open the door, I thank God for once being kind to me with this. "Hey!"

"Hey," Nina says a little quieter than her normal boisterous self.

"Everything okay?"

"I really need to talk and it can't wait."

I push open the door and invite her in. "What's wrong?" She starts to pace, and my nerves grow. Nina is always so easygoing. When things are in crisis, she's the calm one. Seeing her like this is out of character. "Nina?"

"I'm not sure if what I heard is a lie or not, but the rumor is going around and I don't want you to hear it anywhere else."

"Okay…"

This town and their fucking rumors. I'm so tired of it and once again, I'm going to be the center of it. God forbid they get a life and leave mine alone.

"So, Keith was here and apparently, the rumor is that you sent Chastity to get information on Keith."

Well, now I've heard it all. "That's the most ridiculous thing I've ever heard."

"You mean she didn't go to the funeral home?"

"Of course she didn't go! She didn't even know when it was. This is so insane. I'm so tired of this crap. I want nothing to do with that asshole. I've worked so hard to keep Chastity away from him and the poison that is his life and for what?"

"Tea," she says softly. "I saw her."

"You saw who?"

"Chastity."

My heart sputters. "You saw her where?"

Nina releases a heavy sigh through her nose and then shakes her head. "I saw her leaving the funeral home."

This makes no sense.

"She couldn't. She was with Derek."

Nina looks away, she chews on her thumb and then turns back to me. "I know."

"You…he was with her? No, that's crazy."

"All I know is I saw her and then I saw him. I don't know, Tea. I don't know what the story is. Derek didn't tell you?"

No, he most definitely didn't. In fact, he didn't say a word.

"I was going to tell you." Derek's voice fills the room. "I was waiting for the right time."

chapter thirty-six

Teagan

present

I stand, looking at the man I love, wondering what the hell he was thinking. "You took her to the funeral home?" I ask, praying he answers differently.

"It wasn't like that."

Nina walks forward, touching my shoulder. "Call me later, okay?"

I nod, not taking my eyes off him.

I wait, trying to wrap my mind around what she just told me. Derek, who hates Keith, took my daughter to see him. He didn't talk to me, ask me, get my blessing. He just took her? Why? What could possibly be the reason why he would go against something I so clearly was opposed to?

Nina walks around us, her hand rests on his shoulder for a minute and then drops.

"Nina?" I call. "Can you ask the girls to stay downstairs until we get them?"

"Of course, honey."

"Thank you. For being honest as well."

She gives me a sad smile and then closes the door behind her.

Derek straightens his back and his lips form a thin line. I don't care that it hurt, this is far worse. "Before you go ballistic, hear me out."

"By all means…" I say with anger vibrating in my voice.

There's not much that he can say that makes this okay. He took her, behind my back, to see the man that has single-handedly tried to destroy me.

"I was driving down Main Street and saw her walking, which I thought was a little strange, since she said she had to do homework."

I'm going to lose it. She told me that she was going with him and told him she was doing school stuff? Unreal. My daughter is in big freaking trouble, but then again, so is my boyfriend.

"Which led you to…?"

"She was going to the funeral home whether you or I wanted her to or not. I thought it was better for her not to go in there alone."

"That wasn't your decision to make!"

"She wanted to see him, Teagan. She knew he was here, you forbade her from going, and I didn't want her to go in unprotected."

My heart is racing and I can't believe this. "Then you call me! Me! I'm her mother. I'm the only goddamn person in this world who has protected that girl. She never should've seen him."

"You would've rather I did what?"

"Tell her no. Talk to me."

This should be clear as day. He had no right.

"I understand you're mad, I didn't know what to do when I saw her and I didn't want her to walk in there alone. You and I both know she was contacting him."

"You didn't have the authority to act like that."

"So you'd rather I held her captive in the car so you could handle it?"

"Yes!" I slam my hand on the counter and turn away.

I don't know what to feel right now, but betrayal is the one thing that keeps coming to mind. My anger isn't only about the fact that he took her, which is bad enough, but that he kept it from me.

"I'm sorry. I really am. I did what I thought was best for Chastity. I wasn't trying to hurt you."

The thing about intentions is that even while they may be good, they still have consequences. There are things that he's done and I've done that put us here to begin with. I didn't intend to fall in love with him, but I did. He didn't intend to have his wife find the journal, but she did. I also don't know how to reconcile the fact that he intentionally lied.

"No? Then why lie, Derek?"

"She asked me to keep her secret."

"She's thirteen."

"I'm aware of that, but if you and Everly had some secret that wasn't going to harm her, would you tell me?"

I shake my head and start to move. "This could harm her, though. You made a parenting choice when you're not her parent."

He rubs his forehead and moves toward me. "I made a choice as a man who loves you and cares very deeply for that girl. She's not my daughter, and I know that, but she was ready to do it all on her own, and I couldn't let that happen. Was not telling you wrong? Yes. I should've told you, but I'm also trying to win her over."

"Winning her over doesn't mean you conspire against me. Do you see that Keith is the worst part of my life?"

"Of course I do."

"Well, then imagine when Everly and I had our talk the other day that she told me all about knowing our past. Imagine her telling me that you were in love with me during your marriage. Imagine how you'd feel if I kept that from you."

He closes his eyes and releases a heavy breath. "I don't know what to say, Tea. I assure you that I didn't want to walk in there with her any more than you wanted her to be there. The last person I wanted to see was him, and then to see her face after she saw him, broke my fucking heart."

I didn't even get a chance to think about the actual part where Chastity saw him.

"What do you mean?"

"I mean that I had this brave girl beside me, and she walked into that funeral home with her back straight. She was so much like you, ready to show everyone how fantastic she is, and then we get there and he doesn't even see it. He doesn't see that she has his eyes or that she's brilliant. He makes an offhand comment about not wanting to see anyone in this town, while looking at her, and I had to restrain myself from beating the shit out of him."

My chest feels tight as I think about what it must have been like for Chastity to meet Keith.

Chastity has always been steadfast and unfazed by most things that would've sent me into a spiral. She has this ability to shrug things off that I wish I had. However, I don't think she's actually shrugging anything off.

I slump down into a chair, my arms on the table, and let it all sink in.

What if she's not so brave? What if I'm so weak that she has to be strong around me?

Did I do this?

I look up at Derek. I'm so conflicted. On one hand, he acted in a way that I appreciate. Protecting Chastity like a father in some ways. He stepped up, held her hand, walked her through something she was determined to do and ensured she wasn't alone. I appreciate that.

On the other, she never should've walked through it.

They both knew my wishes and the history between Keith and me.

And then he lied.

"Right now, my heart is so torn I don't know what to think. You lied to me, Derek. More than that, I feel like Chastity could be hurting and I didn't know! I didn't get to talk to her about what happened or what it was like to see him. You—"

Chastity opens the back door and looks at me. "I did it. Derek didn't do anything, Mom. I wanted to go see my father. I needed to look him in the eye, and whether Derek went with me or not, I was going."

"You have no idea how much trouble you're in," I tell her as I get to my feet. "You went, after my explicit instructions not to, you've been contacting him behind my back, and then you got Derek involved in your scheme."

She crosses her arms over her chest. "I didn't want to hurt you, Mom, but can you imagine what it's like to have a parent who you don't even know? He's not dead. He's a freaking famous person and people talk about him around here like he's a god. So, yes, I wanted to meet him. I'm sorry that you're mad because I wanted to meet him."

"I'm not upset you wanted to meet him, Chastity. I understand that. I'm upset you lied to me. We don't lie to each other. That has always been the one thing we've promised. You went behind my back—more than once—and I want your phone. You're grounded."

"Fine, whatever. I lied but I had to. You wouldn't listen to me about it! You just told me to stay away. Even years ago when I asked about him! I wanted to know about my father and you never cared!"

"I'm the parent here. I know what's best for you, and *Keith*"—I sneer his name—"isn't good for anyone. I wasn't trying to be mean or whatever else you think, I was protecting you from someone who doesn't deserve you!"

"I can decide that for myself," she yells.

I wish she could. I wish that at thirteen I could've known all the bad shit that was to come. She has no idea what a cruel world it is, and I'd like to shield her as much as I can. "Babygirl, if only that were true, but the bottom line is, you disobeyed me, and you got Derek involved. Hand over the phone."

She hands me her phone and stomps off to her room.

I look up at the ceiling, pushing the tears back. Everly walks through the door and looks at Derek. "Dad?"

"Go on down to the car, Everly. I'll be there in a minute."

I walk over to the counter, putting my hands behind me for support. There's no salvaging tonight.

"You know what kills me?" I say to Derek as he stands there, watching me.

"What?"

"That as angry as I am about all of this, and believe me, I'm fucking pissed, I'm more sad. I had no idea that all of this went on, and here I am, paying the price. I didn't know you loved me a million years ago, and I had to pay the price then. When do I get to make the choices? When is it *my* turn to decide what happens in my life?"

"What do you want, Teagan?"

"I don't ever get what I want."

"Then ask for it."

"I have and what do I have to show for it?"

Derek moves closer, his eyes stay on mine. "Chastity knew what she wanted and went after it. Be proud of that for just a minute. I know you're angry and hurt, but you want to decide, then decide now. What do you want?"

"I don't know anymore."

And that's the thing of it all, I have no idea what I want because suddenly, I feel unsteady. Not because Chastity lied, but because with Derek, my life doesn't feel boxed in. As much as I love it, it's hard not feeling secure. Things aren't as they've always been, and it scares the shit out of me.

With choices comes vulnerability to be hurt so deeply.

He takes a step forward. His fingers wipe the tears that fall down my cheek. "Close your eyes."

My lids lower.

"Don't think, just tell me something real, Tea."

I let his warmth thaw away some of the hurt that's inside of me, and let the visions I've held back for so long come to life. "You and me, in a home, raising the girls and being happy. I want to paint. I want to not be in this apartment, feeling like I'm nothing." I envision myself at the beach, him sitting on the blanket next to me. "I want us to be happy, to grow old together."

His lips touch mine in the softest of kisses. I feel the callus of his thumb graze across my lip when he pulls back. "I see all of that when I close my eyes. I see you in that horrible house of dolls, waiting for me. I see us living a life, building our life, but you have to choose it too."

"I did once."

He shakes his head. "No, baby, you didn't, but you can now. You can choose to see that no one acted in a way that was meant to hurt you. I'm going to take Everly home, you decide when you're ready for me to come back."

He gives me another soft kiss, this time on my forehead and then walks out.

If I could have him stay, I would. It's all I've ever wanted. However, there's a part of me that's so lost in my head because I did choose him once. I chose him the day he married Meghan because I knew that it meant doing what was best for him—not for me.

And now I know that he loves me, wants the same vision that I do, and all I have to do is ask him to stay.

I snap out of it and rush out the door, down the stairs, and through the store. When I get to the street, all I see are taillights.

I stand here, watching him drive away.

I make my way back upstairs where Chastity's music is loud, which means she doesn't really care to talk, which is fine by me.

Grabbing the phone off the table, I go to text Derek, but then I realize it's not my phone, it's Chastity's.

I open the app, wanting to see what exactly she's messaged her father and click the notifications, since I have no idea where the hell the information would be. I look at the image on her page and my heart stops. That's a painting...*my* painting...on here?

Why is she posting my art?

I start to click around and there is photo after photo of my paintings all on here. Comments, hearts, and people tagging their friends to share the posts. I scroll lower and there's one photo with almost one hundred thousand hearts. My confusion grows deeper as I keep going.

Then I click up top and what looks like an inbox appears. There are messages asking about buying them, people wanting to know where the paintings are showcased, and my stomach drops.

These paintings were mine. They were for me and I never wanted to share them.

How could she post them?

"Mom?" Her voice pulls me from the phone.

"How could you?"

"I can explain."

I put the phone down, my hands are shaking. "You better start."

"You wouldn't see how special you are and how beautiful these are. When Everly and I were tasked with the social media project, we had to come up with something that was new and fresh, it was to be taken down after it was over and I thought maybe...I don't know."

"What is this, Chas? Seriously? Because you and I...we don't operate this way. We never have."

She betrayed my privacy. I feel as though someone has punched me in the gut—a second time today. It's not that

I'm not proud of my work, because I am. I think my paintings are beautiful and special, but when I was ready to share them, it would've been *my* choice.

"It wasn't supposed to happen this way."

My eyes meet hers. "What does that even mean? What did you think would happen when you posted them, Chastity?"

Tears with a mix of shame form in her eyes. "At first, it was the only thing I could think of for the project. I thought that maybe it would help us. Maybe you could finally do something you like instead of working in this store." She sniffs and another tear falls. "Then you could be happy, but then you and Derek started dating. It was...I don't...it wasn't all my idea..."

I sit, watching her struggle for words. "Who else's was it?"

"Everly and I thought, that maybe we could, God it sounds so bad, and it is."

"You thought you could break us up?"

She nods. "I like Derek, I really do, but I hated her so much that the idea of having Everly Hartz in my life was so bad, I had to find a way. So we thought, if we could get your paintings seen, and..."

I have never been so upset with her in my life. "Don't stop now, Chastity, what did you think would happen?"

She thought nothing of me, that's for sure. She thought of herself and Everly.

"I don't know. I thought maybe this could help us. I hate this town. You hate this town, it seemed like maybe this was our ticket out. I'm stupid. I'm so sorry. I wanted to tell you, but I couldn't and then, Mom, something happened. People started to find them and love them. We couldn't keep up with notifications. There were inquiries and people asking to buy them…open the app."

I look down at it, not wanting to look at it. Not wanting to do anything but cry.

"Please, I just want to show you," Chastity urges. I do as she asks and then she pushes where all the messages are. "Right there, that came in today. It's what Everly and I were doing downstairs, we were going to tell you today, I swear. At dinner the two of us were going to confess everything and explain."

There is nothing I can say right now. The relationship that Chastity and I have had was always built on trust. Lies weren't welcome. Today, it seems that's all I've uncovered.

"Have I failed you?" I ask. "Was it something that I didn't give you?"

"No, Mom!" Her eyes are filled with tears again. "I'm so sorry. I was just so mad. The idea of Everly around made me crazy. So, we wanted to split you up. Cause a big fight between you two or maybe get your paintings sold so we could move! If we left here, then I wouldn't have to be around her anymore. You didn't do anything wrong and I'm…"

"Sorry."

She takes my hand in hers. "I really am."

"I believe you. I still don't understand why you'd do this. You know my art was private and that I didn't want to share it. I hid it from Grandma, and the last thing I would ever want is it to be public like this. But I know you're sorry."

"It felt like the only way to get out of this town before you marry him."

"I know you hate her, and I get it, but—"

"She's not that bad. We talked a lot the last few days when it went viral. Then there was no way to stop it. It just got more and more out of control."

All of this has gotten out of control. "Can you remove it all?"

"Yes, I can delete the account, but can you read that one message please?"

I wipe my own tears, which fall silently. "This one?"

She nods quickly and opens it.

Dear RealPerspective,

I'm an art curator outside of Palm Beach, FL. I own one of the most prestigious galleries and your paintings have captured the eye of a few of my best clients. We'd like to speak with you further regarding having some pieces displayed and sold here. Please contact me at your earliest convenience.

Best,
Timothy Sterling
TS Fine Art Gallery

"I googled them," she says quickly. "Their last painting sold for over one-hundred thousand dollars!"

My throat is dry while my chest tightens. I'm not ready for this. No one is going to pay that much for one of my paintings. "This is crazy."

"Maybe, but isn't it worth at least replying? This could change everything for us."

That's the problem, what if I don't want everything to change now?

chapter thirty-seven

Derek

present

"How could you do this, Everly? How? You realize that this is a huge invasion of privacy? Do you realize what you two even did?" My temper is beyond reason. Once we got in the car, she confessed everything. I'm so disappointed in her.

I drove to my parents' house in disbelief. We're inside and we need to finish talking, now that I'm calm enough.

I know she's capable of some devious things, but to plan a way to get rid of Teagan and Chastity is beyond my comprehension. This wasn't something they did accidentally, there was a plot to this. They planned and continued on with it for weeks. All the while they were hiding under the pretense this was all for school.

"I thought it would get rid of her! I want to go back home! I want Mom to be alive and…" She starts to sob. "I just want Mom back!"

I pull her into my arms. As angry as I am, I can't watch her cry like this. "I know you do."

"But you don't. You have Teagan now."

Jesus. I can't imagine the pain she must be in. On the other hand, she can't do these things when she's angry. "Just because I'm with Teagan, doesn't mean that I wish your mother weren't alive. I know that the relationship we had wasn't great, and I'm sorry for that. I should've been stronger and left, but I couldn't leave you."

"I know I've been really awful, Dad."

I hear my father's words in my head and pray I can guide her the way he would've done with me. "What are you going to do about it? Because that's what counts. I've made my share of stupid decisions, but it's how you handle it that defines you."

"Can I go apologize?"

I touch her cheek and give her a warm smile. "Yeah, I think we can do that."

She and I head to the door, but there's a knock. I open the door to see Teagan standing there with tears in her eyes.

Everly steps forward before I can speak. "I'm so sorry, Teagan. I really am."

Teagan wipes her face. "It's okay."

"No, it's not. We never should've done what we did."

Her lips turn into a soft smile. "I appreciate that."

I touch Everly's shoulder. "Why don't you go see what Grandma is doing?"

"Sure, Dad."

When she's gone, I step outside, closing the door behind me. "Tea?"

She bolts forward, her arms wrap around my neck, and I hold her tight. She starts to cry, really cry. The last time I saw her this way, she was pregnant. "Hey, what's wrong?"

Her head lifts, eyes red rimmed from crying. "I don't know what I want, Derek. I don't know anymore. I thought I knew. I thought it was all planned out for me. I was meant to be alone, working in that antique store, raising Chas until I could get out. I was prepared for that life and then you came along."

"That's what has you so upset?"

"No." She sniffs. "After you left, I ran after you because you are what I want. You're all I've ever wanted. You're the something real in my life. And now…God, now I don't know how to keep you."

I grip her face, forcing her to look at me. "You don't have to worry about keeping me. I've always been yours."

"It's always about timing. Do you remember saying that to me?"

"Vaguely."

I'm not sure where she's going with this. Teagan takes a step back, shaking her head. "You told me once during college that for some people, it's all about timing, and I've thought about that a lot over the years. I've always figured that our timing was always our problem. And it was, right?"

"Teagan," I say her name, willing her to say whatever it is.

"After you left, I talked to Chastity and she showed me the account. There were so many comments, I couldn't even process it. People talking about how they saw the horizon before, but there was something about the colors or the way the strokes were." She laughs mostly to herself. "As if I have a clue what the hell I'm even doing with the strokes. Then, she made me look at a message from an art gallery in Florida."

Dread fills my stomach. I've had moments like this, when there's a clear vision of what's coming next. This isn't going to be something I want to hear. "Okay..."

"Timing of it was really funny, wasn't it? We find each other, fall in love more than we already might have been, and start to really have this life." I move closer, touching her, because if she's going to end this, I have to stop her. I won't let this be us again. I can't watch her walk away. "I called him, the art dealer, and they want to offer me a spot in their next showcase."

I can fucking breathe again. This is good news, not her ending things. "That's great, Tea."

Then I see the moisture building in her eyes, and I realize...it's not—I'm about to lose her.

chapter thirty-eight

Teagan

present

How do I choose?

How can I walk away from this man when he's every-thing I've ever wanted? I can't pick up and move like this, but...I can't walk away from this opportunity ever.

Someone wants my paintings.

The money that he offered—floored me. To say no would be insane. I love Derek. He's the man I've waited my entire life for. Now, he's here, mine, and in love with me but this is...this is...an opportunity I've dreamed of.

"It means I have to leave," I say.

"For how long?"

I close my eyes, not able to look at him because I can't watch him hurt. "At least a year."

"A year?"

That's not the whole truth. I would have to go for more than that, and if I move Chastity to Florida, I'm not going to move her again. "I don't know because it would be a move and I don't know that I would..."

"Come back."

Is he asking me or finishing my sentence? Either way, I know the sentiment. "It would be a lot to move down with Chastity temporarily."

"And you can't paint from here?"

I sigh. "They need me there for the gala and the opening, there's press, and a tour? It's all so much right now, but he requested that I relocate until at least the first six months of the exhibit have finished. Plus, I need to paint more—a lot more, and it would be easier to paint from their beach. He has these plans, it's not just to sell my art, it's all about exposure and using the social media buzz to launch a long-lasting career. He wants a lot of photos of me painting and hosting events at the exhibit. It's a lot of networking, I guess."

"I see." Derek's voice is filled with disappointment.

"I have to take this."

His eyes meet mine. "I know you do."

"Ever since I found out I was pregnant with Chastity, my life has been hard. Really freaking hard. I've sacrificed everything, lost everything, and now, it's like someone gave me a hand. If I swat it away, I'll regret it forever."

This is the first time that someone has chosen me the first time around. It's a chance to stand on my own, be something more than an assistant manager in my parents' antique store. If I were to marry Derek, I'd go from being my parents' burden to his. Even if he never said it, that's how I'd feel.

Now, I can be my own woman. I can show Chastity that I'm not a college dropout who couldn't do anything with her life.

The only thing holding me back is him.

I have to give up the most incredible opportunity or lose the most incredible man.

Life isn't fair sometimes.

"This is your chance, baby."

It is. "But that means I have to give you up." I choke back a sob.

"Why?"

"Because I have to move to freaking Florida." After I got off the phone with Tim, I asked Chastity what she wanted, and she was ready to pack tonight. I know she wants out of here. Hell, I want out of here, but I want Derek too.

"I'm not saying it won't be hard," Derek turns away. "I don't know how the fuck we'll manage, but we'll do long-distance. We'll make it work."

"I wish you could come with me."

There are a hundred reasons why he can't. Everly, his father, the house he bought, and the fact that we are new, are just a few. How can I possibly leave?

"You know I can't."

I walk closer, placing my hand on his chest. "I know, just as you know I can't turn this down. For the first time, Derek, I won't be nothing."

"You were never nothing."

"No, I am. I have nothing to offer you."

He steps back. "You're all I want. I don't need you to offer me anything."

"Please, listen." I release a deep sigh and try to assemble my thoughts. "I've always wanted more. You showed me once that I could have more, and since then, I've been searching for it. I never shared those paintings because I've failed at every facet of my life. I've been lacking in one area or another, and I couldn't handle one more thing, something I love, to be…unworthy."

Derek's hands wrap around my arms, holding me tightly. "You are worthy of everything, and if I ever made you feel less…"

"No! That's just it, it was never you. It's me! It's my choices and you asked me what I want, and I want it all. I want to paint and make money. I want to be with you and Everly. I want us to figure our shit out and live in that house. All my life I've waited for you, and now…"

Now I have to choose. Do I want love or do I want to finally feel as though I've accomplished something other than screwing up?

"You don't have to explain it." He lifts his hand, brushing the hair out of my eyes. "You have to take this, baby. Not because I want you to leave. Not because I don't love you, but because I love you. I love you enough to wait. I love you enough to let you go because I know"—his voice is filled with determination—"I *know* you'll come back to me."

My lip trembles and I let the tears flow. "I don't want to lose you, Derek."

"Then don't. I'm not going anywhere. I'll be here when you've accomplished what you need to. I know you feel like you've waited your whole life for us, but believe me, I have too. I've loved you, lost you, and I'll be damned to ever lose you again."

Derek doesn't give me a chance to respond, he crushes his lips to mine and I taste my tears along with his vow.

* * *

"Do you really have to go?" Nina asks as she helps pack my suitcase.

"Please don't you start."

I've cried more in the last seventy-two hours than I have in years. My flight is at six in the morning. Tim is going to meet me at the airport and show me the condo they've rented for me and Chastity.

"I'm sad. I'm going to be stuck in this town without my favorite angry person."

I laugh and roll my eyes. "You could come with me…"

"And leave all this?" Nina waves her arms in the air. "No, honey, I'm meant to live and die in this town. But I'm proud of you."

Dropping the sweater in the bag I rush over and wrap my arms around her. "I'm going to miss you so much."

"I'm going to miss you more."

Nina pulls back and shakes her head. "Enough of that. Now, is Chastity with your mother?"

This is another reason I'm struggling. She has another two weeks of school before break, which is when she'll come down. Derek and Everly are going to bring her and spend time with me. I've just never been away from her. A night here or there, but nothing like this.

"I dropped her off an hour ago so she can settle in a bit."

"She'll be fine."

I laugh. "I know, it's me I worry about."

"You have no idea the strength you have inside of you. In the midst of dealing with Keith's bullshit, you raised an amazing child. You've persevered when many would've collapsed. Don't sell yourself short, my friend. I am so proud of you."

"So am I." Derek's voice cuts in as I clutch my chest.

"Derek!"

"You didn't think we weren't going to spend our last night together, did you?"

"Where's Everly?"

"She's perfectly capable of staying home with my parents."

"And on that note." Nina claps her hands. "I'm going to head out and let you two...well, do what you do." She comes over to me, and the tears come again. "Don't you cry, Teagan Berkeley, don't you dare. You're doing something magnificent and I'm so happy for you."

Nina has been my rock over the years. I love her heart and I'm going to miss our daily talks. "This is so damn hard."

She grabs my hand and squeezes. "The things that are worth doing aren't meant to be easy. Call me when you're settled?"

"You can count on that."

She touches Derek's arm on her way out and I hold back as much as I can. I try to be brave and strong because I chose this. I kept saying I wanted to have the power to make choices and now I want to take that back. Choices are dumb.

Give me consistency and Derek.

He makes his way over to me, pulling me to his chest. "She's a wise woman."

I nod, breathing in his musky scent. I close my eyes, committing it to memory so that on the nights I'm missing him, I can remember this. The way his arms hold me just right, his chin rests on my head as I melt into him. There's the faint scent of the ocean that's ever present and then his cologne. It's everything that makes me happy.

"I have a surprise for you," he says after a few seconds.

"Yeah?"

"Are you all packed?"

"Almost."

"I should've figured." He chuckles. "Get your bags because we won't be coming back here."

"What?"

"Just go with it, Tea."

There's so much that I still need to do, but then none of it matters as much as the man in front of me. So, I toss a few more things in the bag while Derek waits patiently. I know I forgot stuff, but he'll be driving down with the girls in two weeks and I can have him bring whatever I need. At least that's what I'm telling myself.

My mother said she's leaving the apartment as is, so when I come back, I don't have to worry about housing.

After ten minutes of checking the apartment over again, I'm as ready as I'll be. We head to the car, both of us quiet but finding ways to touch the whole time. When we get in, I can't keep silent anymore.

"Where are we going?"

"You'll see." I can hear the smirk in his voice.

"You could just tell me."

He turns to look at me, grabbing my hand and lacing our fingers together. "I could, but then I would ruin the fun."

"You and I have a very different version of fun."

I hate being left in the dark. I also know he used to love tormenting me with things he knew that I didn't. The more I pushed, the worse it was.

"Maybe, but you make it too easy to make you crazy."

We drive through town and when we turn down Sycamore Street, I know exactly where we're going.

The house.

Sure enough, he pulls into the drive and releases my hand. "Come on." We get to the front door and he hands me the key. "Open it."

"You want me to open the door to your house?"

He comes around behind me, holding the key with me, and we turn it. I wait for the scary beady eyes to stare at me when the door opens, but they're not there. Instead, the house is completely cleaned out and it smells like fresh paint.

"Go in," he urges.

I enter the space, still waiting for the creepy dolls to pop out, and when he flips the light on, I can't breathe.

It's breathtaking.

The wood is a dark gray stain and the walls are painted a light cream color. Everything has been cleaned and the house looks exactly as I'd dreamed it in my head. "This is beautiful," I say as my hand touches the doorframe.

"I remembered you said something about cream walls so I went with it. Everly picked the exact shade."

I smile. "She did great. When did you do all this?"

He walks forward as if the small distance was too much. "We've been working on it the last few weeks, but we really got busy three days ago."

"When you knew I was leaving?"

"I wanted you to see it before you go."

I close the distance and lean up, kissing his lips. "I'm glad I did because the last time we were here…"

"Freaking scary."

I laugh once and rest my head on his chest. "I'll remember it always."

"Oh, me too, it frequents my nightmares. Come on, there's more to see."

My eyes widen in shock. "More?"

"We've been really busy."

He walks me through the kitchen, explaining some of the work he wants to do to bring it up to a more modern look. "Do you think that'll be good?"

"Me?" I ask. He wants my opinion?

"Well, I fully intend for you to live here at some point."

I'm never getting on that plane. I can't do it. "Don't say things like that, please. Not tonight."

"Why not tonight?"

I sigh and start to pace. "I'm having a hard-enough time even thinking about leaving tomorrow, the idea of knowing that this"—I throw my hands up, waving them around at his gorgeous house—"is what I'm walking away from...I can't do it."

"So you love the house and not me?" His voice is full of humor.

"It's a toss-up."

Derek wraps his arms around my waist, bringing his lips to mine. "I've got one more thing to show you."

"I'd rather us do this," I say as I pull his face back to mine. I kiss him, wanting to pour every emotion I can into it. I want him to feel how much I love him and don't want to leave.

"Baby, I plan to do that in about ten minutes, first let me show you what else we did."

I pout, lip jutting out, and he chuckles.

We walk toward the other end of the house and I'm seriously impressed. I can't imagine how they got all the dolls out, let alone had time to scrub, paint, and refinish the trim. There's a set of double doors with glass planes. Derek pushes them open, his arm extended for me to enter.

"What is this room?"

He walks to the corner and turns the lamp on.

Then, I don't have to ask.

I don't breathe.

I don't move for fear that this will all disappear.

In this room that overlooks the huge oak tree is an easel with a blank canvas in it.

"It's where you can paint when you come home—to me."

chapter thirty-nine

Derek

present

I wait for a reaction, not sure if this was one step too far, but Everly seemed to think it was a great idea.

Come to think of it, the fact that I listened to her is not exactly the smartest thing I've done.

Teagan stands there, looking at the easel, and I move so I'm behind her, inhaling her lavender scent and she leans back, just enough so I can feel her. "Is it the wrong easel?"

"No."

"Is it too much?"

She turns her head, staring at me from over her shoulder. "Yes, but not because of what you think. It's too much because I can't do this. I can't leave you now...I can't..."

This wasn't meant to keep her, this was meant to show her that if she flies, she can always come back. This is her home. This is where she belongs, but I never want to tie her down.

Teagan has to do this, and I'm proud of her for taking

the risk, even if it means we have to be apart for a while.

I walk over to her, wrapping my arms around her, because in a few hours, I won't be able to. I don't know how I survived without her before, but I'm going to have to find a way again.

"No," I tell her. "You're going because that's what you need to do for yourself."

"What about us?"

"Baby," I say, looking down into her gorgeous green eyes. "We're not going anywhere."

Her hands move up my chest and then around my neck. "Make love to me."

"Oh, I plan to, but I want to show you one more thing."

She smiles, her lashes fluttering up and down, making me want her more than anything. I take her hand, leading her upstairs.

I can't show her too much because though we may have cleared the downstairs of the freaky dolls, I couldn't get rid of them until next week, so they're all in one room and I'm talking floor-to-ceiling amounts of these damn dolls.

"I knew this house was special," she says as she touches the banister.

"Which is why I bought it."

She sighs. "Yes, you bought my dream house."

When we make it to what will be the master bedroom, I stop. "I bought our home, Teagan. When I stood here with you that day, I knew that this was going to be ours. I know we have things to work out and I'm not trying to push you." I tell her so she knows, I can be patient.

"You have no idea how much I want that."

"Good." I lean down and kiss her lips.

Then, I open the door for my last surprise. I wanted us to spend the first night here. I worked all day to get the downstairs done with Everly, but came back to do this.

"Derek." She says my name softly.

I laid out a bunch of blankets, like we would on the beach, and surrounded it with candles.

"Now," I say as I pull her to the makeshift bed. "I plan to make love to you."

Teagan grips the hem of her shirt, pulling it over her head. "I'm hoping you have big plans."

I smirk as I pull my shirt off. "You're damn right I do."

She takes a step closer, removing her pants as she keeps her eyes on me. "I like a man with a plan."

I move closer, mimicking her movement. "I'm glad."

She reaches behind her back, unhooking her bra. "And what are your plans, love?"

"Well, you've already taken care of step one by removing most of your clothes."

Teagan's eyes fill with mischief. "I like to think ahead."

When her bra falls to the floor I fight back a groan. She's perfect. Everything about her is desirable. My plan is to love her as much as I can. I want to give her every damn reason to get back on a plane and come home to me.

"I'm grateful for it."

She pulls her underwear down, so agonizingly slowly that I can't do anything but watch. I stand here like a man in desperate need of water and she's the river in front of me. I'm thirsty for her and I can't wait to drink until I can't anymore.

"Derek?" She calls my name after a few moments of me staring.

"Hmm?"

"What's next?"

Next is taking that drink.

I move toward her, my hand tangles into her long blond hair, holding her head right where I want it. I kiss her, pour every damn emotion I'm feeling into her. All my love, hope, desire for the future. *Our* future.

Teagan's hands roam my body as I continue to give her everything. She reaches her hand between us, gripping my dick, and I moan. Everything feels so good with her.

I bring my lips down the column of her neck, loving that she tilts her head to the side to give me better access. "You're perfect, do you know that?"

"No, I'm not."

I bring my hands down slowly, grazing her soft skin. "You're perfect for me, baby. Everything about you makes me want you."

Her eyes close and her head falls back. I pull her down to the blankets so I can adequately love her.

Lying on my side, I look down at her and marvel. She's truly magnificent. Her hair is sprawled out around her, eyes filled with desire, lips are swollen, and I wish I were a painter because she's a vision.

"I love you," she says, looking up at me.

"I love you."

"Please don't make me wait," Teagan pleads.

My hand moves to her breast, kneading and then my mouth follows. I lick, suck, and flick her nipple while her fingers thread in my hair. I move from one side to the other, listening to each noise and loving when she starts to squirm.

"Yes," she moans when I pull a little harder and then bite gently.

I shift so I'm on top of her and then start to move down

lower. I have to taste her. There's nothing like when she comes apart in my mouth.

I slide down, kissing my way and she lets out a small cry of anticipation.

"This is the next step," I tell her before my tongue is on her.

Then, I'm much too busy to talk.

She shifts and pants as I make circles on her clit, driving her crazy, making myself harder than I've ever been in my life. I'm drowning in her and I don't care if I ever come up for air. Her sounds become more intense as I push her higher.

"Derek! God! I can't-I—" She speaks in half sentences and I know she's close.

I slide a finger inside of her heat, increasing the pressure with my tongue.

Her fingers grip my hair, pulling just a little and then I use my teeth and she screams. I continue to extract every ounce of pleasure I can.

Teagan lies there as I make my way back up her body, needing to be inside of her, but she moves to the side. "I have a plan too," she says as she pushes me onto my back.

"You do?"

"Oh, yes. A woman always comes prepared."

"And what does your plan entail?"

Her smile broadens and her lips move close to my ear. "A lady never tells."

I'm about to say something, but her hand wraps around my dick and starts to pump. Words fail me and she takes advantage. She moves down, and I'm going to fucking lose it. Her lips press a kiss to the tip and then she slides her mouth over my length.

"Jesus Christ," I mutter, lifting my head to watch and our eyes meet.

I've had blow jobs before, but Teagan's mouth on my dick is almost too much.

In countless dreams I've envisioned this. Yet all those nights of jerking off as I imagined her mouth sliding up and down haven't prepared me for this.

She takes me deep, using her tongue as she moves back up. Her mouth is hot, wet, and I am about to lose my control.

I try to think about anything other than what she's doing, but I can't focus long enough for it to matter. When it comes to her, I'm helpless.

"Tea," I call her name. "Baby, you have to—"

"Hmm?" she moans around my dick.

"Baby, please. I need you," I fucking beg. I beg because I had plans, dammit. I was going to love her. It was supposed to be all about her.

She pulls off and I'm not sure if I'm relieved or I want to cry. "You need what?"

"You."

Teagan straddles me. "Then have me you shall."

She sinks down and my entire future flashes before my eyes. All the things I want are crystal clear.

I want to marry her, love her, give her kids if that's what she wants. I want to be a father to Chastity and Everly. I want the life that we should've had from the start. Now, I just have to wait for her to come back to me, so we can live it.

chapter forty

Teagan

present

I lie on Derek's chest, listening to the sound of him breathing, wondering how in a few hours I'll find the courage to leave.

Even if it's just for a year, I can't help but feel like it's going to change everything.

I move my head to rest on my chin and stare at his peaceful face. I feel the tears building at the impending separation. I can't look in his eyes and then get on that plane. There's no way I'll actually go.

He says I'll come back, we'll be together and everything will be fine, but he can't know that.

I have to walk away without regrets, and leaving Derek will be my greatest one.

Slowly shifting so as not to wake him, I check my phone. I have an hour before I need to leave for the airport.

My eyes find his perfect face, he smiles in his sleep and I can't help but hope he's dreaming of me. I lean over, kiss his lips, as a tear falls. "I love you," I whisper softly, but pray he hears me somewhere deep in his mind.

I get up, get dressed, and head downstairs. I call for the car service the gallery has set up and now ask them to come here instead of to my house.

Then, I walk around again, admiring all the things he's done, and when I reach the painting room, a silent sob breaks free from my chest. We didn't get enough time together. I never got to sit in here and paint like I've dreamed of. This gift was everything because it meant he believes in me. I want to rush back to the bedroom, wrap my arms and legs around him, and not leave. I feel like I just got him.

I watch as the car pulls up, wipe away my tears and head out. When I reach the door, I close my eyes, hoping he can feel my love.

As I head to the car, my heart feels like it's being ripped from my chest.

One step closer.

"Good morning, Miss Berkeley," the driver says with a smile.

"Good morning."

He takes my bag, placing it in the trunk and then opens my door.

I stare at the bedroom window, hesitating because I want more time. These last few days went too fast. Last night felt like I blinked and it was over.

I hesitate, waiting, praying he doesn't wake up because if he comes after me, I don't think I'll go, but at the same time hoping he does so I can stay.

"Did you forget something inside?"

How do I answer that?

"I didn't forget anything, I'm just leaving something behind."

The driver seems to understand my words. "I see. Do you need a few minutes?"

I shake my head. "No, if I don't go now…"

He gives me a sad smile and I get in.

My eyes don't move from that window. "Please wake up. Tell me to stay," I whisper.

There's no movement in the house and then the driver gets in the car. My heart is breaking and I think about how upset he'll be that I left like this. I wonder if he'll understand that if I didn't, I'd still be wrapped in his arms. The car begins to move and the tears continue to fall as I drive away, leaving my heart in the house on Destiny Lane.

* * *

"So you're through security?" Chastity asks as I'm wandering through the airport.

"I just got through."

"Are you okay?"

My daughter, always worried about me. "Not really."

She sighs. "I didn't think so. Everly told me about what her dad had planned with the house."

Everly told her? Well, that's new. "You and Everly talk?"

"I guess we kind of became friends when we plotted to take you and Derek down."

"Evilness has bonded you?"

Whatever the reason is, I'm glad they have left the mean girl act behind.

"I guess. She sent me a text that maybe we should find a way to bring you back together this time."

I'm glad they're both okay with us dating now. Too bad it didn't happen before this job offer. "At least when Derek brings you down, we don't have to worry about someone killing the other in the car."

Chastity laughs. "Are you at all excited?"

"To see you? Yes. I already miss you." I say the words and my chest tightens. "I've never really been away from you."

"Then why are you going?"

There's a beep on my phone and I don't have to look to know who it is. Derek has realized I'm gone and is calling.

"I'm going because this is an opportunity I will never get again and you want out of that town."

She goes quiet and the beeping starts back up again. I can't answer. I have to stay strong, and if I hear his voice, I'll break. "You know, I always have wanted to, but now I don't."

I stop moving. "What?"

"I thought about it last night when Grandma asked about seeing my father. I never realized it before but living here was hard because I never knew if I would see him or if I wanted to see him or if seeing him would matter. Now that I have, it's not so hard. He's really an idiot."

"Yeah, he really is."

"But all I ever heard about was how great he was. Everyone here makes him out to be this great guy and I didn't understand why you hated him so much. It's been hard. And then Everly came and made my life hell, so I wanted out. But, Mom…" She pauses and my heart races. "I don't think I want to go anymore."

I don't want to go either, but I wanted for just once, to be worth something more. I was finally being told "yes" instead of "no."

"Why are you telling me this now?" I ask with a groan.

"Because if you want to stay, I wouldn't hate it. I would have Mrs. Stinkers and her babies. I can still work with Dr. Derek at the clinic."

I find a chair and slump down in it. This isn't the conversation I expected to have with her. I thought she'd tell me how excited she is and how ready she is to meet me. Now she's talking about staying there and her cat and friends. Right when I think I have it all figured out I'm made aware that I know jack shit.

"Chas…"

"I'm just saying…"

She's just killing me, that's all.

"We will begin the boarding process for flight 445 to West Palm Beach, Florida, in about twenty minutes. Please make your way to gate A-2."

I sigh. "I have to go, Chas. I love you."

"I love you too, Mom. Make good choices." She ends the call before I can say anything else.

I look down at the phone, seeing the missed calls from Derck. He has to be so mad or hurt. I know that I would be if he did that to me, and now I hate myself for doing it to him.

A text flashes.

Derek: I don't know why you left like that but know that I love you.

Me: I love you. I'm sorry, please know that last night

was perfect. You're perfect. I just couldn't go if I had to say the words.

I put the phone away and head to the store by the gate. In the back I grab a drink and a little girl comes over and smiles.

"Destiny!" I hear a woman yell.

I look down at the girl and she turns to the name.

"Destiny, get back here. Oh, God, you scared me!" Her mother yells with that frantic sound to her voice. "I thought I lost you. Don't ever leave me like that, okay?"

My heart pounds as the name strikes me. Someone I love is on Destiny Lane. Someone I left.

Jesus. I need to get a grip.

The woman takes the little girl in her arms and walks off, kissing the side of her head as she goes.

I head out of the store, no longer thirsty, and walk toward the gate. There's a store with a few toys in the window. I stop short when I see the creepy doll.

I quickly take my phone out to take a picture to send to Derek and stop. I have to stop doing this. It was my choice to leave and here I am, seeing all these things that remind me of him.

Instead of sending the photo, I drop my head and walk fast. If I don't see anything, then I can get through this and do what I keep telling myself is what I want.

Florida is where the gallery is. Florida is where I will finally make enough money to get out from my parents' thumbs, give Chastity a better life, and *be* something.

They're already boarding, so I walk straight over to the gate attendant.

The couple in front of me are talking about their wedding and my chest starts to ache again.

"Do you think the girls will be okay?" the woman asks.

"They'll be fine. This is our weekend. Our daughters will be just fine."

She leans her head onto his shoulder. "I can't believe we're finally married."

His eyes are so filled with love it makes my breath catch. "We waited long enough to finally be happy. It's still so surreal. We've known each other forever…"

They start to walk forward and it's my turn. "Miss?" The gate attendant stands there with her hand out.

I look down at the ticket and the tears I was holding back start to flood.

What am I doing?

Why am I here?

This isn't the only chance I might have to do something with my art. There were tons of messages and comments asking to buy the paintings outright.

I'm going to leave for well over a year, and for what? A gallery. A gallery that didn't know of me until that profile was made. I was fine before that app. Sure, I wanted more, but Derek saw the more in me when I couldn't.

He's what matters. He, Chastity, and Everly are all I need. They're more than I could ever ask for.

We could make it through the time apart, I know that. But why make myself wait for the one thing in this world that I've wanted more than anything?

I can paint from that room.

I can sell them on my own.

Hell, I can open my own damn gallery. There's about to be a very empty space above the store that has great views of the ocean.

"Miss?" the attendant says again, snapping me out of my thoughts. "Are you going to board?"

"No. No, I'm not. I have to go."

I race out of the terminal and down to where the cabs are located. Thankfully, I find one willing to take me the hundred miles up to the island. The entire way, I can't stop smiling.

This was the right choice. The only choice. Making a move like this should've been full of joy, but it wasn't. He's my joy. My family is my joy, not a gallery in Florida.

I call Mr. Sterling as we get close to the town limits.

"I'd like to thank you first and foremost. You have no idea how honored I am that you chose me."

He clears his throat. "But?"

"But I can't come there. I have something here, in Virginia, that's more precious to me than anything. You see, I painted those pieces because I never felt like I was on land. I felt as though I were drifting out to sea, looking for the shoreline and the person who sat on that beach. Well, after a very long time, I finally found him."

"You're a romantic, Ms. Berkeley."

"I guess I am," I say with a small laugh.

"I understand. I've been married to my wife for thirty-seven years. I hope you find your happiness."

"Thank you," I say before hanging up.

The car turns down Sycamore Street and my heart is racing. The cabdriver turns left, and Derek's outside, walking to his car.

"Stop here!" I yell and the driver hits his brakes.

I don't wait for the vehicle to stop. I throw the door open and I'm running toward him.

"Derek!" I call his name.

His eyes widen as he sees me rushing toward him. "Teagan?"

The tears that fall now aren't sad. They're tears of relief and happiness. My happiness. I keep moving, crashing into him, and his arms wrap around me.

We stumble a little, but he keeps us upright, just like he's always done. He steadies me when I waver.

"What are you doing here? What about your flight? What about the job?"

"I'm not going. You're what matters to me. You, the girls, this house, I can paint from here. I can paint anywhere, but you're here and you are where I'm meant to be."

He brings his lips to mine, holding tightly and kissing me with his whole heart.

I watch his blue eyes fill with love and contentment.

"I love you," I tell him.

"I love you."

My thumb brushes his cheek and I rest my forehead to his. "Tell me something real." I utter the words that are his and mine alone.

Derek lifts his head, his eyes trained on mine. "I'm really going to marry you."

"Is that you asking me?" I ask with a huge grin.

"No, I already know the answer, it's just what's going to happen."

"Well, I like a man with confidence."

Derek chuckles. "I'm glad. Now, let's go inside so I can show you how much confidence I have."

epilogue

Teagan

one year later

"I'm so nervous I could pee," I say to my husband as we're waiting in the back room.

Derek kisses my temple. "You're going to do great."

"Easy for you to say."

He's not the one who will be judged today in front of hundreds of people. I had to paint an extra ten paintings for this opening. Mr. Sterling believes we'll sell all twenty-five that are being showcased.

"It is easy because I know how talented you are. I know how hard you worked to give this gallery what they wanted, even if it meant you were in that studio while I was getting rid of the dolls, which seemed to multiply."

There wasn't a choice in the matter. Mr. Sterling is also a romantic and offered to still showcase my paintings, but allow me to do it remotely. Of course that came after three other galleries were posting that they were interested as well, but I felt after leaving him in the lurch, it was the least I owed him.

Plus, he came with the best offer.

Derek and I agreed to spend our family honeymoon in Palm Beach and took the very nice check the gallery offered for rights to my next ten paintings.

I smile at the man I love more than anything. "You and I both benefited from my hard work, otherwise, we wouldn't have been able to hire the contractor to put on the addition."

While that house was perfect, it was a bedroom and bathroom short. The girls are getting along, but asking them to share a bedroom was going to put an end to all the progress they'd made. We used my first check to put an extension on the house, giving us another two bedrooms and two bathrooms.

It was the best decision we ever made, other than putting the ugliest couch in history as the centerpiece for my art room. Each day I'm inspired to not create anything that horrible, but then I remember how loved it is, like the people in my life.

"Yes, and I never thought we'd survive the construction."

It took freaking forever to be done, but the last three months have been bliss. "But we did, and now the four of us are living under one roof."

"Now we need to build them separate houses so they stop bickering…"

I laugh and nod. He's not wrong, but they get along so much better, now that they're in high school.

"Well," I say as I wrap my arms around his middle. "I would like that for other reasons."

Derek grins. "And what might that be, wife?"

"I think you know."

"I could use a little help to be sure."

"Could you?"

He brings his lips close. "I could."

"How about I give you a hint?"

I love when we are playful like this, which is pretty much all the time. We haven't had any big fights, not even when the girls are wearing on us. Each day that we're together, we seem to just enjoy. After spending so many years apart, wishing we could be together, it's impossible for us to be angry, because we're finally a family.

"Does it have to do with my impressive and thorough skills in bed?"

I nod. "Oh, most definitely."

"And would it have to do with the fact that you have to bite on pillows when I'm using said skills?"

"You're rather impressed with your skills, husband."

He brushes his lips against mine. "Are you not?"

I kiss him softly. "I'm very impressed."

"Good."

"Do you want to kiss me?" I ask.

"I always want to kiss you." I know the feeling. He's highly addictive and makes me always want more. "However, if I kiss you, I might not stop and then your dress will be wrinkled and you'll be pissed."

Would I? I mean, sex with my husband is a good reason for a wrinkled dress. Then I remember that people are going to want to talk, shake hands, and hopefully buy my art, which would give me the opportunity for another showcase.

"You're right. But tonight…"

He does in fact kiss me, but is careful not to mess my

clothes or hair. "Tonight, I'm going to rip this dress off of you and wrinkles will be the least of your concerns."

I like the sound of that.

I give him a quick peck and take a step back. "I'm *really* looking forward to that."

He walks close, takes my hand in his. "I'm really looking forward to the rest of our life."

Me too, because with Derek Hartz by my side, there's nothing I can't do. And that's something real.

ACKNOWLEDGMENTS

To my husband and children. You sacrifice so much for me to continue to live out my dream. Days and nights of me being absent even when I'm here. I'm working on it. I promise. I love you more than my own life.

My readers. There's no way I can thank you enough. It still blows me away that you read my words. You guys have become a part of my heart and soul.

My editor, Amy Pierpont, and the entire Forever team, thank you for making this book everything I dreamed of.

My agent, Kimberly Brower, I am so happy to have you on my team. Thank you for your guidance and support.

My beta reader, Melissa Saneholtz: Dear God, I don't know how you still talk to me after all I put you through. Your input and ability to understand my mind when even I don't blows me away. If it weren't for our phone calls, I can't imagine where this book would've been. Thank you for helping me untangle the web of my brain.

Christy Peckham: I couldn't imagine my life without

you. You keep me on track in a way that no one else could.

Melanie Harlow, thank you for being the good witch in our duo or Ethel to my Lucy. Your friendship means the world to me and I love writing with you. I feel so blessed to have you in my life.

Bait, Stabby, and Corinne Michaels Books—I love you more than you'll ever know.

ABOUT THE AUTHOR

Corinne Michaels is a *New York Times*, *USA Today*, and *Wall Street Journal* bestselling author of romance novels. Her stories are chock full of emotion, humor, and unrelenting love, and she enjoys putting her characters through intense heartbreak before finding a way to heal them through their struggles.

Corinne is a former navy wife and happily married to the man of her dreams. She began her writing career after spending months away from her husband while he was deployed—reading and writing were her escapes from the loneliness. Corinne now lives in Virginia with her husband and is the emotional, witty, sarcastic, and fun-loving mom of two beautiful children.